on chocorua

Book 1 of the Trailblazer series

Robin Reardon

IAM Books
www.robinreardon.com

ON CHOCORUA
Book 1 of the TRAILBLAZER series

Copyright © 2019 by Robin Reardon

Cover and formatting by Sweet 'N Spicy Designs

Cover photograph by Alex Calder

ISBN: 978-0-9988414-8-9

Praise for <u>WAITING FOR WALKER</u>

"An absolute joy to read. Reardon's characters popped right off the page and enveloped me in their world... deeply felt emotion shining on every page."
— *Camille, Joyfully Jay Reviews*

"A true breath of fresh air. More than a coming of age story, this is a waking up story. This is a book that everyone should read."
— *Meredith, Diverse Reader*

"An exceptional novel that is intelligently written, compelling to read, and emotionally charged. I highly recommend it."
— *Sammy, The Novel Approach*

Praise for <u>AND IF I FALL</u>

"I was captivated the moment I sat down and started to read this novel."
— Rachel, Diverse Reader

"*And If I Fall* has universal themes that depict the complexity of family dynamics, sexual awakening, and human connection. Jude Connor is yet another resilient, admirable youngster among Reardon's impressive body of work."
— *Christopher Verleger, Edge Media Network*

"It by no means follows that a good writer is necessarily a good storyteller, but this author has it nailed. The pacing is spot on, and the story arcs are smooth and well rounded."
— *Cheryl, Sinfully MM Book Reviews*

To my friend John-Michael Lander:

Athlete, actor, teacher, author, and abuse survivor who has blazed his own trail through the uncharted territory of his life with courage and honesty that leads the way for others.

You're the only one you need to prove something to.

— Jeremy Ford, best friend and hiking companion of
Neil Bartlett, brother of Nathan Bartlett

PREFACE

A trailblazer is one who forges a path through uncharted territory, an effort that requires courage, tenacity, and integrity. Although others might follow, only sometimes does the trailblazer have followers in mind.

Nathan Bartlett is a trailblazer—not because he follows established routes in the White Mountains, or on Kaua'i, or on Mt. Desert Island, but because he explores and then follows that inner path that tells him who he is and how he relates to the world around him. Sometimes this path leads to dead ends, or into mazes that confound him, or to the very edge of a cliff. Forging his path doesn't mean he finds all the answers. It means he identifies the questions that matter.

Nathan is a trailblazer on his own journey. And his success will be measured not by how well he follows someone else's path, but by whether he can forge his own.

I have done some hiking in my time. Like Nathan, I hiked the Piper Trail up Mt. Chocorua during a snowstorm one March, my own very first hiking experience. I know what he went through, and I know why he did it.

When we're young, before our brains have developed to the point where we understand consequences, we have an irrational sense of immortality. It's a good thing for me that I was still young enough to be immortal that winter when I was foolish enough to make this ill-advised climb, because otherwise I would likely have died. Like college freshman Nathan, I hiked Chocorua on the Champney Falls Trail the following summer, alone. Like Nathan, I watched some idiot driving golf balls off of boulders at the summit. And, like

Nathan and his brother Neil, when I climbed above tree line I experienced that conviction that I am both infinitesimally small and, at the same time, an integral part of the massive Universe.

In the next book of the *Trailblazer* series, *On The Kalalau Trail*, college senior Nathan will hike along the Napali Coast on the Hawai'ian island of Kaua'i. Although I have hiked a portion of this trail, Nathan will travel much farther down the coast than I did. He will relish the tropical trade winds, marvel at the sheer drop from the trail into deep ocean, shiver inwardly at the cairns erected to commemorate lives taken with sudden force by an unpredictable, capricious ocean. He will travel through a land so rugged that places where a helicopter might land, even in an emergency, are few and far between. And he will meet people who, once they arrived on The Kalalau, could not bring themselves to leave: the Kalalau Outlaws.

The title of *Trailblazer's* third book, *On The Precipice*, refers to an extremely dangerous climb up the eastern cliff face of Champlain Mountain on Mount Desert Island in Maine. Although I have climbed Champlain from the western approach and have stood at the top of the Precipice Trail, I have never scaled the cliff side. Many have; and each year, at least a few of them fall to their deaths. It is a dramatic, exposed ascent, profoundly affected by weather. Expert climbers can make disastrous mistakes if they take the trail for granted or lose focus as they climb. Nathan, out of college and contemplating the rest of his life, must make a choice. He must weigh the power of his body, his strength of will, and his readiness to take a life-altering risk, and then decide whether the precipice life puts before him is worth it.

Note that while reading all three of the Trailblazer books in order will take you on Nathan's journey with him—his first love, his successes and failures, and the maturity he gains along the way—each book can be read and enjoyed individually.

— *Robin Reardon*

CHAPTER ONE

This climb is for you, Neil.

The summit of Mount Chocorua is an odd place. With a tree line lower than most peaks in New Hampshire's White Mountains, the rocky top makes it seem as though the mountain is taller than it is (just under three thousand five hundred feet). Its neighbors are taller—some significantly—and they qualify for the four-thousand-foot club, a glory that hikers can claim if they've made virtual notches on their hiking boots after climbing all the mountains in the Whites that have an elevation of four thousand feet or more. Chocorua doesn't qualify. Even so, it looks impressive. It's sometimes called "Little Matterhorn" because of its bald pate.

It's odd for another reason, too: the types of people who climb it. For example, as I sit here on the open rock face, looking south and westward toward where the September sun is beginning to descend, about twenty feet to my left is a guy with a golf club, driving balls into the forest below. This ought to be illegal, and probably it is; I mean, if you're going to die on this mountain, you should do it like I nearly did, not by getting beamed with a golf ball.

From where I stand, near the official summit marker on the jumble of boulders and crags, I can see the tops of trees below. Some wear the brilliant colors of autumn, while some—the mountain pines—are a green so dark they appear almost black against the oranges and golds. All looks peaceful, all looks like it is as it should be. And yet my head feels as jumbled as the rocks on the mountain-top—part vindication, part contrition, and maybe just a small bit of

1

pride. When I'd been to Mount Chocorua the first time, last March, my first hike ever, I hadn't made it to the summit. And maybe, in part, that was because I made that climb for all the wrong reasons.

This time I'm here because I felt the need to dedicate my climb up Chocorua to my brother. Neil had put many virtual notches on his hiking boots, representing the many summits he'd achieved. But although he had asked me more than once, I'd never hiked anywhere with him.

This mountain had nearly killed me last March. A few months later, a different one killed my brother.

So often I've heard about someone dying, and people say, "He died doing what he loved." Like that makes it okay. Well, Neil died on a hiking trip. He loved hiking. He lived for it. But I'll bet he didn't like the way he died.

Sorry. Can't dwell on that right now. It was only a couple of months ago.

I nearly died because I fell for a guy I had no hope of winning, and then I took an active interest—feigned or otherwise—in whatever interested him. One of those things was mountain climbing. Much as I adored my brother, we went different ways in the outdoors. Even skiing; he did downhill and wasn't interested in Nordic, which was the only kind of skiing I did.

But I didn't lust after my brother. I lusted after Daniel Cooke. So when he said *Come hiking with me*, that's what I did. Together, we hiked Mt. Chocorua.

Daniel wasn't gay. Not exactly. He knew I was—or, I told him eventually. And he said that didn't matter. At first I think he hung around with me after he met my sister Nina. Maybe he thought hanging out with me would give him an advantage with her. But after a while, I realized that wasn't it. He just liked me. The sad part was I didn't just like him. I wanted him.

For her part, Nina wasn't especially interested in Daniel, but he was attractive and convenient, which is probably why she didn't outright reject him—at least, not at first. She kept him in her shadow for a while, and that kept him in my life.

How attractive was he? Let's see... dark brown hair with a nice wave to it, a little long on his neck and forehead; smooth skin the most beautiful bronze color (he was part Cherokee); a long, slender nose that didn't hook but that came to a refined end above sweetly-shaped lips the color of dark cherries; deep brown eyes; a body muscled in a way that wasn't bulky but that showed sleek definition whenever he needed to lift or pull something.

Oh, and there was something about him that I found compelling, as though he knew all kinds of secrets he'd be happy to tell you if you would but ask the right questions. I couldn't understand why Nina didn't fall head-over-heels for him. God knows I did.

For this climb, today, my second up this mountain, I did not follow the Piper Trail, the one Daniel and I had followed. That climb had nearly ended my hiking career the same day it had begun. Instead I hiked Neil's favorite trail up this picturesque mountain, the Champney Falls Trail. But I will visit the Jim Liberty Cabin, which sits just below the summit on the Liberty Trail. That cabin had been Daniel's intended destination, the place he'd planned for us to spend the night on that hike that was my first, that hike that he suggested, that hike where I lost my hiking virginity.

The Piper Trail is the easiest on Chocorua, in terms of steepness of grade, but it's not the shortest. Daniel chose it because despite his own expert standing as a hiker and ice climber, I was a novice. Oh, yeah, and it was March. In New Hampshire. Cold. Snow. Ice. Blizzards.

I met Daniel in the very beginning of my freshman year at

college. Despite the fact that Neil had graduated from UNH—the University of New Hampshire in Durham—the previous year, and even though Nina was starting her second year there, I was anxious about my first year.

I'd been assigned a roommate over the summer, and he'd been the first to reach out. He'd sent me an actual letter, hand-written and everything, in a blue envelope that had arrived one rainy day in early August. The return address, from Lewiston, Maine, was from a person who identified himself as "L. Speed."

Nina thought this was a riot. "El Speed! Is he Latino? El Speedo... maybe he looks good in swim trunks!"

It turned out the L stood for Lawrence, or Larry, as he was usually called.

On that swelteringly hot day when Gram drove me and my few boxes of possessions and clothes down to Durham from our house in Concord in her old, green Honda, I was a mess. I'd packed and re-packed my clothes maybe three times in the previous few days. Before leaving that morning, I'd sat in my desk chair biting my lower lip for maybe fifteen minutes, rocking back and forth the whole time. I'd nearly thrown up my breakfast as we were loading the car.

Everything I was going to have to do in the next couple of days piled up in a mental heap in my brain, each new task coming to the fore in turns. I was going to meet El Speed. I'd need to get along with him, to agree on who got what side of the room we'd share. I'd have to figure out where my classes would be, meet all kinds of people I didn't yet know, navigate the dining hall without looking like the loner I felt I must be, figure out the best place to sit in each class, try and suss out the instructors so I'd know how much I'd be able to get away with in terms of studying—basically figure out all kinds of stuff I'd never had to do. I'd lived in the same house since I was too young to know the difference, so this upheaval was of a major kind.

It helped only so much that I had some familiarity with the campus, having visited a couple of times while Neil had been there. I knew I could count on no help from Nina. She and I were never enemies, but for reasons I never understood, the bond between us was pretty thin.

These are all things that might plague your average incoming college freshman. I had an additional layer of concern, sort of a foundational anxiety on which all the others rested: Should I come out now?

So far only Neil knew. I'd been able to keep it hidden at high school, but I was going to *live* at college. For all aspects of life, I would be immersed in the campus environment. Could I live *that* life, too, as a lie, as I'd lived so far? Or should I believe what I kept hearing about one's college years, which is that it's a great place to reinvent oneself?

Of course, I wouldn't be *re*inventing anything. I'd been hiding, and now I had the option to stop.

What might the consequences be? I mean, it was 2015, which was a lot further down the road of acceptance than when I was born, but just how far down that road were we? Would my roommate request a transfer? Would other students around the dining room sneak glances at me and whisper? Would no one take the seat next to me in classes?

I'm pretty sure that the decision I'd made the week before the semester began was what was making me nauseous. I'd decided that I would be honest about who I was, that I'd reveal it when it was appropriate. And if anyone didn't like that, then fuck 'em. And that would include Nina, though I didn't expect our paths would cross much.

Neil had been at Hunter Hall for all four years of his UNH career, and now he was in his first year of graduate school in Colorado. I suspect I'd chosen Hunter for my dorm because it would be familiar, one less thing for me to have to figure out, but it's also possible that I saw it as maintaining my relationship with my brother. You know, like having something in common with him, something that was with me now that he was so far away. He'd been like a father to me, after our parents died. I don't know of anyone who was like a father to him.

El Speed, very tall and very blond and very solidly built—that is, my exact opposite—turned out to be pretty laid back about life in general. He didn't seem at all embarrassed when I caught him sniffing his day-old underwear to see if another wearing was possible.

"Why not?" he shrugged. "Why waste the time and the water and the electricity to wash something that doesn't need it?"

I just shook my head and wondered if his girlfriend knew. He'd started talking about Ellie, who was at the University of Maine in Orono, right after we'd met, and he'd said he had his car here on campus and would be driving up to see her frequently. At first I thought he might have picked up that I was gay and wanted to set the ground rules immediately. There were a few minutes where I tortured myself trying to decide whether to say anything. I finally decided I might get into more trouble by trying to hide who I was from him.

"I don't have anyone like that in my life. Not yet, anyway. But it wouldn't be a girlfriend." I busied myself with something in my closet, afraid to see his reaction.

His response sounded like a gentle shrug. "I'm cool with that."

So I came out of the closet. "Great. And, uh, y'know, I'd kind of like to be the one who tells anyone else."

"Got it."

Definitely easy going. He even got a kick out of my calling him El Speed, both because it was so similar to his girlfriend's name and because he thought it was a little ironic.

Chuckling, he shook his head. "Not much about me that folks are likely to call speedy."

It was because of El Speed that I met Daniel. I'd been complaining, the first couple of weeks, about two things. One was my calculus professor, whose habit of scribbling equations and formulas on the board with his right hand while talking about them, and erasing them with his left hand as he went, was not helping my comprehension. The other was not having enough spending money.

El Speed had no solution for the professor. But as to the money: "So why don't you get a job?"

"Here?" Now that I was here, even though I'd surmounted some of the obstacles that had made starting my freshman year seem so daunting, the idea of asking for, applying for a job intimidated me. At home I'd worked summers and many school-year weekends, often using my need to make money as an excuse for why I wasn't asking girls out. But all those jobs had come to me by way of Gram's connections. She'd lived in Concord all her life, and she was seen as a wonderful person, having raised her late daughter's three children alone. So competing with other people who might want the job I was applying for, trying to impress a potential boss enough to make them choose me, maybe being rejected—it seemed like a lot.

Not to El Speed, evidently. "Sure. Like, maybe at the dining hall. You know that digital scrolling bulletin board they have there? It said they need people."

So I girded my proverbial loins, marched myself into the dining hall office, and applied. As I filled out the form, one of the options was whether I preferred to work on the serving line or in the dishroom. There was no option for the kitchen; maybe they didn't let students cook the food they served. Too dangerous, for everyone. I was about to check "Serving Line" when I realized I really didn't want to stand behind the steaming food cases and have someone ask me what I was serving, to which I'd have to reply, "Salmon loaf," at which point they would say, "What?" to which I'd have to reply, louder this time, "Salmon loaf." Nope; that wasn't for me. I checked "Dishroom," figuring if it turned out to be awful I could always quit.

I started my new job the very next week, my third week at school. Gram was nervous.

"Are you sure you aren't taking on too much? You're just getting started in your classes."

I pictured her sitting at the kitchen table: short and very slender, her fluffy hair now more silver than the nearly-black she'd been born with. We were on the phone, Gram and I, about every third or fourth day in the beginning, though of course it thinned out as the semester wore on.

Her anxiety had an odd effect on me; it took mine away. I told her, "But I'm taking mostly intro subjects right now. I'll be fine. And if not, I'll quit."

But once I'd started the job, I didn't want to quit. I'd met Daniel.

The first person I met when I showed up for my lunchtime shift, though, was Eva, a tiny drill sergeant of a woman, probably in her late fifties. She was dressed all in white, her more-salt-than-pepper hair confined by a white net, and she ruled over the entire dining operation—serving line, dishroom, and kitchen.

"Nathan, this is Daniel Cooke. He's the dishroom foreman," she told me without a shred of irony. It occurred to me to ask why he wasn't in the kitchen, preparing food, with a name like that. But he stood beside her, and when I looked into his eyes, I was speechless.

We shook hands. "Welcome, Nathan. Glad to have another pair of hands in here. Come on; I'll show you the ropes."

I'd have followed him anywhere. It wasn't that he was gorgeous, though he was certainly attractive. But there was something about his face, something in his eyes maybe, that affected me powerfully, something that pulled at me. At first it didn't seem sexual. And, with most people in the world being straight, I didn't immediately wonder if he was gay, though it didn't take me long to begin hoping.

If it hadn't been for Daniel, I'd have been tempted to quit after my first shift. The dining hall itself was air-conditioned, but there was no way the climate of that white-tiled cave of a dishroom would be anything but hot and steamy. And there was no way to avoid the odd mixture of smells: a little garbage almost hidden under a layer of chlorine.

The room was partially bisected on the diagonal by a stainless-steel sheathed, tunnel-shaped behemoth that said "Hobart" on the end I could see. It was positioned between a spot near the rear right corner of the room and a spot most of the way toward the front left. It hissed and steamed in a rather intimidating way, and without seeing inside it I could tell something was grinding its way through the tunnel. But Daniel led over to the rear left corner of the cave, ignoring the bluster of that steel monster. He stopped on the near side of a long, waist-high, steel, shelf-like thing that extended from the wall on the left about fifteen feet into the room. He pointed me toward a position to the right of a girl who looked like she was probably also a freshman.

Daniel had to raise his voice to be heard over the din. "I'm going to have you work next to Lori here. Lori? Nathan. Jeff?" He pointed to a guy to my right, who stood at the end of the long steel thingy, then over at two guys on the opposite side of the steel thingy. "Dave? Aaron? This is Nathan."

Each introduction brought a nod from each of the others; apparently no one dared stop what they were doing long enough to give anything more by way of acknowledgement; the march of the trays, coming along a conveyer belt that flowed into the room from an opening in the left wall, all with gloppy, sticky, gunky stuff on them that had to be dealt with, was relentless.

Daniel gave me a quick rundown of my mission, which was to stand near the right end of the metal shelf, or counter, or whatever, and grab anything that the others had missed. They had specific tasks: crockery, flatware and paper, glassware, and trays. I was to grab any renegade item they might miss and place it on a rolling cart that someone else would replace as it got loaded.

I donned the rubber gloves Daniel handed me and stepped closer to my work station. Immediately I nearly fell. The conveyer belt with the trays flowed from left to right, but there was a sluiceway between me and it, full of water that flowed from right to left. It was amazingly disorienting.

Daniel caught me from behind. "Yeah, you'll get used to that." I don't want to, I thought, but of course he wasn't talking about our physical contact. "It makes some people dizzy, with the conveyer belt and the water going opposite directions."

Daniel draped his right hand on my left shoulder and leaned his face toward my ear so I could hear him better. With his other hand he pointed at the wall to the left.

"See over there? That opening? The trays come from the dining room from two directions and merge there onto the single conveyer belt in front of you."

I nodded, hoping he'd keep talking; I could feel his breath on my ear. He obliged me.

"And see the low, plastic pegs along the belt? Ideally they keep the trays separated from each other as they merge. But sometimes...." He gave my shoulder a light pat, chuckled, and stepped away. "You'll see."

I wanted to watch him walk away, but I also wanted to impress him. I turned to my task. Immediately I saw that Lori and the guys on the other side of the belt had started to let a few things slide through their frantic efforts to clear everything off, so I had no choice but to get going.

It took me several minutes to get used to the contrast between the belt and the water, but finally my brain managed to stabilize. It was hot work, I had to move quickly, and the din of the room discouraged small talk. So I felt like some kind of automaton. But I didn't let anything get by me, and I didn't break anything.

At one point, there was just too much stuff on the belt, and Lori hit a button on the wall. The belt stopped, and everyone scrambled to deal with what was in front of them. I knew that the longer that belt stayed still, the worse the load would be when it started back up. And, indeed, as soon as Lori hit the button again, the belt carried in trays stacked on trays, and she had to turn it off once more. Finally the lunch crowd thinned out enough that there were empty slots on the belt between trays, and one of the guys across from me left to do something else.

And Daniel was back. "How'd it go, Nathan?"

The room was a little quieter now, and I could hear a roundness in his voice that was sultry and seductive, even though I couldn't believe he was consciously going for that effect. When he wasn't shouting, his voice was deep and resonant.

"Okay, I guess." I wasn't thinking fast enough to make a more interesting reply; at that moment, my brain wasn't doing anything other than taking him in. He wasn't tall, I realized, maybe a couple of inches taller than me. About Neil's height, actually. And under the white, work overalls I was sure his body was trim and finely tuned. Also like Neil.

His laugh was low and soft. "You didn't break anything or send a fork into the disposal, did you?"

"Disposal?"

He pointed in the direction where the water was still flowing, toward the wall. "At that end, on each side of the belt, the water sinks into a garbage disposal. You didn't hear it go on and off? Lori had control of the switch. By the way, for future reference, if you do drop a fork in there and you need to reach for it, make sure whoever's closest to the switch knows what you're doing. Don't want to chop up any fingers."

The room had been so noisy that although I'd been vaguely aware of an occasional whining sound, I hadn't given it any thought.

"I'm giving you a bit of a break today, Nathan. Starting tomorrow, I'll have you help with the cleanup. For today, just stand someplace out of the way and watch what the others are doing. Tomorrow you and Jeff can work together, and after that you'll have your own territory."

He smiled and started to walk away, but he stopped about five feet from me.

"Nathan? Glad to have you." This time I did watch as he walked away. And I really liked what I saw.

As I was about to leave the dining hall for the day, Eva approached me.

"I hope you had a good first day, Nathan."

"Yes, ma'am."

She smiled, and it seemed genuine and friendly. "We rely on Daniel quite a bit. He does a great job in there."

I saw an opening for learning a little more. "Is he a senior, or something?"

"Oh, Daniel isn't a student. He's taking a year off, actually. No, this is his job. He was at a school in New Jersey, I think, for two years, and he's taking some time to decide whether to change majors."

"Oh. I—so, why here? What's he doing in New Hampshire?"

She grinned and leaned a little toward me as though sharing a secret. "I think he likes the mountains."

INTERLUDE I

Life with Neil: I'm Comin' Out

I wasn't the sort of kid who got teased about looking gay, acting gay, seeming any more gay than my male peers. If I was picked on, it had more to do with the fact that I refused to pretend I was dumber than I was. And occasionally some cretin would take issue with my obvious Chinese heritage, diluted though the characteristics are with a couple of generations between me and my Chinese maternal great-grandmother.

Sometimes in middle school I heard the word "fag" thrown at me, but it never seemed to have any authority behind it. For sure, I didn't take it seriously. In fact, when I got to tenth grade and fell head over heals in love with Riley Shapiro, I was as surprised as anyone else would have been if they'd known.

Riley, of course, wasn't gay. I don't know what he made of the fact that my eyes followed him everywhere, constantly terrified that he'd realize it. I couldn't say whether he noticed that I developed a sudden passion for attending swim meets, when it was only because he was on the team. I prayed he didn't pick up on the fact that I'd developed an odd friendship with his girlfriend, or that the time I spent with her was all about encouraging her to talk to me about him.

In other aspects of my obsession, I felt safer. He couldn't know I dreamed about him, or that that he had any part in the mess I made of my sheets most nights. He didn't have any idea that the feelings he aroused inspired me to browse a couple of online men's fitness sites, from the laptop in my bedroom, so I could ogle the dense thighs, bulky biceps, and ripped midriffs of men who were definitely not swimmers, while struggling to keep my breathing quiet as I caused a part of my own anatomy to swell and throb.

The summer before my senior year of high school Neil was getting ready for a hike along part of the Appalachian Trail where it cuts through Vermont. One afternoon I had been... um... admiring two particularly attractive men working away on machines, side-by-side and grinning at each other, when Gram called to me from downstairs. Without closing the browser, I shut my laptop to go see what she wanted, and when I came back upstairs Neil was standing at my desk, laptop screen open, the gorgeous men in all their glossy glory essentially ogling each other.

Maybe if I hadn't left the hand lotion dispenser right there beside the laptop I could have played innocent. Or maybe if I hadn't been painfully aware of what was certainly a beet-red blush right up to my ears, I could have assumed an irritated expression at the intrusion. Then I could have said, "Need something, Neil?" or "How would you like me to spy on your computer?" and faked my way through it.

The truth was, though, that I had been dying to tell someone. It might be more accurate to say I had been consumed with the need to tell someone. And there was no one in my life I trusted more than Neil.

We stared at each other for a good five seconds before he said, "Nathan?" His tone was confused and pointed at the same time.

By way of ending the standoff, I sat on the edge of my bed. He turned the desk chair to face me and waited.

Shoulders hunched, hands clasped between my knees, I looked at him from under my eyebrows. "So."

"So." And again he waited.

"I suppose you want to know about that."

I'll never forget how soft his voice was. "I want to know about *you*."

I didn't mention Riley. He was unimportant. What was important was that Neil understood, that he believed me, that he accepted me. I told him about my feelings, my worry about being discovered in the wrong way by the wrong people, and my near terror when I thought about the future, about living life as a gay man. Would I ever fall in love? Would anyone fall in love with me? Would it ever be possible for me to settle down and maybe even have a child with someone, if that's what I decided I wanted to do? My options seemed severely limited by society's determination that there was something wrong with me that should be hidden, or at least that they shouldn't ever have to deal with it.

Neil let me vent, let me go on and on. I can still see him: elbows resting on his thighs, hands clasped together loosely between his knees, head slightly tilted, eyes intent on mine. He was fully present, completely there for me. And when I finally ran out of words, he smiled.

"You know, there's a kind of unwritten law that no one should ever 'out' anyone else. And I believe in that rule. Even so, I think Jeremy would be fine with me telling you that he's gay."

My brain screamed, *Jeremy Ford? Your best friend who goes hiking with you?*

What I said was, "So... so you don't think it's terrible?"

"That you're gay?" He gave a quiet snort and sat back in the chair. "The terrible thing is how I've seen Jeremy treated by some total idiots. I don't want any of that to happen to you, but you need to be who you are."

Be who I am. It sounded so simple. Even if you're not gay, though, I think it can get very, very complicated.

CHAPTER TWO

After that first dining hall work shift, I had maybe forty-five minutes before psych, my next class, and I wanted to head back to Hunter Hall and take a shower. But my phone rang. I would have ignored it, but the screen displayed a photo of Neil and his tall, blond hiking buddy, Jeremy Ford, arms draped on each other's shoulders as they beamed smiles at whoever was taking the shot. Behind them, I knew because Neil had told me all about it, was the famous knife edge at the summit of Mount Katahdin in Maine.

"Hey, bro," I said into the phone, my mind silently registering how much Jeremy looked like El Speed.

"Hey, yourself! Why aren't you in class?" His tone was teasing.

"Bustin' my balls, eh? Why aren't *you*?"

I heard his laugh, an honest, open sound. "Say, listen. I just got off the phone with Gram. I hope you're talking with her as often as you can. I think she's lonely, now that her youngest—that would be you, in case there's any doubt—has flown the coop."

"I've been talking to her!" It felt like an accusation, one I didn't think I deserved. I willed my fingers not to clench the phone so tight. "I can't call her every day, you know."

"Just keep in mind that she's going to be reluctant to call you. She doesn't want to be a pest."

"Are you giving Nina this sage advice, too? I'm not the only one who—"

"We all need to call her. So, yes. But you know you're her favorite."

"Am not!"

"Well, you're the baby, then."

I let that hang in the air; it didn't deserve a response. The next thing Neil said sounded like he wanted to get back on my good side.

"Seeing anyone yet? Any handsome young men on the horizon?"

"Not yet." I almost said, *Not really,* thinking that maybe possibly potentially there had been some vibe coming from Daniel, but that would have brought more questions from Neil, ones I didn't want to answer. Or, at least, that I wasn't ready to answer.

"Okay, well… you know you can call anytime you need to, right?"

"Yeah." An odd combination of irritation and something kind of like relief fought for attention inside me.

So Neil thought Gram was lonely? I supposed that wasn't unreasonable. And, after all, she was our de facto mother. Had been for years. And now, none of us kids lived at home any more.

I decided I didn't quite have time to get back to Hunter and shower. I had the materials I needed for my next class in my pack, and I had a few minutes, so I found a bench under a maple tree, its leaves brilliant reds and oranges in the autumn sun. A light breeze brought the occasional leaf twirling gently down around my feet or onto my shoulder as I let my mind wander.

Guess where it went.

I closed my eyes and relived the feeling of Daniel's hand on my shoulder, his mouth close to my ear. In my imagination, I could feel the warmth of his body as I turned my face toward his, bringing our lips so tantalizingly close that neither of us could resist having them meet. So many emotions fought for attention. Confusion: Was it terrible of me to have these feelings about a straight guy? Or about any guy? Fear: What if Daniel figured out that I felt like this? What if other people figured out that I felt like this? Amazement: Fucking A, but that felt GREAT!

I heard my own sharp intake of breath as energy shot into my dick, and I opened my eyes. A couple of girls walking by gave me a brief glance. I cleared my throat and sat up straighter.

When I'd told Neil I was majoring in psychology, his response had been: "Um… why?"

I had no good answer. Or, at least, no answer that I felt I could articulate. The truth was that during my senior high school year, after Neil had been so cool when I'd trusted him with my truth, I'd tried hard to improve my perception of myself. All those dreams I'd had about Riley had served to deepen the shame I'd already accepted as my due. And even if he'd been gay, I don't think I would have had the nerve to approach him; shame wasn't something I should be sharing.

But Neil's support had made me take another look. It had made me lift my head up—a little anyway. And when I did that, even as I pushed shame into the shadows where it belonged, I could still see all those things that had caused me to buy into that shame.

I had fallen deep into some odd combination of envy and fury. All around me, there were girl-boy couples, holding hands, kissing when they thought they could sneak one in, going places together, talking—even bragging, sometimes explicitly and sometimes with veiled meaning—about things they'd done together.

I couldn't do any of that. It wasn't that I wanted to brag about going at it in the back seat of a car with some guy. I just wanted to be able to respond to the perennial question, "So, what did you do over the weekend?" with something better than a shrug and, "Not much. Worked." Especially since I felt obliged to add, "You?" and then listen to them talk about their heterosexual activities, conquests, whatever. And all the while I'd know that even if I'd had the best weekend ever with someone I cared about, I wouldn't be able to say a word about it. I wouldn't even be able to identify who I'd been with.

ON CHOCORUA

Sometime around March of my senior year I hit some kind of wall. I came so close to telling Gram I needed to talk to someone, like, you know, a professional. But I didn't see how to do that without telling her about myself, and also I knew that she'd be worried sick for a variety of reasons. So I just kept telling myself, *Hang on; it'll be different next year. College will be the place where you can be yourself.*

And college would be the place where I could take psych courses that would help me help myself.

Sitting on that bench, letting the crisp, autumn air refresh me after the sweltering dishroom, I watched a few more colorful leaves drift down from the maple tree behind my bench, little patches of orange and yellow swaying back and forth on their descent through the still air. One particularly gorgeous yellow specimen caught my eye, a veritable slice of sunshine, and I followed it on its journey to where it landed on a bright red version of itself on the ground near my feet. Beside the red one was a brilliant orange one with red and yellow spots.

I leaned over, picked all three up and held their stems together, and as I settled back onto the bench I heard a girl's voice.

"That's a beautiful combination. Love the freckled one."

Her own face was a beautiful combination of sparkling blue eyes, arched eyebrows an intense brown, and lots of freckles. She wore a bright green cardigan over a white blouse, and jeans that looked too new. In her arms was a collection of books and notebooks, and a brown shoulder bag hug near her hip. In another age, she could have modeled for Norman Rockwell.

Her smile was genuine and friendly. "Are you going to take them with you?"

Knowing she meant the leaves, I shook my head. "I don't have a better place for them than right here."

She laughed. "So you'll leave them with their friends! I like that."

She moved on, gazing around her as though wanting to commit absolutely everything to memory. I loved the freshness of her appearance. I loved the open, friendly attitude that had nothing in it of guile or flirtation. I thought, *If I weren't gay, I'd maybe go after her, chat with her, see if we could meet up later.* But I was gay. And although it might be great to have her as a friend, I knew that would mean telling her the truth. I couldn't predict her response. If it was negative, it might bring that shame crashing in again. I wasn't quite ready to deal with that.

That night, I dreamed of Daniel. We were alone in some environment that looked like the dishroom but wasn't. He was on the far side of a phallic-shaped metal thing, a substitute for the Hobart, which looked for all the world like a silver dick pointing out from the back wall. The head of the erection was near me.

Moving slowly from where he stood near the back wall, Daniel made his way along the dick, sliding one hand slowly along it as he went, his eyes locked onto mine. I couldn't move, so I just watched as he got closer to the exposed head, which he caressed. He stood still, watching me, as his hand traveled around and around in a motion that was part loving, part teasing. My own dick responded as though his hand were caressing me.

Suddenly he plunged a finger into the hole on the end of the metal dick.

I woke up, panting, a soggy mess at my crotch.

Had El Speed heard me? Did he have any idea what had just happened? I strained my eyes to see whether he lay still, and the sounds of gentle snoring floated through the dark air.

It was probably an hour before I could fall back to

sleep.

Coming out of the dining hall a few days after the dream about Daniel and the metal dick, feeling a little bummed because Daniel was pretty much leaving me alone in the dishroom now that I knew what I was supposed to do, I nearly bumped into my sister. She and a couple of her girlfriends were standing on the sidewalk not far from the door.

I figured she wouldn't have any particular desire to introduce her kid brother to her coterie, so I just nodded. She looked at me long enough to nod back, but instead of turning back to her friends, her eyes focused on something behind me. When I turned, I saw Daniel.

Now Nina was willing to talk to me. "Who's your friend, Nathan?"

I was still gazing at Daniel, who was gazing at Nina in a way he would never, I was now sure, gaze at me.

Daniel stepped beside me, his eyes still on Nina. I said, "Nina Bartlett, this is Daniel Cooke. He's my boss in the dining hall."

Nina looked at me. "Dining hall?"

In what were no doubt his richest tones, Daniel said, "How delightful to meet you, Nina Bartlett. Yes, Nathan does a great job for us, in the dishroom. You're his sister?"

He smiled at her, and she examined him from the corners of her eyes, head tilted slightly. I found myself wishing our Chinese ancestry had given me as much capacity to look exotic and sultry as it had given Nina.

"I am," she said to Daniel. "I hope you aren't letting Nathan get away with anything." She smiled at him but turned back to her friends as if to signal to Daniel that the exchange with him was over.

Nina's group moved off slowly. I watched Daniel. He watched Nina. I sighed inwardly.

"Nathan." Daniel's voice startled me. "Is your sister

seeing anyone exclusively?"

"Not that I know of."

"Could I get her number?"

I can't say his request surprised me. I had no doubt that Nina had deliberately followed her sultry look at Daniel with the sight of her gently-swaying backside walking away, the subtext being, *Pursue me.* Her behavior was a stark contrast to the Norman Rockwell model who'd been excited by autumn leaves.

A voice in my brain suggested that if Nina and Daniel started seeing each other, I might get to see even more of Daniel. The face of Riley Shapiro's girlfriend flashed through my brain. I shook it away.

"Probably," I told him. "I'll ask her."

I consoled myself with the thought that if Daniel had any inking that I lusted after him, he wouldn't have asked for my help with Nina. Small consolation, but I took it. And there I was, alone again.

When I got back to the room, El Speed was deep into some heavy-duty conversation with a guy I didn't know. I'd heard their voices, not loud but intense, from the hall. When I opened the door they stopped talking abruptly. El Speed was in his desk chair and facing mine, where the other guy sat, facing El Speed. They were both leaning forward as though that would help press whatever points they wanted to make. They looked at me.

"Interrupting?" I asked. "Should I go away?"

El Speed sat back, evidently trying to demonstrate how relaxed he was. "Nothing goin' on here," he said, but he was glaring at the other guy.

The other guy stood and turned toward me, his hand out. "Gordon Wellington." He was tall and skinny, reddish blond hair cut short, a face that could only be described as sweet.

"Nathan Bartlett," I replied as I shook his hand. "Seriously, I could go to the library or something, work on my psych project."

Gordon smiled. "Your roommate was just trying to convince me that I shouldn't pledge."

El Speed chimed in, "I said you shouldn't pledge Nu Lambda Psi."

I hadn't paid any attention to the frat recruitment. Neil hadn't pledged a frat, so it hadn't occurred to me to do it. Now that I say that, it seems dumb. But I wasn't really interested in frats, anyway.

"Why shouldn't he?" I asked El Speed. "What's wrong with that house?"

He lifted an arm and let it fall again, not quite a shrug, not quite dismissive. "They have a bad reputation. Hazing. Last year some pledge drowned."

Gordon didn't want to let that stand. "That wasn't here. It was on a campus out west somewhere. Or in the south. I forget. And anyway, they never proved that it had anything to do with hazing."

"Bullshit."

I asked Gordon, "Why that house?"

The silence in the room said worlds. This seemed to be the crux of the matter.

Finally, Gordon answered. "Well... because one of the brothers... one of the brothers wants me to."

That didn't satisfy El Speed. "Because one of the brothers wants *him*."

My head snapped toward El Speed and then toward Gordon's blushing face. So he was gay. I wondered if I was blushing, too. I wondered if I should say anything.

But all I said was, "Why do you need to be in the frat, though? The brothers are allowed to consort with lowly non-Greeks, aren't they? Or with members of other frats?"

"Well, sure, but—you know."

I didn't, not exactly. Maybe I lusted after Daniel, but I

didn't start working in the dining hall because he was there. I decided to change the subject.

I glanced at El Speed. "So how do you guys know each other?"

"Gordon is Ellie's best friend."

El Speed's girlfriend. So all three were from the same town.

Gordon turned on El Speed, his voice pointed as he asked, "Did she tell you to stop me doing this?"

"No, Gordo. She told me you were doing it, and she told me she was worried. So am I."

"Well, I'm not. And I'm going to do it."

So much for changing the subject. I watched as Gordon left, shutting the door a little harder than necessary.

El Speed still had his eyes on the door when I turned back to him. As I resettled my chair at the desk, I asked, "You're really worried?"

"Ellie and I both are." He stood and resettled his own desk chair. "Seems like almost every year, some pledge from that house gets into trouble. And, like I said, last year one of them died."

"Well, maybe that will make them more careful this year."

He glared at me. "Not something I'd risk *my* life on."

The next day, during my lunch shift in the dishroom, I half expected Daniel to ask about Nina's contact info, which she'd texted me permission to give him. But he greeted me in his usual way, which was just a quick "Hey, Nathan," and said nothing else. So at the end of the lunch shift, after doing my assigned clean-up, I caught his attention.

"Got something for you, Daniel."

"Cool. Let's grab a coffee or something and sit in the dining area for a few minutes, eh?"

It was challenging for me to sit across from him, to

look directly at him, and not to let myself get carried away by lust. What was it about this guy that got to me like this? I couldn't have said. Maybe we never know what it is about someone else that pulls on us. I'd never understood what it was that had pulled me toward Riley. Was he smart? He was, actually. Daniel seemed smart, too. Was Riley's body nicely put together? Well, yeah; he had a swimmer's body, not bulky, but sleek and trim. Daniel's build was very similar, but I knew that was just gravy. Was Riley attractive? Not really. Daniel's face was nicer, but it wouldn't have got him any modeling jobs. All I knew was that something about the way Riley moved, the way he held his head, the way he used his hands stirred something in me. And I felt the same pull, for essentially the same reasons, from Daniel. What called to me from each of them was something visceral, something about the way they made me feel. And I couldn't have said what that was.

I pulled out my phone. "You wanted Nina's contact info."

He pulled out his phone. "Shoot it to me." He called out his phone number, waited for my send, and put the phone away. Didn't even look at the information. "Thanks, Nathan." He seemed so casual, so unconcerned, that I wondered if he'd changed his mind about Nina.

We sipped our coffee for maybe fifteen seconds that seemed like forever to me. I felt awkward; I don't think Daniel did.

I felt the need to talk. It was Friday, so although the question was mundane and trite, I asked, "Doing anything special this weekend?"

His eyes followed the coffee cup as he set it down onto its saucer, and then he looked at me. "Anytime I can, I go to the mountains. I have to work this Sunday, because someone else can't, but tonight I'm headed north. Think I'll do the Carter Dome to Mount Hight loop tomorrow. Hight all by itself doesn't give you a four-thousand notch because of the way the summit is configured, but it has the best views. And when you add Carter Dome to it, it counts. It's still early enough in the season that I can stay tonight at the Carter Notch Hut and get fed."

"That's a couple of hours' drive, isn't it?"

"Do you know the loop?"

"What? No, I've never been hiking. But my brother's crazy for mountains. I'm from Concord, so I have a vague idea where you're going."

He sat back in his chair, a friendly scowl on his face. "You've never been hiking? How could your brother let you get away with that?"

I shrugged; there was no good answer, because he'd offered to take me but had never pressured me. Instead, apropos of not much, I said, "I do Nordic skiing, though. Bushwhacking is kind of a specialty of mine."

Daniel laughed. "Well, shit, I love that, too. Only I prefer to think of it as trailblazing. Maybe this winter we could take a weekend and go." He stood. "Meanwhile, I've gotta head out if I want to make the hut before it gets too dark."

And just like that, our chat was over. Seemed unlikely he'd be calling Nina this weekend.

When I got back to the dorm, El Speed was huddled in front of his laptop while Gordon stared at the screen from over his shoulder. They barely heard me come in.

To the room in general, I asked, "What's so fascinating?"

Gordon glanced briefly toward me and back to the screen. "TM." I don't think he meant to sound cryptic, but he did.

I had no idea what that meant. "TM? What's that?"

"Come look." He held his arm out toward me, fingers flexing as though to pull me over.

Standing behind El Speed, huddled close to Gordon, I felt a wave of warm sensuality that seemed to have nothing to do with sex. It made me a little dizzy, in a good way. I tried to concentrate on the laptop screen.

The larger type was easy enough to read: Learn Transcendental Meditation.

"Meditation?" I tried to keep my tone neutral; meditation had always seemed kind of like hocus pocus to me.

Without glancing away from the screen, El Speed corrected me. "*Transcendental* meditation."

"Ah," I said, unable to remain completely noncritical. "That makes all the difference."

El Speed turned around in his chair. "Actually, it does. They give you something to focus your mind on so you can get into a meditative state quickly and stay there more easily."

"Meditative state...." I echoed.

"Don't be so quick to dismiss it," he said. "It gives you more energy, lessens your stress, makes concentrating on things like classwork easier, improves your sleep quality—all kinds of stuff. Might not hurt you to get a little meditative, y'know."

"Me? What's wrong with my concentration?"

"Well, I want to try it. Can't hurt, and it might help."

Gordon seemed excited by the idea. "I have this friend who's doing it, and he swears by it. Says it's made a huge difference in his life!"

I chuckled. "Would this be the same friend who wants you to join Nu Lambda Psi?"

By way of answer, Gordon blushed. But El Speed came to his rescue. "You can learn from anyone, Nathan. Anyway, we're thinking of going to the free intro session in Portsmouth on Sunday. I'm not going home this weekend. D'you wanna join us?"

"Oh, I don't think so. You can tell me all about it when you get back. Now, I have to get ready for my next class."

El Speed turned back to the laptop. "I told you to drop that one. Who wants a class on Friday afternoons?"

I ignored him, grabbed my backpack, and headed over to Paul Creative Arts Center. I was enjoying this class—Introduction to Acting—and I didn't mind that it was on Friday afternoons. What was I going to do with my Fridays otherwise? It wasn't like I went home every weekend like so many students here did. Besides, I was hoping the class would help me feel a little freer to follow Neil's advice and be who I am.

INTERLUDE II

Life with Neil: "Little Man"

I don't remember much about my parents, or about the day they died. Of course, I was all of a whole year old at the time, so I can be forgiven. I do know the details, however, or as many of them as I need to know.

Neil had been born five years ahead of me, and Nina had come along four years after him. Then me. Then, a year later, the accident.

Gram had stayed with "the kids" at home one hot, July day so Gramps could drive his rebuilt 1953 Studebaker Champion—bright red, white roof, whitewall tires—to Moultonborough for an antique car show. Mom and Dad had been with him, traveling up Route 106, when a farm truck almost as old as the Studebaker and hauling machine parts had lost its brakes coming off the Daniel Webster Highway outside of Laconia. There were no survivors.

Gram had been Mom's mother, so when the three of us kids were growing up, there was always explaining to do for why our last name was Bartlett but hers was Dixon. The confusion was exacerbated by the fact that Gram had been only nineteen when she'd had Mom, and Mom had married young, so Gram looked young enough—barely, but still—to be our mother.

Neil had been all of six when our folks had died, but he'd been called "little man" for long enough that he took his seniority seriously. He could have been obnoxious about it, and certainly there were times he was. But mostly he was responsible beyond his years. Nina chafed at Neil's assumed role more than I did, maybe because she had at least some memory of our actual father. I didn't.

In many ways, Neil was "Dad" to me. The first incident in my memory that demonstrates this relationship was when I was starting first grade. Like, the first day of class. Gram had taken each of us out individually (and only now as I remember this does it occur to me how much patience that must have taken) to get school supplies. Looking back, I suspect that it was because each of us had different needs, and also because Nina was a bit of a little terror, which must have required a lot of Gram's attention in public.

Anyway, the only item I remember purchasing for school was my Spiderman lunchbox. And I remember that because I *loved* Spiderman. (Sidebar: I kind of like spiders in general.) I made a big deal out of it the night before school started, and Nina (about to start second grade, obviously much older and wiser than me) teased me about caring so much about some dorky fictional character. Neil didn't step in to help me, even though I was ready to punch my sister.

Neil was going into sixth grade, at middle school, but Gram had made him promise to walk me home (less than half a mile) the first week. So at the end of my first day, I was waiting obediently in front of the school for Neil, even though Nina had already dashed off with a couple of her friends, when a kid named Billy (later to be dubbed Billy the Bully by classmates) decided I looked like easy pickings. He was a year older than me, and bigger overall than most kids his age.

He saw me standing alone, and with the one teacher who was stationed outside busy with some other kid's questions about what bus to take, my vulnerability was more than Billy could resist.

"Waiting for Mommy, are you, little baby?" His voice oozed ridicule.

I tried to ignore him, but he stepped up to me, mere inches away, towering over me (or so it felt like), blotting out the very sky.

"Go away," I told him, my voice shaking despite my

efforts to appear unaffected.

"Go away? Ha ha! Oh, I'll go away. And I'll take that stupid lunchbox with me."

He grabbed at it, but I clenched my fingers around the handle as hard as possible, teeth gritted with the effort. Billy placed one hand on my shoulder and wrenched harder with the other, and after a bit of a struggle he managed to pull my prize away from me.

He turned, laughing, and ran. Right into Neil.

Neil grabbed his arm. "Where do you think you're going?"

Billy tried to wrestle away from Neil's grasp, but my lunchbox, as well as his own pack, hampered him.

With his free hand, Neil grabbed one of Billy's ears hard enough to hold on but not hard enough to make him cry out or stop struggling.

"Drop the lunchbox."

"Make me!"

And then there was a wail from Billy as Neil pulled and twisted Billy's ear with one hand, and with the other he twisted hard on the arm holding my lunchbox.

Neil's voice didn't get any louder. "Drop it."

Billy, evidently realizing he'd met his match, tried to throw Spiderman onto the pavement, but Neil's grip on his arm prevented that. It hit the ground, but it wasn't damaged.

Neil let go of Billy's ear, and as he let go of the arm he pushed Billy just enough to send him on his way. As I rushed to pick up my lunchbox, I saw Neil wave to someone behind me, and when I looked I saw the teacher as she reappeared from the other side of a bus. She'd missed the whole thing.

"Hello, Neil!" she called, smiling. "Enjoying middle school?"

"Yes, ma'am!" he called back. Then, to me, "Ready to go?" It was as though nothing had happened.

As for Billy, he went on to torment other kids, but he mostly left me alone.

CHAPTER THREE

The acting instructor, Lena Harrison, had us do all kinds of things I'd never done before. It was kind of like in the beginning of that movie, *Tootsie*, where Dustin Hoffman's character does things like have two people face each other, and one of them has to imitate what the other is doing—scowl, stick their tongues out, laugh, cry, whatever. Or maybe one person has to stand alone in front of everyone else while shaking their body and whining. Lena said if we could bring ourselves to do stuff like this, we'd be able to open up enough to be creative with our personal presentation in the world, on and off stage.

That Friday, Lena had us do something we'd never done before. And she started with me and another guy in the class, a sophomore. Alden Armstrong was tall, his limbs slender but with nicely-defined muscle. He had sandy hair that was a little long, grey-blue eyes, and a wry grin. I'd had a few conversations with him and liked him, at least as well as I could without knowing him better. I was glad Lena had teamed us for this exercise.

Each of us had to choose a fear without revealing it until the other person figured out what it was, and we had to do this by acting out an impromptu scene. We couldn't just ask, "What are you afraid of?" It didn't have to be a fear we had ourselves, as long as it was reasonable that someone would have the fear. At first I thought about clowns, because I do think they're kind of creepy even if I'm not actually afraid of them. But somehow I wanted it to be deeper. So I changed my idea to dyslexia.

Lena had me guess Alden's fear first, and we stood in front of the class.

"You look terrified," I opened. "Are you all right?"

He shuddered and pulled a chair away from the wall. Before he sat on it, he checked underneath, running his fingers under the seat edges. I pulled a chair forward so I could sit, too, but he jumped up, obviously scared.

"Wait!" His voice was a little panicky. "You need to be sure."

"Sure of what?"

"Look underneath! Check every crevice!" As I did so, he went on. "It's the worst, man. I mean, once it happens, it's kind of all over. Good luck recovering!"

I pretended to check as he had done, wondering what I was supposed to be looking for. Finally he calmed down a little, and we both sat.

I glanced at our audience, a.k.a. the rest of the class, and made a face like, *Is this guy whacked, or what?* Their quiet laughter was gratifying. To Alden, I said, "What is it you can't recover from? What does that mean?"

"It's forever! You're never free again."

"Free from what?"

"You don't know?" He was sounding frantic again. I shook my head, and he nearly shrieked, "Then you're probably already a goner! You haven't been checking anything, have you? Oh, my God!" And he slapped a palm against his forehead.

He gave me a horrified look, stood, moved his chair farther away from me, and sat down again. He didn't speak. He was so convincing, I was getting a little creeped out about this nameless mystery.

"So if I already have this thing, you could get it by just being too close to me?"

"Well, yeah. I mean, it's not contagious like the plague or something, but—well, they hide, and they spread, and they infest, and they hide some more."

"What do they do to you?"

"You aren't itchy anyplace?"

"I—no, I don't think so."

"You don't think so? Don't you know? Lift up the leg of your jeans. Go on."

I did, and he stood and came a little closer to me, obviously not wanting to be in the path of whatever danger I might be in.

"No itchiness?" he asked. "No red spots?" I shook my head. "Lift your shirt."

"What?"

"Seriously. Let's see your stomach."

We had the full attention of everyone in the room. I pulled up my shirt, wishing I had a six-pack of muscle there, and Alden and I both stared at my skin.

He reached out a finger, coming close but not quite touching me. "What's that?"

"A mole, or something."

"Does it itch?"

"No."

"Are you sure? You haven't stayed in a motel or anything recently, have you?"

And it hit me. Should have hit me sooner, really, but now I knew. It was bedbugs. That was his fear. But I decided to play along a little further. "What about you?"

"Me?"

"Yeah, you! Lift *your* shirt. Let's see *your* stomach."

"Well...."

"Go on! What if you're the one who's infested and not me?"

Either he was embarrassed to expose his midriff, or he was a pretty good actor. Scratch that; he was a really good actor. Slowly, his eyes on me and then on his belly and then me and then his belly again, he lifted his shirt.

"Ha!" I shouted, pointing at nothing as though it were a gaping wound. "You've got bedbugs!"

Applause and laughter called an end to the scene, and Alden and I bowed in acknowledgement and then switched roles. I felt a little heady, even a little bold, from the fun of guessing Alden's fear and from my class members' laughter.

I sat on my chair, and Alden sat on his. I looked down at my hands, clasping and unclasping them in my lap, and said nothing.

"Something's weighing on you." Alden's voice was gentle, even tender. "You're not—you're not afraid of me. There's no reason you would be."

I gave a tiny shrug. "Maybe a little."

"But it's not me. Not really."

That was a little close to asking the question we couldn't ask, but Lena didn't interrupt. I shook my head, eyes still downcast, and said nothing.

"You're—are you ashamed of something?"

My head snapped up, a kind of sad anger coursing through me. Alden saw it on my face. He said, "No, not shame, exactly. Or, not a shame you agree should be shame."

I shook myself visibly, spread my fingers across my thighs, and held my head up defiantly. I stared at a spot over his head. "I'm not ashamed."

"But do others think you should be?"

I felt my nostrils flare, and my breathing grew shallow and rapid. "I don't care."

Alden and I regarded each other silently for a few seconds, and in that tiny slice of time some deep recognition flashed between us. He said, "I think you do."

I shook my head rapidly three or four times, back and forth, deliberately communicating that I was in some kind of denial.

We sat there, him looking at me with a concern that seemed genuine, me not quite looking at him.

Alden leaned forward and slowly, sweetly even, laid a hand on my knee. "It's okay, Nathan. I'm left-handed, too."

As if on cue, we stood and embraced. He'd guessed wrong. And he'd guessed right. So had I. We were both gay.

After class, I was packing things up to head back to my dorm when I realized Alden was standing close to me.

"Hey," he said. "Wanna grab a coffee or something?"

"Sure." Why not? Better than going back to hear more about TM.

He stopped at the door, smiled, and held his arm out for me to go first.

From behind me, I heard, "How about Zeke's?"

"Great."

We headed in the direction of the library, where the café was. I was trying to act cool, and like this was the most natural thing in the world—two guys going for a snack together. But was I right? Was he gay? And had he really sensed the same from me?

Yes. He had. The giveaway was that he'd known it was *necessary* to guess the wrong fear. And when I'd accepted it, I'd confirmed his true guess. So it wasn't just two guys going for a coffee. It was two *gay* guys going for a coffee. This was epic. My head felt like it might explode. As we walked, I calmed myself by repeating a phrase like a mantra they might assign people in TM: *College is where you're supposed to do this. College is where you're supposed to do this. College is where....*

Alden ordered a cookie and a caramel macchiato and then shrugged at me. "Sweet tooth. What can I say." I got a muffin and a café Americano as Alden poured a prodigious amount of sugar into his cup, and then we nabbed a table.

Again, Alden took the initiative. "I'm not left-handed. Are you?"

We locked eyes. "No." I grinned. "And I'm not dyslexic, either."

He nodded. "Ah. So that was the real thing you didn't want to be ashamed about. Neither am I. But we have something else in common. Something much more important." It wasn't quite a question, but I nodded. His voice quiet but confident, he asked, "Are you out?"

"Uh, well, a little. Some people know. What about you?"

He chuckled and waved a hand in the air. "Oh, I think anyone who knows me at all knows I'm gay. I came out in high school. Got the scars to prove it."

His voice was so dry, so matter-of-fact, that I couldn't tell if these were literal scars. He took a huge bite of his cookie, so I had to wait after I said, "Scars?"

When he could speak without sending crumbs across the table, he said, "You saw my belly. Nothing much. But you should see my back."

"Your back."

"I had the temerity to ask a boy to junior prom. I'd though he was gay and closeted. Turns out he wasn't gay at all. I see that, now, but at the time I think I was just so determined to like him, and to get him to like me, that it blinded me. Anyway, he and a couple of his best buds took me for a walk in the woods. Forced march, more like. They stripped down a poplar branch, then stripped me down, and—well, like I said, you should see my back."

Something stopped me from asking what happened to his tormentors; maybe it was the casual way he described this event. It was like he wanted to believe—or maybe wanted me to believe, or both—that it hadn't been especially important. I'd have been willing to bet, though, that he'd been hospitalized.

Instead, I asked, "In our little acting scenario back there, would you have shown your back if I'd asked?"

"No." Simple. Calm. Final. And he polished off his cookie.

"Is there a reason you decided to tell me about it now?"

He lifted his coffee cup and nearly emptied it before setting it down. His hand held onto the cup. His elbow was on the table, which made him lean just a little toward me rather naturally. His eyes found mine and stayed there, and he tilted his head and half smiled. "Yes. Because I'm hoping you'd be willing to see my back. And maybe the rest of me."

He waited. He waited while my brain bounced around my head. What was he saying? What did he want?

"Are you—are you asking me out?"

Alden chuckled. "Nothing so prosaic. I like you, Nathan, but I'm not talking about romance. I'm asking if you'd like to fuck."

Without meaning to, I sat back in my chair, away from the table, away from Alden, away from this suggestion that he seemed to think was so casual. I was barely able to resist glancing around to see if anyone else had heard him despite the low tone he'd used.

Did I sputter? Yes, I'm sure I did. Alden's expression didn't change. And then he laughed, quietly, gently, not making fun of me at all. "All right, I can tell that took you too much by surprise. No worries. But think about it. Have you fucked a guy before?"

All I could do was shake my head.

He nodded. "Sorry, then; I thought you probably had. Your fear? In class?" He shrugged. "It seemed like you were drawing on a real fear, but that it was somewhere behind you. I didn't realize how gutsy you are, to let the whole class see that fear when it's still so close to you. I hope—I really hope you're not offended."

I shifted in my chair, relaxing a little, moving closer to the table again. Closer to Alden. "I guess I'm flattered, really. I mean, no one's ever asked me to be with them before. Guy or girl." Hell, I'd never even kissed anyone. What a child....

He downed the last of his coffee. "So let's just be friends, then. Can you do that, even though I might have creeped you out?"

"Yeah. No problem."

"Good. 'Cause I like you even more now, and I'd hate to think I'd ruined that." He grinned, and I grinned, and we got up to leave. He went into the library, and I went back to my dorm.

Correction. I danced back to my dorm. An older, experienced, attractive guy had asked me to have sex with him! I felt ecstatic. I felt terrified. I felt *alive*.

It had never occurred to me that it might happen like that. I mean, I'd never exactly had a clear picture of what it might be like to approach sex with someone, but I'd expected it to have something to do with feeling the way I'd felt about Riley Shapiro, or how I felt about Daniel Cooke. And then I laughed out loud, right in the middle of the walkway that goes through the trees between where I'd been and where I was going. I stood still, and I laughed. A couple of girls, walking together toward me, gave me an odd look as they passed, but I didn't care.

I laughed because Alden had just told me how much trouble he'd gotten into by approaching a guy who'd turned out to be straight. Straight, like Riley. Straight, like Daniel. It was almost like Alden had known and was trying to point out the dangers that lie in that direction. And then, on the heels of that warning, he'd propositioned me. He'd given me an alternative to lusting after straight guys. And I'd turned him down.

Another correction. I hadn't actually turned him down. I'd just been too shocked to get a sense of how I felt about it.

And now that I was over that shock, how did I feel about it?

I stood at the edge of the walkway and stared sightlessly at the back of the student union building. In the dusky light, I drew an imaginary picture of Alden's face, his greyblue eyes, his half-smile, and I admired his I'm-okay-with-life-and-things-roll-off-my-mutilated-back attitude. Maybe he had that attitude because he knew that whatever was going on here, at college, nothing was going to be as bad as what had happened to him before.

Wait… wasn't there a tree called an alden? Or, no, it was alder. Close, though. At least they hadn't beaten him with that.

As I turned back onto the path, my mantra sounded again in my head: *College is where you're supposed to do this.*

Despite the unspoken lesson from Alden about not fixating on straight guys, I fixated on Daniel all weekend. I imagined him hiking up Mount Hight (odd name for a mountain, anyway, and why was it spelled like that?), after scaling Carter Dome.

In my mind, his pack was black, with straps and edging and zippers of different colors—yellow, blue, green, red, orange, purple—a veritable rainbow. By the time I realized he'd never have anything like that, it was too late to change my image.

In my daydreams, he wore khaki hiking shorts that allowed my eyes to linger on the swelling of his thigh muscles as he planted his boot-shod feet on one rock after another. Neil often said that many White Mountain trails were little more than dried-up stream beds lined with rocks of various sizes, and that with every step you ran the risk of having the rocks wobble and shift beneath your weight. I'd asked him once why he kept hiking there if it was so bad, and he'd said, "Are you kidding? I accept the challenge. It's fun!"

For a special treat on Sunday while El Speed was in Portsmouth learning how to sit quietly with his eyes closed as he silently repeated some secret mantra and hoped to fall between the sleeping elephants of the thoughts that otherwise bounced around his head (okay, yeah, I looked it up just to see what it was about), I pictured what Daniel would look like hiking ahead of me. His ass was at my eye level, the fabric of his shorts strained over the muscles as they clenched and released, and I must have come three times before we reached the summit of whatever imaginary mountain we were on.

And then I felt guilty. Because, I mean, how would he feel if he knew some gay kid was lusting after him, beating off to the sight of his ass, wishing it had been him instead of

Alden who'd propositioned me? And all the while maybe he's lusting after my sister?

So I tried to come again while picturing Alden instead, but either I had nothing left to give or Alden just wasn't doing it for me.

Christ! Why does this have to be so complicated?

Just before El Speed and Gordon were due back, someone knocked on the door, and I opened it to possibly the most gorgeous guy I'd ever seen. His nearly black hair was just long enough to curl over his forehead and behind his ears, his eyes were the kind of intense blue that almost had to be tinted contacts, he had one of those chiseled jaws that should never be covered by facial hair, and his smile nearly made me melt onto the floor.

He leaned one arm casually on the door frame and spoke in a voice that was low and quiet, the kind of voice that makes you believe you have his complete attention. "Hey. Gordon here?"

"Gordon.... Oh, um, yeah. I mean, no, not at the moment."

"He told me to meet him here. I'm a little early. Mind if I come in?" His arm dropped as he moved forward. I hadn't agreed he could come in, but he seemed to know I wasn't likely I'd stop him.

Even as I told myself the guy was probably a total asshole, and that in any event he was way too aware of his looks, I couldn't think of a damn thing to say.

He held his right hand out. "Byron Moreno."

Shaking hands is automatic enough that I didn't need to recover my composure before offering my name.

Byron chatted easily as he walked in and sat in my desk chair. "I'm over at Nu Lambda Psi. You pledging anyplace?"

"Not really my scene."

"You never know till you try! And you have only a

little time left before we send out bids."

"Are you giving Gordon a bid?"

His smile was cryptic. "I'm not at liberty to divulge that information."

The look he gave me was part tease, part come-hither. Even so, there was something about him that left me feeling he wasn't gay. I strained my memory: had anyone actually said he was? El Speed had said something about a frat brother who "wanted" Gordon, and for sure I'd picked up that Gordon wanted that someone back, but was the guy just leading Gordon on? And was that the same guy who was sitting in my desk chair right now, or was there someone else involved?

I wanted to know if he was the meditator. "Are you the brother who does TM?"

"That's me."

"'Cause that's where Gordon is now. At some intro session. With my roommate."

"I know. But not you. You didn't go."

"Not me."

"Why not?"

I could feel my eyes narrow of their own accord. "Sounds like your mission in life is getting people to join things. Or join in on things."

"Busted!" His laugh was loud, and I was aware of a kind of push-pull going on inside me. Byron was appealing in so many ways, but something about him set my teeth on edge. And it wasn't just that he seemed to know how charming he was.

Before I could zero in on what bothered me, I heard muffled voices approaching from the hall, and then El Speed and Gordon appeared.

Gordon froze and stopped talking mid-sentence when he saw Byron. Then, "Oh! You're here already. I guess we are a little late."

Byron smiled. "Nope. I got here early to meet your friend's roommate," and he turned toward me, "the one you said was so attractive."

Everyone looked at me. I'm sure I blushed. I'd never thought of myself as attractive, and I didn't imagine El Speed or Gordon had, either. But then I noticed that Gordon's face had more flush than usual. He looked down at the floor and shrank, just a little. Talk about being busted....

Byron stood and said, "Gordon and I have a dinner to go to."

Gordon nodded and they were gone about as quickly as Gordon had arrived.

"I don't like him." El Speed's voice was nearly a growl.

"Yeah, but do you know why not?" My own opinion was still puzzling me.

"Well, shit, yeah. He's leading Gordon down some garden path. He doesn't give a fuck about the kid. Just wants to prove a point."

"And that point is—?

"Byron says he rhymes with his name. Bi. And he doesn't think there are enough non-straight guys in his house. Whether he's right or not, I don't care. I just don't want to see Gordon get hurt, and I know things are headed that way."

So he was bi. Was that what had made me leery? But why would it? I nodded like I agreed with El Speed, and in principle, I did. But it was the sort of hurt we all had to live through. And maybe Gordon would take a valuable lesson from whatever pain he got. At least his back wouldn't be scarred for life.

El Speed wasn't done. "Gordon's helplessly in lust. I don't get it. Bi Byron looks like his face was put together by a focus group of teenage girls."

After I stopped laughing, he added, "Plus, like I said before, that house has a bad rep. Hazing."

"Yeah, you've said. What do you think they'll make Gordon do?"

"No idea. And if I have my way, they won't make him do anything."

INTERLUDE III

Life with Neil: Beautiful Notes

When I started high school, I was told to pick a couple of elective courses. Over the summer, Neil had told me about a couple of electives he'd chosen and how they'd helped him decide that he wanted to study the environment. He'd taken biology or zoology and I forget what else. But I was having trouble deciding on my choices.

"How did you decide?" I asked. "I don't want to take any more science courses than I have to."

"I took those because I had some idea what I wanted to do."

"Yeah, well I don't know what I want to do."

"Well—then, what do you *love* to do?"

Good question. What did I love to do? I hadn't a clue.

Neil said, "You love to sing. What about music?"

That was it. I decided on chorus, and I added private singing lessons, and I loved both. I sang first tenor in chorus, but my voice teacher had other ideas. I'll never forget my very first lesson with her.

She sat on a bench at the keyboard of her upright piano, and I stood facing her, the funny pattern of wooden slats and the mechanics of the piano's back all I could see of the instrument. Her fingers played an easy, running scale down from one note, and I sang the notes. She started on a slightly higher note for the next scale, and I repeated the run. At some point she began to play little runs up and down, and down and up, and I repeated everything. Then she started to play them higher, and higher, and higher. I don't have perfect pitch, but I realized she was taking me into a range I'd never sung in before, and I stopped.

"What are you doing?" I asked, puzzled.

She grinned as she played scales up and down, higher and higher. "I'm just trying to figure out how long it will be before you can sing the Queen of the Night aria from Mozart's *The Magic Flute*."

I'd just started to figure out that I might be gay, and at first I thought she was ridiculing me. "I don't ever want to do that!"

She laughed quietly. "I know. And you never will. Not really. But, Nathan, I wonder if you know that you're not really a tenor."

"Then—what?"

"You have the makings of a fine countertenor. Your range goes well into that of a second soprano. And if you're willing, I can help you find out if that's right for you, and you can decide if you want to work in that range."

She lifted her hands off the keyboard and sat still, her eyes on my face.

I was confused. "I don't know what that means."

So she told me. And the more she talked about it, the more the idea appealed to me. We decided I'd keep singing tenor in chorus, because the quality of my countertenor voice might not fit in well with all the girls singing alto there (not to mention what might happen to me if I "sang like a girl"), but in my lessons she would take me as far into countertenor territory as I wanted to go.

I went pretty far. I practiced and practiced at home until Nina told me I was driving her crazy. When Neil was home from college for Thanksgiving, I practiced even more, and Nina couldn't stop herself from making some snide comment.

Neil stopped her cold. "Nina, shut the hell up. You don't hear anyone making fun of your interest in fashion design, do you?"

"But what Nathan is doing is stupid. It's a waste of time."

"And what you're doing is superficial and vain. It's a waste of time *and* money."

"It is not!"

"And why not? Because you love it? You've never criticized me for playing acoustic guitar. Wanna try it and see how that goes over?"

She pouted at him, but she never said another word about my singing, good or bad.

But there was another problem: the end of semester recital, when all my teacher's privates students would sing one song for an audience of family and friends. For sure I didn't sing that Mozart aria. But I sang a gorgeous song by Fauré, "Les Roses d'Ispahan," arranged for alto voice.

No one from school was required to attend, other than my teacher's other students, but I was worried. These students would, I was sure, tell everyone else that I sang like a girl. But, dammit, I loved that song. I loved singing that song. I *wanted* to sing that song. And on some level I wanted other people to hear it.

So I practiced. And I sang that song at the recital, in my countertenor voice, and everyone there was bowled over. Maybe that was partly because they weren't expecting it, but that wasn't the whole reason. Neil was there, home from college for winter break. He and Jeremy had plans to go ice climbing, but he made Jeremy wait until after the recital.

After the singing was over, there was a reception. I heard a couple of snide comments more *about* me than *to* me at the snacks table. I was sure I'd sung better than any of them had, but I didn't know what to do. Should I say something? Should I ignore them?

Neil had just stepped up beside me when one of those kids said to the other, "Fucking fag."

Neil looked right at him and laughed. Both kids looked up at him, and loud enough for half the room to hear, he said, "Jealous isn't a good color on you."

I never forgot that statement. It worked on so many

levels. I claimed it as mine, and although I didn't have very many occasions to use it, it was my friend for the rest of high school.

Nina might not have been my biggest fan, but Gram was, and Neil wasn't far behind her. One day, the anniversary of the crash that had killed Gram's husband, daughter, and son-in-law, she dug out a large, paperback music book, a collection of songs from many years ago. Its cover had swirls of vivid blue on it and large, red lettering. She opened it to a song she said my grandfather had sung to her many times: "What Are You Doing The Rest Of Your Life." She remembered the tune, so between her humming and my limited sight-reading ability I managed to work on it enough to sing it for her. It made her cry, and I thought she wouldn't want to hear it again. But she hugged me.

"Oh, Nathan, you have such a wonderful voice. And there's something about it that makes that song come alive."

I handed her back the collection, and she started to take it. But then, "Tell you what. Why don't you look through here and see if there are other songs you'd enjoy."

Not wanting to make her any sadder, I nodded and carried it upstairs, thinking that at some point I'd put it back. But it kept appearing under piles of other stuff on my desk, its blue swirls seeming to beckon me, to tempt me to open it. So I did.

One snowy Sunday afternoon, I was in my room, the songbook open to "The Pajama Game." I was humming along, learning the melody to see if it was a song I wanted to learn. I was so engrossed I didn't hear Neil come in after a day of skiing. It wasn't until I heard my door creak open that I knew he'd been listening.

"Those are Gram's songs, aren't they?"

I might have asked how he knew, but I didn't. "Yeah."

He stood there, his hand still on the doorknob, his face full of a kind of admiration. He said, "You sound really good, Nathan. I think your voice is great for that kind of song. Why don't I learn the chords of a few of them on my guitar?"

I stared at the inside of my door for some time after he'd shut it on his way out into the hall. That was the start of my love of torch songs.

CHAPTER FOUR

Monday when I showed up for work, Eva found me right away. "I'm putting you on the serving line today, Nathan. We're short a person, and I thought you'd like a change."

A change. Well, no, I wouldn't. Not only did I not want to have to stand there in a white smock with a flimsy net on my head, but also I wanted to be where Daniel was. I wanted to ask him about his hiking weekend.

I almost suggested to Eva that perhaps someone else would love an opportunity to serve, as it were, but the way she was smiling at me told me she saw this as some kind of privilege. Somehow I knew it would insult her if I resisted.

The job was at least as bad as I'd expected, especially when people I knew came through the line. When anyone looked twice at me or acknowledge that they knew me, I grinned and shrugged. If there was an opening, I said, "Lost a dare." I wanted to give the impression that I didn't care who saw me. But I did.

At the end of the shift, when those of us on the serving line had finished our after-meal tasks, I went to stand in the doorway to the dishroom. It was obvious that my absence had meant more work; they were still in the early stages of clean-up. I grabbed an apron and a pair of gloves.

I'd finished swabbing down the conveyer belt on the back wall when I heard Daniel's voice.

"Nathan! Wow, man, you don't have to do this. But we really appreciate it."

I grinned at him over my shoulder as I continued to scrub. "I'm not really that fond of the serving line. Eva seemed to think she was doing me a favor."

He laughed. "I'm sure she did. Anyway, thanks. Oh,

and I was going to ask someone else, but given your volunteering efforts here, any interest in working dinner shift tonight?"

Dinner shift. Did Daniel work breakfast? If so, it was unlikely he also worked dinner. But even if he weren't here, it would give me more brownie points with him. "Sure. What time?"

"Anytime between four thirty and five. See you then."

Excellent.

I was there by four forty-five. Daniel was at the Hobart, showing another guy how to load and unload the giant dishwasher.

"Nathan! Great. I can teach both of you at once. This is Bud. He's starting on nights this week."

Bud grinned and held up his hands, sheathed in thick, black gloves that went half-way up his arms. "Can't shake; sorry."

Daniel talked him through getting the square, plastic trays full of dishes or glasses or flatware onto and then off of the conveyer belt that went through the Hobart. The trays were nearly two feet per side, and depending on what was in them they could weigh maybe fifty pounds each, and because they were both heavy and awkward there were a few tricks to lifting and carrying them safely. Mostly, though, it was just brute strength.

Daniel had me try it next, and it was both easier and harder than it looked: easier, because it meant working directly with Daniel; harder, because although fifty pounds doesn't seem very heavy, setting the trays correctly into the Hobart was a challenge.

I worked at the Hobart for a while that evening, and my reward was more of Daniel's time. After clean-up, he waved at me across the dishroom.

"I'll be done here in about five minutes. There's still

one coffee machine working; they'll clean that before breakfast tomorrow. Wanna grab some dessert?"

Did I! I couldn't imagine why he'd suggested this, and I didn't care. If it had more to do with Nina than with me, I'd take what I could get.

There were a few diners lingering over their own desserts and coffees when we sat across from each other at a small table. We'd each taken a piece of chocolate cake, and before touching mine with my fork I opened the conversation.

"Hope the hike was great."

"Oh, yeah. I mean, the weather was perfect, and the views were fucking amazing. I'd expected to see lots of people on the trail, but there weren't many at all." He stabbed at his cake. "There was this one guy, at the hut, who made me wonder what I'll be like in forty years."

He described this man who was probably in his sixties—long, gray hair, mostly woolen clothing with holes from moths or tree branches or both, boots beaten and scarred by countless rocks and boulders and tree roots, and a frame pack that was nearly falling apart.

"This guy had the most dented-up white kerosene stove I've ever seen. But it was still working, and damn if that guy wasn't still hiking. He said he'd done all the four-thousand footers, some of them more than once, and I believed him. He's hiked in the Rockies, and in Austria. He also said he'd done the whole Appalachian Trail when he was fifty, as a kind of pilgrimage."

"Sounds like his whole life is a kind of pilgrimage."

Daniel's hand, around his coffee mug, stopped halfway to his mouth. "Damn. I wish I'd thought of that. I wish I'd said that to him. Because you're right. Anyway, I asked what he did for a living, and he just smiled at me as though I'd said something amusing that didn't require a response."

"My brother could end up like that guy, he's that fond of the trail."

"And yet he never managed to get you onto it." I was

surprised and flattered that Daniel had remembered. "By the way, Nina's coming with me to a movie Saturday. So, thanks for acting as intermediary."

Maybe that's why he'd suggested coffee? "Don't thank me until you know her a little better." I grinned to cut through any negativity.

"Really? Do tell."

I shrugged. "Just pulling your leg, really. She's a girl who knows her own mind and doesn't scruple to share what's on it."

"'Doesn't scruple.' You, uh, majoring in literature, maybe?"

"No. Psych." I had considered English lit, actually; if I hadn't believed it to be a pipe dream, I'd love to have become a writer. "Lit was tempting. So was music."

Daniel's mouth dropped open. "You are a man of many talents, it would seem. Do you play an instrument?"

"Not really. I love singing. But I don't have the voice for a performance major, and I'm not interested in teaching. Or composing."

"So you want to be a psychologist?" I couldn't tell whether his voice hid amusement.

"Right now, I just want the undergrad degree. Then we'll see." Each of us took a forkful of cake, and as Daniel picked up his mug I asked, "How about you? You're not here as a student, is that right? But you were?"

"Right, but not here. I was at New Jersey Institute of Tech. Industrial Design." He draped an arm over the back of his chair. "I was thinking it would be nice if we built structures as much in harmony with the environment as possible."

"Did you graduate?"

"Finished two years. But," and he shook his fist in a jesting way toward what I presumed was north, "those goddamned mountains kept calling to me. So I'm trying to figure out if I should transfer here. I'm really tempted by the Wildlife and Conservation Biology program."

He shifted in his chair and leaned his arms on the table, an intense look in his eyes. "I can just see myself trekking through the Rockies in search of cougars to collar and track. Following a wolf pack through Yellowstone sounds like heaven. Can you imagine it?"

It could have been Neil talking. I nearly shivered with joy at this connection Daniel was making with me. My inner voice said, *Down, boy.* My audible voice said, "Well, for sure you sound lots more excited about wildlife than industry, environmentally friendly or not."

He sat back. "Yeah. I do, don't I? Well, I've given myself until the end of December to figure it out. Because if I decide to transfer, I'll need to get that process started."

I polished off my cake and was draining my coffee mug when he turned the conversation my way. "You sing, eh? What do you sing?"

"Tenor. High tenor. And—well, really, I'm a counter-tenor. Or so my high school voice teacher tells me."

He laughed. "I meant what kind of music. What's a countertenor, anyway?"

"It's the highest range of male singing voice. Some say you're a countertenor if you sing in that range in natural voice and a male alto if you go into falsetto for the upper registers. I don't know which I'd be yet, but I do like to sing in falsetto."

"Really." His tone gave nothing away; was he confused? Creeped out? Fascinated? "So, what music do you like to sing the most?"

If I told him the truth—that I love torch songs—would he assume I'm gay? And did it matter whether he knew that or not? I mean, why was I hiding myself from him? I could never have Daniel in any way that I dreamed about, so it was a question of friendship. If I lost a friend because I'm gay, what kind of a friend would that have been anyway? So why not just tell him the whole story?

Oh. Right. Nina. She doesn't know. And she and Daniel might become an item.

I shrugged and sat back to gain a few nanoseconds. I waved a hand in the air. "Oh, lots of stuff. I like singing French art songs, like Fauré. And some Mozart is fun. But then I'll sing along with folk singers on recordings."

"Are you still taking voice lessons?"

"Not right now. My voice is nothing great. It's just fun to sing."

"Well, heck, you know what a countertenor is. Might even be one. I'd love to hear you sing sometime."

I shrugged again. I didn't see that happening.

Nina wasn't as impressed with Daniel as I was. I put this down to a flaw in her character.

She texted me on Sunday afternoon. *Went out with your friend. He wants to live in the wilderness. I want to live in NYC.*

You never know, I texted back. *And it's not like he asked you to marry him.*

I guess. And he is eye candy.

So you'd see him again?

Probably. But, evidently, not enthusiastically.

Early Tuesday evening I was trying to study in my room, but the distraction of El Speed texting on and off with Ellie was too much. They were planning something for his dad that evidently involved some complicated logistics. I gave up and went to the library and wasn't doing much better in terms of focusing when I got a text of my own: Alden.

Hey got time to grab an ice cream?

I didn't even have to think. *Absolutely*

Candy Bar ten minutes. Hoof it they close at 9

I was there in eight. It was kind of warm that evening, so I waited outside. I didn't know which direction Alden would come from, so I did my best to look like I was just hanging out. It was dark, but the street was well lit, and when I saw a tall, blond guy approaching, hands in his jacket pockets, loping along like he didn't have a care in the world, I knew it was Alden.

He saw me and raised his chin.

"Hey," he said when he was close enough.

"Nice night for ice cream," I said, and we went inside. So far, pretty casual.

Alden ordered the most disgusting concoction of chocolate ice cream with banana slices, strawberry slices, cashews, chocolate sauce, and whipped cream in a monster-sized cup, to go. I stared at him in disbelief, and he shrugged.

"I have weird tastes."

I got mundane pistachio ice cream, double scoop, and we headed back outside. Alden led us along Main Street to Madbury Road and took a left onto it. We didn't say much right away; too busy eating. I, of course, was also too busy getting off on the fact that Alden had invited me to meet him. I wasn't quite ready to say I wanted to accept his invitation to fuck, but just hanging out with another gay guy who seemed totally comfortable in his skin felt like Paradise. I don't think I tasted one mouthful of my ice cream.

Finally he'd consumed enough of his mess, which wasn't all of it, and as we passed a trash bin he tossed his cup into it. I'd emptied my ice cream so quickly I was on the verge of an ice cream headache, and I threw my cup in as well.

"You didn't finish," I said. "Was it as disgusting as it looked?"

"Nah. Just had enough."

We walked back in the general direction of Main Street for maybe half a minute, and then he said, "Thanks for meeting me. I didn't feel like going right back to my apartment."

"Where is it?"

"Half-way to Dover."

"You must have a car, then. The campus buses don't run very late."

A few steps later he said, "My dad owns a dealership. Specialty cars."

"Nearby?"

He laughed. "No. I guess that was a bit of a disconnect, wasn't it? I'm from St. Louis."

"Missouri?"

"The same."

"But—you didn't drive here from Missouri, did you?"

He laughed. "No. I bought a car here. I'm not making much sense, am I? It's just that the mention of a car sent me back to last summer when I got to drive a Lamborghini Spyder around the sales lot, and my mind went all gushy." He sighed. "One day that car will be mine."

I glanced at him, trying to decide whether he was hoping to impress me, or bragging, or maybe just being his natural self.

He changed the subject. "Where are you from?"

"Concord. Not quite an hour west and a little north of here. And I do not have a car."

"You're in a dorm?"

"Hunter."

"Roommate, or a single?"

So I told him about El Speed, and Ellie, and Gordon, and TM, and Byron. He laughed out loud at how El Speed got the name. "Your sister sounds like a hoot. Is she your only sibling?"

So I told him about Neil. I told him about my parents dying and about how Gram had raised us. Then I told even more about Neil, and a little about Nina. And more about Neil, including that he hiked a lot, and I'd never gone.

When I finally paused for breath at the corner of Garrison and Main, Alden came to a stop and faced me. "You really love your brother." It wasn't a question. "He sounds like a terrific guy."

"He is."

"Does he know about you?"

I knew exactly what he meant. "He's one of only three people who do. You're one. And El Speed."

Alden turned along Main. "I'm parked in B lot, off Mill Road, kind of past your dorm."

"Great." We were quiet for a bit as we walked, and then I asked, "Do you have a roommate?"

"Nope."

He offered nothing more, so I asked another question. "Brothers? Sisters? I can't be the only one gabbing about my family."

He chuckled. "I loved hearing about your family. Mine is pretty boring. No siblings. My mom is a surgeon."

"A surgeon? Really?"

"Yup. Cardiac."

We chatted about acting class after that, nothing else really personal, and as we approached Quad Way we grew quiet again.

Alden came to a stop. "So I guess I'll see you Friday, in class."

"For sure."

He smiled and turned toward the parking lot, and I felt an irrational disappointment. I watched him walk away, asking myself if I had expected anything else. Had I thought he'd hold my hand? Hug me? Kiss me? No; I had not. And yet....

Friday afternoon's class was much less interesting than the previous week; no skits, no acting. I had arrived early, and when Alden got there he didn't sit near me even though there was an empty seat. I glanced his way several times, but it never seemed as though he'd looked my way. But as the class ended, somehow he was behind me as I headed for the door.

"Going home this weekend, Nathan?"

I shook my head. "There's really no good way to get from here to Concord except by car. I have a friend with a car who goes home some weekends, and I ride with him sometimes, but not this weekend."

"K. Well, see you next Friday." He grinned and walked away.

I watched him, feeling rather like I had on Tuesday night when he'd left me and headed to the parking lot.

El Speed was already gone, on his way to Maine, when I got back to the dorm. I had dinner with a couple of guys from down the hall, and then I headed back to my room, thinking I should do some classwork but knowing I was more likely to kill time browsing on the internet.

I spent a lot of time browsing the internet that weekend, though I also got a lot of classwork done. By Sunday evening I was bored and feeling a little lonely, despite having a feeling of accomplishment.

I was at my desk, browsing photos of various guys' packages (as it were), expecting El Speed's return at any time, when I got a text. Alden.

Planning to watch the lunar eclipse?

I stared at my phone. Was this the same guy who had left me standing awkwardly outside of acting class Friday afternoon?

Somehow this felt different from being asked out for a casual ice cream. But was it?

There was only one way to find out.

Forgot it was happening. You?

I'm on campus. Wanna watch it?

Sure why not

Alden was waiting for me outside Hunter. It was a clear night, but chillier than Tuesday. He had a leather jacket that was much nicer than the one I wore, which was a hand-me-down from Neil, but I figured that kind of thing wouldn't matter to Alden. After all, it must have been obvious from what I'd told him Tuesday that I didn't come from money, even if he did.

He didn't say Hi or Hey or anything else by way of greeting. Instead he looked up at the moon. "It's already underway. The eclipse. The initial penumbral phase is nearly over."

I looked at the moon and then at him. "Penumbral?"

"In a total eclipse, which this will be, it's the very beginning. The earth has just started to cast its shadow onto the moon."

He started walking toward a car I'd never seen around the dorm before, a white BMW. Two doors. A convertible. With the top down. And, unbelievably to me, he opened the driver's side door and got in. I shook off my initial shock; after all, this guy came from money.

We headed west out of town, past the athletic fields. My leather jacket had been enough for the weather until the wind started whipping heat away from me.

I looked at Alden, who appeared so comfortable behind the wheel of this beautiful vehicle that it almost seemed like they had merged somehow. "Aren't you cold?"

I watched the side of his face as a faint smile sent the corner of his mouth up a little. "Yup. I like it. Sometimes, anyway. Sometimes I do this when it's cold to feel the real world. To feel alive." He let two or three beats go by. "And I want to feel very alive tonight."

He didn't look at me, just held onto that smile that now felt both cryptic and insinuating.

Alden turned onto a side road that went past some open fields and pulled over to the right at one end of what appeared to be a long, narrow body of water. He repositioned the car in a couple of deft moves, and I wondered what he was doing until he killed the engine. Directly in front of us was the moon, now with a tiny sliver of its glow replaced by Earth's shadow.

We got out of the car and I followed Alden as he moved closer to the water.

He said, "The position isn't quite right to see the whole eclipse reflected in the reservoir, but I thought it would be fun to see what does reflect."

We gazed at the doomed moon, the moon that would be devoured by Earth. Alden stood beside me, hands in his jacket pockets. "The full part of the eclipse won't begin until eleven minutes past ten. It will last just over an hour."

It wasn't quite nine-thirty now; how long would we be out, I wondered. "So it will all be over then?"

"Oh, no. No, just the full part of the eclipse. We won't see the entire moon again until midnight."

Midnight. Would I feel any warmer by midnight?

We stood in silence for a couple of minutes. Then, maybe because neither of us knew what else to say, he started talking about the stars.

"Are you a star follower? Constellations, that kind of thing?"

The life in his voice gave him away; he was definitely a star follower. How to answer his question and say *No* without sounding uninterested.... "I don't know very much."

"I won't bore you with a lecture. But there are a few things worth pointing out. We won't be able to see a lot of stars with this amount of moonlight. But they'll be easier to see during the full part of the eclipse."

He put a hand on my shoulder and leaned down a little toward me, his eyes on the sky. He pointed to a spot overhead. "I can barely see one of my favorites. Cygnus. The Swan. If you don't know what to look for, you probably won't see it now."

I tried to follow as he pointed, naming the stars around some shape only he could see. I had to admit, "Nope; you're right. I see night sky and some white dots. That's it."

He chuckled. "I'll point it out again when the sky is

darker. And over here," he pointed in a different direction, "is one for us."

"Us?"

"Pavo. The Peacock." He raised an eyebrow at my puzzled expression. "Peacock? Gay men? No?"

I laughed. Of course! Duh. I almost told him I was kind of new at this gay thing, but I didn't want to seem like a babe in the proverbial woods.

"My favorite, though," and he changed direction again, "is Aquila. The Eagle." He let his arm fall.

Was it my imagination, or was his face closer to mine with each new constellation?

"Why that one?"

His cheek was so close to mine I could feel his warmth.

"Most people tend to think 'male' when they think of eagles. But Greek mythology says Eagle represents the goddess Aphrodite. Goddess of love and pleasure. At the same time, Eagle is said to carry thunderbolts for Zeus. So Eagle possesses very powerful characteristics, both masculine and feminine."

He pulled away from me just a little, and we faced each other. We were almost close enough to kiss. Would that happen? Did I want it to happen? What would I do if it happened? What *should* I do?

So close. But no; he broke the tension with a smile and stood beside me again, facing the moon. Once more, we were silent. A car approached along the road, its headlights creating odd shadows on the trees around us as the car progressed, making the very familiar seem very unfamiliar. Maybe this was far from the first time I'd seen headlights on greenery, but tonight it brought on a feeling that was part eerie, part exciting. And definitely unfamiliar.

We watched the gradual disappearance of the moon, another familiar object that light was changing into something new. With the moon, of course, it was light disappearing, rather increasing with the man-made lights from a car. But that difference did not cancel out my feelings of anticipation. Anticipation of what, though? There was the question of whether Alden would make a move, because I would not, largely because I knew what I'd kind of like to do but not how to do it. But the bigger question was how I'd feel about it—not just how I'd feel about Alden, but how I'd feel about having something I'd only dreamed about come to life. That "something" would be passion between men, passion that was good and right and decent and maybe even loving.

Every few minutes Alden made some comment that involved words like penumbra and umbra. I shifted my feet to try and keep them warm, careful not to make Alden think I was moving away from him, while he explained that the yellowy-silvery moon would take on a reddish color as the eclipse progressed.

Time passed slowly, and it passed quickly. I was in some kind of alternate reality where anything might happen, or nothing might happen, and I had to wait it out to know which it would be.

The moon got redder as Earth's shadow progressed, and finally it was totally red. It gave off an odd light that made things around us look eerie. Alden checked his watch a few times and eventually declared it official. "Here we are. Full mid-eclipse. From this point on, Earth will begin to release Moon from her shadow."

"Regurgitation."

His head turned toward me. "What?"

I shrugged. "Well, the moon got eaten. But now it's being regurgitated."

Alden laughed. "Of course. So you're a student of mythology?"

I blinked. What was he talking about? "Not that I know of."

He laughed harder. Good; I hoped that meant he didn't mind that I wasn't a student of anything, really.

"Actually, Nathan, you might be one without knowing

it. There are many cultures that developed myths to explain eclipses, and lots of them involve some animal—a dragon, a snake, or something else—devouring the moon, and then regurgitating it back onto the dark blanket of sky."

With the moon's light interrupted by Earth, I couldn't see Alden's face very well, but I could tell how close it was to mine. Now? Would something happen now?

But no. Alden turned rather suddenly back to the eclipse. "This is as dark as it's going to get. Can you see Cygnus now?" He pointed and mentioned a few details to help me.

I wasn't convinced I was even looking in the right place, but I said, "Oh, yeah."

He turned again, this time toward the Peacock. "Pavo," he said, and then added what he could to help me see it. I thought I almost maybe saw that one.

"And there's my Aquila. That powerful mingler of male and female, of all things called life."

I saw it. I saw it almost before he gave me any hints. I nodded.

And then I shivered. It was part from pleasure and part from cold.

"Hey." Alden turned toward me. "It's fucking freezing out here. Come on."

I thought he'd put the top up on the car, but instead he fetched a blanket from the trunk. He opened the passenger door and folded the back of the seat forward.

"Let's sit in here for a while." He gestured for me to climb into the back while he unfolded the blanket. It was plaid, I think in various blues and greens—hard to tell in the dark—with a cream background. As he laid it across my lap I felt the thick softness of the wool.

Alden climbed in beside me, and we arranged the blanket so it covered both of us, chins to ankles. The seats weren't actual bucket seats back here, but there was a raised, hard surface in the middle, probably with cup holders or something like that in it, so we weren't hip-to-hip.

Several minutes went by as we sat under the blanket and watched the sky, and then a tiny whitish shape like the slice of a trimmed nail appeared on the side of the red moon, the opposite side from where the digestion had begun. We were now into the regurgitation phase.

I surprised myself by speaking. "What kind of animal is eating this one, do you think?"

"Oh, a dragon. Definitely. Dragons have massive power in many areas. They can manipulate the weather—hurricanes, typhoons, floods—so it's a dragon up there. A red dragon, I think, and when the moon is fully red it's shining from the inside of the dragon's belly. But the moon is too cold for the dragon, so he spits it out again."

Alden's arm reached behind me while he spoke in a movement so subtle I was barely aware of it until he caressed the outside of my ear with a finger.

Should I look at him? Should I pretend this isn't happening? Should I reach a hand over and touch his thigh? Should I pull away?

God! What should I do?

"Nathan?" He waited until I turned my head toward him. "If you're not okay with this, just say the word. But I'm going to kiss you."

I said nothing.

Alden was tall enough, and slender enough, that he was able to lean across that barrier in the car seat. And, okay, yeah, I helped him by leaning in his direction. And then I closed my eyes.

The earth didn't move. The sky didn't erupt in fireworks. But after the initial tender touches of his soft lips on mine, he took my lower lip between his teeth. Tingling shivers went up the back of my thighs as I felt Alden run his tongue slowly back and forth on my captive lip.

At first I couldn't breathe. And then I managed a gasping, shaking in-breath, and it was at that point that Alden placed a hand behind my neck and began to explore the inside of my mouth with his tongue.

He didn't do anything quickly. In fact, the way he kissed was very much like the way he moved generally, with a slow, easy grace that implied confidence and calm. Alden pulled away slowly, and I opened my eyes on the first man who ever kissed me. The first *person* who ever kissed me.

I wasn't sitting on the seat of Alden's car any longer. I was flying, up in the sky with that moon. And like the moon, I had undergone a magical transformation. Alden, the dragon, had taken me into his mouth and released me again, and the experience had changed me—into what, I didn't yet know. But one thing I did know was that it was a good change. A necessary change. An enthralling, terrifying, confusing change. And in a very important way, I would never be the same.

Alden watched me for a few seconds. And then I said, "Please, sir. Can I have some more?"

My memory of what happened in the back of Alden's car as the light around us changed with the reappearance of the silvery moon is as clear as it is vague. The clear part is that I wanted this experience, and I wanted it with Alden. The vague part is that although we ended up massaging each other's crotches—a move he began and one that I reciprocated only with an amount of courage that equaled my arousal—no clothes were shed (blanket not-withstanding). But there was a lot of kissing, and a lot of caressing, and a lot of harsh breathing before Alden pulled away and threw himself back against his own side of the car seat.

He allowed himself a few more loud exhales. "I've wanted to do that since I saw you."

"Saw me? Not since our skit in acting class?"

"Oh, make no mistake. I wanted this even more after that. But I've wanted you since I laid eyes on you."

The offer he'd made over coffee and cookies came back to me, and I prompted, "You wanted *me*. But not romance."

I watched his face so long that I could almost track the recovering moon's reflected progress on it. Then, "We'll see."

When I got back to the dorm, El Speed was deep into classwork.

"Hey," I said quietly as I shut the door behind me. I didn't know if he'd be up for a chat, or if he'd neglected his classwork in favor of quality time with Ellie all weekend and was desperate to catch up. I was hoping for the latter; I was still flying from my make-out session with Alden, and I was sure I must look like a blushing day-old bride who'd been a virgin until the pervious night.

He turned in his chair as I moved into the room. "Hey. Um, didn't someone you know climb Carter Dome recently?"

Time warp. "Yeah. That would be my dishroom boss, Daniel. He did both Carter Dome and Mount Hight, just last weekend. Why?"

"Did he tell you about it?"

I sat down on the side of my bed, at least partially out of his sightline, hoping to hide enough of my face so that he wouldn't ask me why I was glowing. I recited much of what Daniel had told me about the hike, about adding Carter Dome to Hight to get credit for four thousand feet, about the mountain nomad Daniel had met, about how much Daniel loved hiking, how he could imagine himself chasing wolves around Yellowstone—I went on and on. I knew I was babbling to some extent, but it was a cover-up so El Speed wouldn't pick up on what was really on my mind.

As I spoke, El Speed got up and came to sit on his own bed, facing me, and when I finally shut up, he said "Okay. Well, I was really wondering whether he'd talked about the trail itself. Like, how experienced a hiker would need to be do to it safely. A friend of Ellie's is thinking about doing it."

"Oh. No idea. But Daniel has done a lot of hiking. Like

my brother."

El Speed regarded me with an odd look on his face. "This guy, Daniel. Does he like you, too?"

My ears felt hot. "What do you mean?"

"Well, it's obvious you like him, the way you talk about him. I just wondered if you two might get together." His smile was somewhere between *I'd like to think of you in a good relationship* and *I don't really know how to talk about this*.

"Okay, look, he's straight. He's going out with my sister."

El Speed stood and went back to his desk. "Got it."

But I wasn't convinced that he was convinced.

INTERLUDE IV

Life with Neil: Through the Haze

By the time Neil was a junior at UNH, he and Jeremy had climbed several of New Hampshire's four-thousand-foot mountains. They'd started with Mount Liberty as soon as one of them was old enough to drive, and they'd kept going. These mountains are scattered across the upper mid-section of the state, so the boys grew very familiar with the routes, the trailheads, and the terrain. They encountered other four-thousand-foot hikers who'd done summits Neil and Jeremy hadn't yet climbed, people with information about those as-yet-unknown peaks, and their knowledge of the area grew until it seemed encyclopedic to me.

This familiarity did not, however, breed either contempt or lead Neil to take the mountains for granted. He was an adventurous climber, but one who planned and executed cautiously. Jeremy was, if anything, even more careful.

Sometime in late October, when Neil was home for the weekend (I think it was Nina's birthday), he told us about a frat hazing gone terribly wrong. I don't think he would have mentioned it, but Gram had seen the story in the news and wanted to know everything.

Nina had gone out with her friends for the evening, and Gram, Neil, and I had hot cocoa and sat by a small but respectable fire in the living room fireplace.

"Neil," Gram opened, her voice carrying a hint of concern.

He looked at her from under his eyebrows. "Gram."

"Tell me about that young man who died on Mount

Washington. Help me understand how that happened."

Neil's deep sigh was almost silent, and his eyes closed. He opened them on the fire, not looking at Gram or me. He didn't ask why she wanted to know, he didn't try and pass it off as unimportant, he didn't do anything to try and avoid the truth I came to understand later: Mountains can kill you. And they don't care.

"It was a frat hazing. They drove a bunch of pledges up the auto road and made them find their own way down."

"Down the auto road?"

"That was one option. Takes a while, almost three hours. Over seven miles. But it's the safest way. They'd be met at the Glen House."

He set down his mug. "Or if they wanted, they could descend along the Lion Head Trail to Tuckerman's Ravine and end up at the Joe Dodge Lodge, south of the Glen house on Route 16. They'd wait there until everyone coming down the auto road had arrived at Glen House, and then they'd get picked up."

He paused, and Gram urged him on. "That sounds incredibly dangerous. Very ill-advised."

"Everyone going down the road was okay, barely. The weather was great when they dropped the pledges off. But you know the mountains."

I repeated something I'd heard Neil say many times. "They make their own weather."

"And that's just what this one did. Washington's notorious, actually, and just past noon a snowstorm hit the summit. I heard that some of the guys walking down the road slipped and fell on ice, and one of them had to get picked up because of a fractured kneecap. Cell phone coverage is spotty, and he waited nearly four hours. One of the pledges waited with him and got rejected from the frat because he insisted on riding down with the injured guy rather than walking alone in the dark."

Wood sparking and crackling in the fireplace was the

only sound for a couple of minutes. I polished off my cocoa and set the mug down as quietly as possible.

"And the one who died?" Gram prodded.

"Yeah. Well, there were four guys who decided to do the trail rather than the road. Three of them made it down. Again, barely, and one of them wandered in alone long after dark, not in great shape."

He drained his mug and set it down. "They'd gotten separated in the storm. One of them got totally disoriented and walked right off a cliff somewhere. The guys didn't know where they were, blinded as they were by the snow, so they weren't sure exactly where he'd fallen from. Rescue crews recovered his body, so they have some idea, but they can't be sure where he went over."

As I listened, images formed in my head. Gram had always refused to drive up Mount Washington, despite my pestering to go many times when I was a kid, and she'd clicked her tongue at any "idiots" who plastered one of those "This Car Climbed Mt. Washington" stickers on their bumpers.

"I guess those stickers are a good thing," she was famous for saying. "I'll know to avoid buying any used car that has one on it."

The auto road is much longer than any of the hiking trails, because cars can't climb at too steep an angle, and a steep descent wears out the brakes and/or the transmission. From the base on Route 16, the road meanders along the tops of ridges, through forested areas, emerging above tree line, and finally ends up in a parking lot at the top, with unbelievable views from six thousand, two hundred and eighty-nine feet above sea level.

Of course, those views disappear in a nanosecond whenever cloud cover settles over the peak, or in heavy rain, or in heavy snow, and any of that can occur at almost any time. One August Neil and Jeremy had climbed up Mt. Madison through the Great Gulf Wilderness and camped near the summit overnight. In the morning, they'd had to knock a few inches of snow off their tent before they could pack it.

I'd been outdoors in enough snowstorms to know that yes, it is entirely possible to become disoriented with enough of the white stuff blowing around you, especially if everything else around you looks pretty much the same in every direction anyway, as would have been the case on the Lion Head Trail. In my mind, as Neil told of the ill-fated frat pledge, I twirled and twisted, looking for the trail, looking for a landmark, looking for the direction I'd come from and unable to discern even that. And then, the cliff. Oh, yes; it was definitely possible to die there.

I'd gone up to bed later with these images still fresh in my mind, and I couldn't sleep. After tossing and turning for maybe half an hour, I got up and stood outside Neil's door, listening for any sounds. Hearing nothing, I opened the door and went in. I sat on the edge of Neil's bed.

I couldn't see much. His face was buried into the pillow, his back toward me, the nearly-black hair—a color Nina and I shared with him—easily visible on the lighter pillowcase. For maybe ten minutes I listened to the sound of his slow breathing, and then I placed a hand on his shoulder, and he jerked awake.

"What? What is it?"

"Promise me you won't ever do that."

He rolled toward me. "Do what, Nathan?"

"Die on a mountain."

I heard him exhale. "Don't be silly. Go back to bed." And he turned away from me again.

CHAPTER FIVE

I didn't hear from Alden again, and I didn't contact him, for the rest of that week. In acting class, he arrived a couple of minutes late and sat near the door. When the class ended, he was the first one out. He never even nodded in my direction.

Was this what he'd meant by "We'll see," and was he waiting to see if he still wanted me after giving our eclipse "date" a little space? Was he giving me space to do the same thing? And how much space did I want?

More than that, was this feeling of being pissed at him reasonable?

To help myself figure out what I wanted, I consciously brought Daniel to mind. Yeah, he was straight, but I'd had the hots for him. Did I still? Or had the prospect of having my interest or passion or whatever returned in kind, from someone who was actually gay, knocked Daniel out of my wet dreams?

In the dishroom, all this past week I'd been aware of where Daniel was most of the time, as usual. And when I'd looked at him, I'd still felt drawn to him physically; his body was perfect, more perfect for me than Alden's tall frame, and he was—as Nina had put it—eye candy. But what about the man himself? Was he still as appealing as he had been?

I still felt compelled by his sense of humor, by the depth of his gaze, and by that sense that he held some secret knowledge. And, about those dreams—I'd had one that had stood out, where my partner had the body of Daniel, but I'd called him Alden.

In short, I was confused.

The next Tuesday, Alden texted me in the morning to ask if I had any time open in the afternoon for a walk. I replied immediately, we set the time at four thirty, and all my insecurities floated to the surface. "For a walk." Was that anything like when one person says, *We need to talk*, and you know they're breaking up with you? What did I want him to say? Did I want romance, or did I just want a roll in the hay now and then? Did I want roll in the hay with Alden at all?

I was pretty sure I did.

But did I want it to be romantic? Did I even want to be involved with a guy who made out with me one day and totally ignored me a few days later? And was he going to brush me off this afternoon anyway, so none of the time I spent wondering what I wanted would have been anything but wasted?

All afternoon I tried to block worries about what a walk with Alden would mean. I didn't do very well.

He was waiting in front of Hunter when I got there after classes, sitting on one of the granite benches in the middle of the quad, eyes closed and face held up to catch the late-day sun. I stood in front of him, casting a shadow, and he opened his eyes.

"Hey, Nathan." His voice was soft, with nothing in the tone that made think he had bad news.

"Let me dump a few things. I'll be right down." I could have asked him to come in with me, but without knowing what he wanted it felt awkward.

As we headed up Quad Way toward Academy Way, I asked if he had a destination in mind.

"Let's see if we can spot the swans on Mill Pond. I don't think they've gone anywhere yet for the winter."

We made our way down quiet streets past houses where some faculty members probably lived, and I couldn't stop myself from keeping what felt like awkward silence at bay.

Without knowing what Alden might want to talk about, what this meeting was for, I babbled on about Gordon and Bi Byron and how nervous El Speed and Ellie were about the frat.

When we got to the pond we walked over a grassy area and stopped as close as we could reasonably get to the water. Alden glanced around the pond, evidently looking for swans.

"Do you see them?" he asked.

"Not yet. Maybe they'll swim by."

Alden bent over and pulled up a handful of grass, which he proceeded to pick apart in his slow, graceful way.

I decided to offer the opening bid. "Are you uncomfortable being in acting class with me?"

He dropped the grass bits, and I heard him exhale. It did not give me a good feeling.

"That's not—I mean, no. That's not what's going on."

"What *is* going on, Alden?"

"We, um...." He hesitated, exhaled audibly, and then continued. "Okay, so that first time we had coffee and I came on to you, all I was thinking was that we'd be great fuck buddies."

"Fuck buddies?"

"Yeah. Like, friends with benefits. Nothing romantic, just good friends who sometimes have sex."

He thrust his hands into his jacket pockets. I thought he might turn to face me, but he didn't. "I've been trying to tell myself that's all we're going to be, if even that. And I've tried to convince myself that my interest in you is completely casual. But it isn't working."

Now he turned toward me. "And I need to ask how you feel. I think you enjoyed—we'll call it the eclipse—as much as I did. Nothing about that night would necessarily mean more than something casual. Except that I can't stop thinking about you."

I watched his face, wondering if he'd say more. But no; he was waiting for me. What did I want to say? Well... how *did* I feel? And it hit me that the truth is in dreams. Maybe it wasn't Alden's body that attracted me. Maybe it was Alden.

"And I can't stop dreaming about you." I added a wry smile, and one of my eyebrows might have lifted upward just a little.

He blinked, maybe unsure how to take that, and then he threw back his head and laughed.

I remember not being entirely aware of any part of my body, except that my head felt very light. What had I just said? Had I just told someone that he aroused me in a way that I couldn't control? What would he say? What would happen next?

Holy shit! What had I done?

I looked out across the pond, eyes focused on nothing, and then back at Alden. "What happens now?"

He leaned over and kissed me. It was a sweet, tender kiss. "Let's see where this thing goes."

The Monday after Columbus Day weekend, El Speed got back to the dorm around ten at night and thundered into our room.

"That little twerp!" He dropped his pack with the last word. "I'd call him worse, but I blame that asshat more than I blame him."

I'd been kind of waiting for El Speed to get back. Alden had texted me over the weekend and invited me to his place for dinner the next night, Tuesday. I anticipated another make-out session, at the very least. And although I hadn't yet decided whether I was ready for more, I wanted to tell El Speed about it so he'd stop thinking I was lusting after Daniel. But after his opening, I had to ask, "That 'asshat' being one Byron Moreno?"

"Obviously. Do you know what they've made the pledges do?"

"Obviously not. But I'd be surprised if it turned out not

to be something reprehensible."

He went on as though I hadn't spoken. "Ellie told me. They started with stuff I might have predicted. Like, you know, mooning from the front yard for maybe three minutes at a time. Big deal. Then they progressed to the scatological, and Gordon and another pledge had to carry buckets of shit, contributed by the brothers, into College Woods. Then they had to record each other, first painting each other's faces with it and then burying the rest."

"You mean—actual shit?"

"I mean actual shit."

"That's gross."

"And illegal."

"The face painting might be. But when Neil's hiking, he buries his."

"Whatever. Anyway, that's just the beginning. There's another fun thing they did to some of the pledges. They haven't done it to Gordon, but they could have. They might. It's called 'Naked and Afraid.' Like the TV show. They take a blindfolded pledge into College Woods at night, strip him completely, tie him loosely to a tree, and leave him there."

I decided against asking El Speed if he knew whether the pledges had created makeshift loin cloths out of leaves and grass, once they worked their way free, so they could get back without being arrested. I said nothing.

El Speed had more to say. "Ever heard of the 'Elephant Walk?'"

"Not in this context."

"The pledges had to traipse around the frat house in a line, going from room to room, upstairs and down, naked, holding the dick of the guy behind them and keeping their thumb up the ass of the guy in front."

I think my mouth dropped open. Against my will, horrible though I knew that hazing was, the image made me very aware of my dick. And my ass. My voice sounded hoarse. "They did that?"

"They did that. But that's not the worst of it."

He stood there staring at me, his breathing audible, his eyes beginning to bulge. I didn't want to hear any more, but I knew that didn't matter. So I asked, "Then what is? The worst of it, I mean."

He sat down hard on his desk chair and leaned his elbows on his knees. His voice low but sharply focused, he said, "They forced the pledges to lace each other's beer with drugs. If a pledge got caught doing it, he was the one who had to drink the beer. And the drug? The *drug*...." His eyes closed for a few seconds, and he swallowed hard. "That was fentanyl."

"They—they can't do that!"

"They bloody well did, though. Gordon's had at least three of them."

"Why didn't someone report them?"

El Speed rubbed his hands into his scalp. "No one there would dare, I guess. So it's up to me. I don't know how Gordon will react, but I have to do it. I'll start by going to campus police. Ellie agrees with me."

"I'll go with you." I don't know where that came from, but it came out fast. I had no real skin in this game, other than being El Speed's roommate. I wasn't invested in Gordon at all. And yet I wanted it to stop. I wanted all of it to stop.

El Speed stood and looked at me with an expression I couldn't quite read. I stood, too, and immediately his arms wrapped around me. It was brief, but it was real.

He sat down again. "Like I said, I'll start with campus police. But I'm not above going to the Durham police if I have to. So what's your schedule tomorrow?"

We landed on three forty-five as the best time for us to go together.

I think "ironic" is the right word for the fact that the University Police, as they refer to themselves, are housed in a building on the edge of College Woods, where so much hazing takes place.

I arrived a few minutes early to the place El Speed had said to meet so we could walk over together. As I waited inside the Academic Way entrance to Paul Creative Arts Center, I was grateful for the shelter in the pouring rain. Folded black umbrella dripping onto the floor at my feet, I stared out at the beaded curtain of water and hoped El Speed would take a suggestion I planned to make.

I had done some research about hazing in general since last night and had discovered that UNH has a hotline for reporting hazing incidents anonymously. I was thinking it would be a better idea to do that. But I also didn't want El Speed to think I was a moral coward. I didn't want to think of myself that way, either, but....

El Speed appeared suddenly on the wetter side of the glass doors, his navy blue anorak looking soaked through. As he stepped inside he threw the hood backwards, sending a spray of water behind him.

"Ready?" He looked ready, rain or no, anonymity or no.

"Before we go, I wanted to let you know what I found out." I stepped closer to the wall out of the way of anyone brave enough to venture outside or wet enough to hurry in through the doors.

"K. Shoot."

"I looked up hazing on the campus website, and—no surprise—it's illegal, not just by campus policies, but also by state law. It's also illegal not to report it if you know it's going on. Not sure how they figure out who should be arrested for that, but that's not our problem. We're reporting. But here's the thing. There's a hotline. Anonymous. Specifically for hazing."

"I don't care about being anonymous. And anyway, if they're willing for us to be anonymous on the phone, we could probably remain just as anonymous if we go in person. I mean, the police aren't exactly going to throw their arms around our shoulders and post selfies on Instagram."

"But we wouldn't have to walk all the way out there through the rain."

"Look, Nathan, if you don't want to do this—"

"No, I do. Really. It's just—"

"See, I want to look them in the eye—the police—when I tell them. I want to be sure they believe me, and I want them to tell me what they plan to do about it. A phone call won't do it for me."

Fine. I nodded and gestured with my umbrella toward the door. "Got it. Let's go, then."

It was a long walk in pouring rain, nearly ten minutes. It felt longer, because we weren't saying much of anything. El Speed kept his hands in his pockets and his head bent forward. I peered sideways at him a few times from under my black bat-skin, hoping his pack was waterproof, contemplating how effectively umbrellas keep people separated. But my pack was definitely not waterproof.

That meant ten minutes to think. What was I doing, anyway? What was my objective, or my mission? What was my intended end state? World peace, of course, but beyond that, what?

I truly did think hazing was a seriously fucked-up thing to do. I did want it to stop. I knew a little something about the horrific opioid epidemic, and I wanted *that* to stop. Last night I was committed to helping stop all of it. That was still true today, even on this uncomfortable walk. But with only the sounds of rain splatting onto my umbrella, with only my own thoughts to focus on, I had to admit that the reason I was here beside El Speed had to do mostly with him.

I wanted El Speed to respect me.

This realization came when we were maybe two-thirds of the way to our destination. It swirled around in my head for a few minutes. And then, just before we stepped onto the wooden ramp leading up to the door of a massive, ugly, single-story building that looked as much like an industrial barn as anything else, a motivation that I had tried to hide from myself finally escaped from under the other reasons. It was El Speed, sure. But even more? It was Neil. It was Neil's respect I craved. And this was kind of a crazy way to get that.

I shook my umbrella off outside the door, more to fling away uncomfortable thoughts than to avoid bringing rain water into the building. El Speed just walked inside, apparently oblivious to his water-logged condition, or at least uncaring.

The African American woman behind the desk looked very comfortable in her police uniform, which was such a dark blue as to be nearly black. I tried to pay attention to what El Speed was saying, but I missed much of it, still focused on the disconnect between my brother and Gordon's hazing experiences. I couldn't even imagine describing them to Neil.

I followed El Speed and the officer into a small room where a table and a few folding chairs occupied most of the space. She motioned for us to sit and then left. El Speed shed his dripping jacket while I gazed at the back of the room where a few more folded chairs leaned their faces against the wall doing "time out" for unknown offenses. El Speed seemed alert but not nervous. I was nervous.

After maybe three minutes, a huge white guy in a dark navy blue campus police uniform came into the room. As El Speed and I stood, I could tell the cop was about six-one—as tall as El Speed—but he was maybe twice as wide, more dense than fat. He had one of those haircuts that leaves about a half inch of hair sticking up on the top of his head, with the sides buzzed almost to nothing. There was so little hair I had to look at his eyebrows to see that they were light brown and extrapolate from there. I guessed his age at around thirty.

He shook El Speed's hand, then mine, and then perched his massive self, somehow, on the seat of that folding chair. "Officer Kemper. And you?"

El Speed hesitated just for a second and then said, "Joe Anonymous."

Kemper exhaled audibly and then asked, "What can I do for you?"

I was glad El Speed took the lead; Officer Kemper's voice was so different from his appearance that it stunned me momentarily. It was high and a little nasal and didn't suit him at all.

I listened as El Speed explained why we were there. He mentioned Nu Lambda Psi but didn't name any people. He described the hazing he'd told me about the night before. I watched Kemper's face as El Speed got to the elephant walk, expecting a response—disgust? horror? righteous indignation? But his face was as unreadable as concrete. He didn't react to the fentanyl, either.

The first thing he said was, "You could have called the hotline. Did you know that?"

El Speed sat a little straighter in his chair. "I wanted to know who I was dealing with. I want to make sure you believe me, and I want to know what you'll do about it."

They locked eyes over the table. Kemper broke the moment. "First, we take this kind of thing very seriously. And I'm not saying this is the case with you, but some people make false accusations. Maybe they didn't get in the frat, and they want revenge. Something like that."

"Rest easy. I've never pledged anywhere. Don't care to. But the reason I know what's going on is a guy who's like a kid brother to my girlfriend is pledging there, and this is what he says is happening."

"Did he get in?"

"He got a bid, yes."

"His name?"

"Jack Anonymous."

Kemper shook his head. "That's for you, not for them."

"He didn't instigate this. He didn't buy the drugs. He didn't make anyone do anything. He's a victim, here."

Kemper made some motion that would have looked like sitting back in the chair if there had been less of him.

"Why I ask, it's kind of hard to investigate without an 'in' of some sort. A place to start."

He waited, I waited, but El Speed was silent. Kemper gave in. "Okay, then, here's where we are. We can't raid the place on your say-so. We have other ways of investigating situations like this, but it's better if I don't describe them. In case, you know, you're talking with your friend 'Jack' and you let something slip."

He stood, and we stood. He extended his hand to shake again. "Thanks for coming in. I assure you we'll look into this."

I decided it was time to step up. "How will we know?"

Kemper looked at me as though he'd forgotten I was there. "Pardon?"

"When you've done your investigation, and let's say you find something, will you contact us or something?"

His grin was barely on the friendly side of patronizing. "This is anonymous, right? Can't have it both ways. How would we let you know?"

"We could come back, if you tell us when. A week? Two?"

Kemper shook his head. "If there are developments, your friend will probably tell you about them."

I could tell El Speed wasn't thrilled, but rather than say anything else he pulled his soaked nylon anorak back over himself.

As we moved toward the door, Kemper lifted a pamphlet from a plastic rack on the wall beside him and handed it to El Speed. "In case your friend gets enough fentanyl to need help. Signs to look for, where to call, that's in here."

Back outside in the deluge, I popped my umbrella, El Speed flipped his hood over his head, and we stood there, staring into the wall of water as though each waiting to see if the other would speak. Neither of us did, so we trudged back, a longer walk this time because Hunter Hall was a good four minutes on the other side of Paul Arts from here.

As soon as we were in the room, El Speed started stripping. I tried not to watch. He said, "Gotta take a shower."

"I might, too. Warm and wet is better than cold and wet."

He shook his head as he wrapped a towel around his midriff. "I feel dirty."

I didn't feel dirty, just chilly and wet. Barely had time for a quick shower before leaving for Alden's.

El Speed didn't pay any attention to me as I fussed over what to wear. He lay on his bed, arms crossed over his chest, legs crossed at the ankles, and stared at the ceiling as I considered my options. Jeans were a given. What shirt to wear? I laid one after another on top of my navy cotton bedspread, rejecting a couple and then un-rejecting them, rejecting them again in favor of something else. Each one felt either too casual or too formal.

Finally I stood still and closed my eyes to steady my mind, and when I looked back at the selection on the bed I reached for a soft, baby-blue, pinwale corduroy shirt with pale mother-of-pearl buttons. I put it and the jeans on, and it felt right. I topped the look with the distressed leather jacket of Neil's that I'd worn the night of the eclipse. He'd given it me, as he'd said, "to get started right on campus." I wasn't sure what that meant, but I liked the jacket, and the rain had stopped.

El Speed glanced at me as I was about to open the door. "Going someplace?"

I decided this wasn't the time to go into details. "Out for dinner with a friend. I might be back late."

El Speed's eyebrows shot upward, but I left before he could respond.

Alden had said he wasn't going to be back in town until Tuesday afternoon, which meant he wouldn't be on campus, so we'd agreed I'd find my own way to his place. Short of hitchhiking, I'd need to take the 3A campus transit, the run that left around five.

On the bus, I took a window seat and stared kind of sightlessly at the trees on the side of the road, the skeletons of bare branches looking a little sad now that the brilliant colors of earlier in the season had mostly fallen to earth.

I let my mind wander to a few things Alden had told me on our walk back from looking for swans. For one thing, although his folks accepted that he was gay, they still occasionally moaned about wanting grandchildren, as though that were out of the question. He'd taken a year off after high school and spent it in Canada for reasons he didn't make clear, even when I'd asked; all he'd said was, "Have you ever seen the polar bear invasion in Churchill?"

My mind went back to that first time we'd gone for coffee. He'd asked if I wanted to fuck. I'd been so surprised. What a naïve little kid.

Since then, despite the development in our relationship, there'd been no mention of fucking. But how likely was it that he'd want this next step to happen tonight?

Christ, but I wish my own feelings were clearer! Did I like the guy? I did. Very much. Had I enjoyed kissing him? Very much. Had my body responded in the appropriate way? It had. Indeed it had. I knew I was gay. I knew Alden was gay. We really liked each other. So what the hell was my problem?

Did straight people go through this? Didn't most of them get over their first-time jitters in high school? I'd avoided talk of romance and sex in my own high school years, mostly out of fear that people might figure out the reason for my lack of that kind of experience.

And was this feeling tonight nothing more than first-time jitters? How would I know?

ON CHOCORUA

I hadn't come prepared. I mean, I hadn't brought any condoms. (I'd never even *bought* any condoms.) It seemed likely that Alden would have some on hand, and the idea of what we'd be doing if we needed them felt both alluring and terrifying.

Smokescreen, Nathan. Back to the question.

The only way to figure this out was to let things happen. So would I do it?

Maybe.

Yes. Maybe.

Yes.

What if he was waiting for me to say something? If he didn't bring it up, would I?

... Maybe.

Yes.

CHAPTER SIX

I got off at the Arrowbrook Road stop and, as instructed, walked north a short distance to an old Colonial with Alden's car parked off to the side. There was just enough light left in the day for me to tell that the yellow house Alden had said was his was actually yellow. A few almost-bare trees and a couple of pines stood between the house and the road, and Alden's white BMW was there, top up.

The house looked like maybe it had been built in the early eighteen hundreds. It wasn't in terrific shape; a couple of shutters had been painted dark mustard maybe a few years ago, while other windows had dark green shutters—sometimes only on one side. At some point someone had added a narrow, covered porch to the front of the house. There were a couple of wicker rocking chairs on it, a small table between them.

I saw "A. Armstrong" on the upper of two buzzers, rang it, and waited. I heard someone coming downstairs from inside the house, and the door opened.

"Hey, Nathan. Come on in."

I followed him up the stairs, allowing myself the luxury of watching his backside, even though my stomach was sending flutters of anxiety through my body.

Alden led the way through an open door at the top of the stairs on the right, and suddenly the environment was different. Subtle oriental rugs mostly covered the polished hardwood floors—not the wide pine boards of your typical colonial, but narrow, contemporary flooring. To my right, with some windows looking to the side of the house and some toward the road, the living room had furniture of dark wood and navy upholstery, all of it looking fairly new and expensive. Exposed beams in the ceiling gave the room an old-world elegance.

Yup; there was money, here. I'd guess lots of it.

"Honestly, Alden, I don't know why you don't want to live in a dorm. I mean, my furniture's at least as nice as this stuff."

He chuckled. "I'm making a martini. You want?"

A martini. What did I know? I'd never had one. "Sure."

"Dirty? Olives? Lemon?"

Christ, I didn't know. "Whatever you're having."

He hadn't kissed me, and I hadn't kissed him. I wondered who was waiting for whom. Or maybe a kiss right away would have been too forward? Maybe neither of us should presume that much? Fuck. I had no idea how to handle this.

I wandered around the living room, picking up occasional knick-knacks, which—I was pretty sure—were small pieces of art. I was particularly intrigued by a piece of dark green stone, maybe six inches high, that kind of almost maybe looked like a human figure. It reminded me of Gorignak, the giant rock monster that chased Captain Jason Nesmith around on the planet of the little blue devils in *Galaxy Quest*. Neil had made me watch that film. By now I'd seen it maybe four times.

Speaking of art, there were some paintings on the walls that looked like originals, though I guessed they came from art fairs rather than art auctions.

On the wall between the two front windows was a tapestry. There were slightly abstract mountain shapes in lots of colors, obviously an autumn scene, with the blue of a lake in the lower right. I was admiring it up close when Alden approached from behind me.

"That's a Sarah Warren. Amazing weaver. Lives up in the northern part of the state." He held a glass toward me, a classic martini shape with a thin, cobalt blue spiral inside the stem. It contrasted in a lovely way with the bright yellow twist of lemon. "I always use vodka. Hope that's okay. Gin leaves me feeling toxic."

"Thanks." Would he kiss me now?

No.

He took an upholstered chair that sat at right angles to the couch, where I sat. I took that as a sign that if he had anything more than drinks in mind, either he was gonna get me drunk first, or he was waiting for me to make the first move. I told myself not to be nervous, though it did little good. This drink, this sophisticated grown-up drink in the beautiful, fragile glass made me feel even more out of place than Alden's apparent wealth did.

Maybe it was nerves, or maybe I really was hungry and thirsty, but I polished off the drink faster than he did, sipping between handfuls of salted nuts piled in a dark green bowl on the coffee table. And what did we talk about? I can't say that I remember very much until he emptied his own glass and set it down on the table beside him. Then he looked at me, seeming perfectly relaxed, and waited.

"Um," I opened, "what time's dinner?"

"Eight. And we're going out."

Eight. And it was only—what, a little after six now? And why hadn't I noticed until this moment that there were no cooking smells? "But—I won't make the last bus back."

"Not to worry. I figured I'd give you a ride."

But I did have another worry. "Um," and then I couldn't decide what to say next. How much would my meal cost? Should I say I didn't have money for a nice place? Should I say I didn't bring enough with me? Finally I managed, "What kind of restaurant?"

"A place I like. A real restaurant." He scoured my face and must have figured out where I was coming from. "Nathan, *I* invited *you*. This is my treat."

Some part of me wanted to protest. Another part of me didn't want to put any kind of stink on the evening. I decided to let him have his way. This time.

And now, we had plenty of time for us to do whatever. Plenty of time for me to get up the guts to suggest something, if that was how he wanted to play this. And that made sense; he knew I was a virgin, or had been at the time of that first coffee together, and he'd taken the initiative on tonight's meal. Somehow I knew the rest was up to me.

He looked a little sideways at me, and smiled. "Would you like another drink?" I shook my head. "More nuts?" I knew it was a loaded invitation; he'd give me more food if that's what I wanted, but he looked ready for something else.

I took a deep breath. "I might like yours."

He threw back his head, just like he had at the swan pond, and laughed the same way. It was a great laugh, kind of deep, full of life and fun, and nothing of ridicule in it. I waited, fighting my own laughter.

"Nathan, you are a delight." He stood, and I stood, and he took my hand. "I'd love to show you the bedroom. How does that sound?"

It was all I could do to say, "Lead on." My entire body tingled, and it was tough to know how much was pleasure and how much was anxiety. But I knew I wanted this.

We walked through the kitchen, which was a big, open room all across the back of the house, and continued around to the opposite front corner room.

Neither of us spoke at first. We stood just inside the doorway, facing each other, and Alden wrapped his hands slowly around the sides of my head. He opened his mouth just a little and touched my lips with his, and something about his slow grace kept me from doing what my libido wanted me to do, which was to glom onto his mouth with mine. Instead, I let him lead.

He flicked the insides of my lips with his tongue, sending prickles of excitement in both directions between my ass and my dick. I barely had time to register—scratch that; to celebrate—that *I was kissing a guy*, when one of his hands moved to my shirt buttons and began undoing them. So much of my attention was… well, elsewhere that I barely noticed he was doing that until he pinched one of my tits. Hard.

An ecstatic cry came from my throat, and suddenly—not slowly any longer—he was behind me, his teeth grazing the left side of my neck, his right hand wrapped around my throat, pushing my jaw up and my head back against his shoulder. The way his hips pressed against my ass made me want to scream. As I reached back to grip his hips and pull them as close to me as possible, his left hand grabbed my tit again and held on. And twisted.

I panted. I moaned. I nearly squealed. I was ready to come—*dying* to come—except that I wanted this feeling to go on forever.

He released my tit, flattened his hand against my belly, and worked his way under my waistband. Two of his fingers found the creases at the tops of my thighs, then descended and massaged the flesh on either side of my balls.

I heard myself pant, "I can't… I can't…."

Alden lifted his head from my neck and laughed. "Yes you can."

As quickly as he'd grabbed me, he released me, and I nearly fell to the floor, I felt that weak. He spun me toward him and grabbed my waistband, working it open.

"Unless things have changed," he said, his voice low and sultry, "this will be your first time with a guy." He pulled his head away far enough for me to see him smile. "I'll be gentle with you."

He was. He undressed both of us, and I watched as this process revealed his tall, slender frame. It wasn't a body like Daniel's, but it was perfect for Alden. And then the rest of it became almost irrelevant as his full cock appeared. I nearly laughed; it was so different from ogling other guys' dicks in the locker room. This dick wanted me.

Alden threw the bedcovers back to expose spring green sheets, lowered me onto them, and—his left hand twisting first one tit and then the other—wrapped the fingers on his right hand around my cock.

I'm just gonna pause here and remember what that felt like. Except that I'm not sure there are words that can do justice to the sensation of having someone else—someone other than me, someone who *wants* me—touch me there.

He massaged me to orgasm, and if there were any thoughts in my brain it was just amazement that this older, sophisticated man was about to see my "O" face.

And there it was. I barely recognized the sound I made, it was so much more intense, so much more spontaneous than anything I'd inspired with my own hand.

I was barely aware that he grabbed my right hand with his left. He guided me to his hard dick, at the same time spreading my cum onto it so I could use it like lube.

Again, this new sensation—this time having someone else's dick in *my* hand—was insanely wonderful. I had come, so I could take my time with him as I fingering the wrinkles and taught areas that were like mine and not like mine, thrilled that it made Alden moan. He was on his back now, and as I worked he turned his head side to side in what could only be called abandon.

I cupped his balls the way I liked to hold my own, one at a time and then both together, squeezing until I heard him suck breath in through his teeth. I ran my thumb around the head of his dick, poking and teasing, tapping it in irregular rhythms and pressures. I did to him the best things I've done to myself until he was incapable of saying "God!" any longer and could manage only "Ga!" He came silently, his breath stopped in his throat as effectively as if I'd been choking him. It was maybe ten seconds before he allowed himself to breathe, and when he did he panted several times before his breathing relaxed. He barely opened his eyes to look at me, and his smile told me all I needed to know.

Alden pulled me down into the crook of his arm, I pulled the covers over both of us, and we lay there quietly for a long time. He smelled like wool warmed by the sun. It wasn't cologne; it was Alden.

I must have fallen asleep, because the next thing I was aware of was Alden, fully dressed, standing beside the bed. A bedside table lamp was on. This was the point at which I realized I hadn't seen the scars on his back; maybe next time.

He smiled. "You look so charming when you sleep. I hope I'll be seeing that again soon."

I sat up and looked around. The room was furnished in a style very similar to the living room, only with lots of dark green. The king size bed fit in here easily, and two overstuffed chairs flanked the side window.

"What time is it?"

"Seven fifteen. Just time for you to do a quick wash-up, and we can head out to dinner."

As we drove in the BMW into Dover we looked at each other on and off, smiling the kind of smile that says *You are amazing.* I was flying high, nearly overcome by the thought that I'd arrived at a whole new stage in my life. That stage was one where I was finally living in a way that was true to who I am. It's one thing to say, "I'm gay." It's quite another to be able to prove it and to love the proving of it. I'd loved having another guy manhandle (love that word) my dick, and I'd loved holding his captive. It had surprised me how much I'd loved holding his balls, teasing his balls, *feeling* his balls. And maybe best of all, I'd loved how he'd responded to the way I'd touched him. I couldn't have said whether it was ridiculous or not, but I felt as though I'd earned that sophisticated cocktail. (I love that word, too. So insinuating.) I felt as though I wasn't just gay. I was a gay *man*.

In the restaurant, the hostess smiled at Alden like she'd seen him a number of times before and led us to a table in the corner, out of the way of traffic, and pretty private. I wondered how many other guys Alden had brought to this exact spot. Was it likely he'd come here alone? And if I asked whether he enjoyed dining out alone, would I sound like a jealous harpie? For the first time (yeah, another "first") it hit me how fine that line is between relaxing in the glow of someone else's regard and worrying that the glow was something he shared with others. I told myself to knock it off. I told myself to enjoy what was happening right now, tonight. It mostly worked.

The prices on the menu were not outrageously high, but they were high enough that I was glad Alden was paying. He ordered a beer, showed the inquiring if apologetic waiter an ID that must have been forged. I didn't have anything that would get me a beer, so I ordered a ginger ale.

"You're welcome to some of my beer," he said as I perused the menu. And then, "I'm going on the assumption that you enjoyed this afternoon as much as I did."

"Understatement."

"Excellent."

I wanted to hear more. I wanted one of us to say this would happen again, soon. But our waiter arrived back before either of us could say anything else. He gave me my soda and then set a pilsner glass and a bottle beside Alden. He poured some of the brew before taking our food order.

The waiter left and Alden asked, "So, how are things going with that kid who's pledging? Gordon, right?"

So much for more talk of our wonderful afternoon. Maybe it hadn't been quite as wonderful for him; I hadn't been his first.

Relax, Nathan.

"Oh, well..." Where to start? "He got a bid from the frat. But El Speed is just finding out now what the brothers forced the pledges to do." My voice quiet, I described the acts, holding the lacing of beer till last as El Speed had done. I took a swig of Alden's beer before adding, "And they had to lace each other's beers with fentanyl."

Alden's body jerked. "Keep your voice down." I didn't think it had been much above a whisper, but Alden seemed shaken.

"What is it?"

His face was tense, his mouth pulled into a thin line. Something like a twitch moved between his eyes. He seemed very un-Alden-like.

Our food arrived, giving Alden a little more time. He poured the remaining beer into the glass and ordered another bottle. As the waiter left, Alden drained the glass and sat back in his chair. Eyes closed, he pinched the bridge of his nose for a second and then shook his head.

As he reached for his water glass, his voice low and hushed, he asked, "Do you know how many laced beers Gordon has had?" He seemed to look anywhere but at me.

"Not really. A few, at least. Why?"

His eyes locked onto the water glass he gripped, and even though it was still on the table, it seemed like it might be shaking just a little. "Do you know if he's used it at other times? Other than those hazings?"

"Alden, what are you getting at?" My own voice was now nearly a whisper. Something was wrong.

"That's a really bad drug. Gets into you in a deep way and won't let go. And it can happen really, really fast." He filled his lungs with air and let it out slowly. "How close are you with this guy?"

"Not at all, really. My roommate is, though. Why?"

"Has Gordon moved into the frat yet?"

"No; it's just a bid at this point. Will you tell me what's going on?"

He took another mouthful of water. "See, Nathan, the thing is, once you get into that stuff, it's nearly impossible to get away from it again. And you'd better believe that if the brothers were using it as a hazing tool, it's already well established in the house overall. I can't say whether there'd be pressure for Gordon or anyone else to keep taking it if they didn't want to, but I can tell you that if he does want to, it's there. And once he does want to...." Alden's voice trailed off and his eyes gazed across the room, unfocused.

The flatbread Margherita pizza we'd ordered to share as an appetizer smelled so good my mouth watered, and the second bottle of beer had arrived. Alden seemed not to have noticed.

I decided to prompt him. "Um, should we dig in?"

And immediately he was with me again. "Oh. Sure. Of course. Like another swig?" He pushed the beer glass toward me.

He pulled a couple of pizza slices away from the platter and onto his plate, and it felt like some nasty spell had been broken. I stuffed the pointy end of a slice into my mouth, wondering if I could move the conversation away from fentanyl without seeming like I didn't care. I cared, I guess; I just didn't know what to make of Alden's behavior. And I sure as hell didn't know what to do about Gordon.

Alden solved the conversational problem. "Tell me more about your brother. How come you've never been hiking with him?"

I shrugged and gave him an explanation that had little to do with reality but that sounded at least superficially reasonable. "It was like Neil's thing. Plus, if I'd gone and hated it, I didn't want to get pushed into going again because 'it would be better next time.'"

It was possible I'd love hiking. My fear was that I would, and I'd want to hike *and* spend time with Neil, and he'd get tired of having his kid brother tag along all the time. I didn't think I could take the rejection. To Alden, I said, "Do you hike?"

"No way. I'm all for a good gym workout, but you won't find me anyplace where I don't have a hot shower, a warm bed, and the option to pay someone else to cook my dinner if I don't feel like doing it."

Alden asked me a few more questions about Neil, and I ended up describing how I'd come out to Neil before anyone else. "His best hiking buddy is gay, as it turns out."

"I think I like your brother."

By the time I'd finished my thick-cut pork chop and a piece of Boston cream pie, it was after ten. As we walked out of the restaurant, Alden laid a hand on the back of my neck. At first, I wasn't sure I liked that; it felt a little possessive. But he gave me a quick squeeze and then dropped his hand, which told me he wasn't being possessive, just affectionate.

We didn't talk for the whole first half of the ride, but the silence was comfortable, like we were both relaxing into the same warmth. But Alden did have something he wanted to say.

"Hope I didn't come across too intense over dinner. About the fentanyl."

I looked at the side of his face. "Not a problem."

"It's just that it's really nasty stuff. Are you worried about your friend?"

"I—he's not really my friend. More of an acquaintance." Hadn't I made that clear?

"Right."

"And anyway, El Speed and I went to the campus police this afternoon to let them know that fentanyl had been used in hazing. Did you know there's a regulation that if you know about hazing and you don't report it, you're in trouble?"

"I hadn't heard that, no. That's not why you went, though."

"No. I went to support El Speed, and he went because I think his girlfriend really wants him to watch out for this kid."

"Did you give the police any names?"

"Not one. Not even ours. You can report hazing anonymously, so we did."

He nodded. "Probably for the best." Almost a minute later he added, "Will you let me know how Gordon does?"

On campus, Alden pulled over to the side of the road that led to Hunter Hall, put the car in park and pulled the handbrake, and then turned toward me. There was enough light that I could see him smile.

He reached a hand around my neck and leaned toward me for a kiss. And then another. After a really deep one, he pulled away and laughed. "That's it for now, or we'll have to climb into the back."

I grinned at him, thinking he must have parked away from the door to avoid being seen as we explored the insides of each other's mouths.

"Worse things could happen." I climbed out before either of us could say anything more. Except that just before I shut the door, I said, "Thanks for dinner. Thanks for everything."

He smiled and nodded, and I floated on warm air all the way to my room.

On Wednesday El Speed and I ended up having dinner together, with no one else at our table. I decided it was time to let him know about Alden.

"I'm glad I ignored your advice about acting class," I opened.

"Why's that?" He was gazing down at his plate, coaxing black beans and corn kernels onto his fork.

"I, uh, I met someone there. Someone I'm seeing now." That got his attention. "Wow. Okay. What's his name?"

I really liked this guy. How many straight roommates would have asked that question so casually?

"Alden."

"So you've been out with him? And this is the first I'm hearing about it?" He seemed more amused that pissed off.

I chuckled. "Yeah. Sorry about that. A few times. That's where I went last night, actually. Dinner."

"Dinner." His tone said he knew that was only part of the story.

I wasn't about to provide any details that my hot ears didn't give away. Instead I described his apartment, and El Speed picked up on something that hadn't occurred to me.

"So if his apartment is so nice, what's it doing in that house? You've said the outside is not in great shape."

He was right. I didn't have a clue. "Dunno. Maybe I'll ask, next time I see him."

"He sounds like a good guy. Better than wasting your time on Dishroom Daniel."

I tried not to grin. I failed.

INTERLUDE V

Life with Neil: A Halloween Sacrifice

I loved Halloween. I loved coming up with a costume, I loved helping Gram make my costume. She helped all us kids with costumes every year; she could sew, and she didn't want to spend money on ready-made costumes. So she turned the effort into a fun family project.

The year I was seven for Halloween, which would be on a Sunday, Gram and I worked extra hard on my costume. It was... you guessed it: Spiderman. It was not a simple costume. Gram went to at least three stores to make sketches of Spiderman costumes. My part in the effort was to make the spider web bits that we'd attach with fabric adhesive, and she taught me to crochet a simple chain stitch with black yarn. I made yards and yards of it while she worked on rest of the costume, and then I helped her glue the "webs" onto the finished outfit. Fitting the head portion was a little tricky, but Gram was able to make adjustments so that it mostly worked.

I don't now remember what Nina's costume was, or Neil's; I was as self-absorbed as anyone else that age, so it was all about me.

The plan that year was that twelve-year-old Neil, for the first time, was free from the tethers of going trick-or-treating with Gram and his younger siblings and instead was going out with Jeremy and a couple of their friends. They would, of course, go much farther afield than Gram would take Nina and me.

On the morning of October 30, a Saturday, I woke up to the sounds of someone throwing up in the hall bathroom. As I approached the door, which was mostly closed, I could see that it was Gram. She kneeled on the floor, arms wrapped around the white ceramic bowl of the toilet, head fallen forward as though she didn't have the strength to hold it up.

I turned and ran to Neil's room. "Gram's sick!" I announced loudly to the lumpy form under the covers.

Neil's sleepy face appeared. "What?"

"She's throwing up in the hall bathroom!" This alone was odd, because the master bedroom, which she used, had its own bathroom.

He jumped out of bed and ran down the hall, then knocked gently on the bathroom doorframe. Gram didn't hear, because she was heaving again, so Neil pushed the door all the way open and went in.

I watched as he did all the things it wouldn't have occurred to me to do: feel her forehead and declare it hot; wet a washcloth and wipe off her face; hold her away from the toilet enough so he could flush it. Then he sat on the floor.

"Gram? How long have you been in here?"

She shook her head weakly. I could barely hear her answer, "Not long. I threw up in my bathroom and thought I'd be okay, so I—" and here she leaned over the toilet again and heaved, though nothing came out but some drool. Her breath was shallow and labored, and it was several seconds before she could continue. "I thought it was over, so I thought I'd go downstairs." She tried for a smile and failed. "I didn't make it."

Neil planted Nina and me in front of the television with threats of what he'd do to us if we moved from the spot other than to get water, have bowl of cereal and milk, or go the bathroom before he got back, and he took Gram in a taxi to an emergency clinic. They declared her sick with the flu, gave her a couple of bags of IV saline, and sent her home late in the afternoon with medicine and instructions, which included bed rest and liquids.

Neil lined a wastebasket with a plastic bag and told me to place it beside her bed in the event she upchucked again.

He went into her bathroom to scrub the toilet.

"She made a mess?" I asked

"The nurse said to do this. What Gram has is very contagious. Don't use the hall bathroom until I've cleaned that one."

When he finished upstairs, he gathered us in the kitchen. "We all need to help Gram." He showed us a piece of paper. "Here's the schedule. Two-hour shifts. Nina, you take the first one."

She didn't like that. "Why not you?"

He glared at her without responding to her question. "Your job is to check on her every fifteen minutes. If she's thrown up, you need to replace the plastic bag."

"EEEWWWW!"

"Tough noogies. You will take her temperature and write it down on the pad I'm going to put on the bed table. And you need to check her medication list." He set another sheet of paper on the table, the medicine schedule. "You'll need to give her a clean cup, or a clean spoon, and make sure she takes anything on this list when it's time. Then you need to clean the cup and spoon or whatever for the next time. Got it?"

"I can't do all that!"

"Nina, you're eight years old. You can absolutely do this. Nathan can do this, and he's younger than you. You should bring something to read, or write on, something like that. Now, I'll take the shift after Nina, and then Nathan, it's your turn. Then I'll take another shift, and then it's Nina's turn again. I've set Gram's cell phone to vibrate every fifteen minutes so it won't wake her up."

I asked, "What if she wakes up and has to go to the bathroom?"

Neil blinked at me and was silent, which told me he hadn't thought of that. But it didn't take him long to solve that problem.

"I'm going to bring the dining room chairs upstairs and

place them so she can lean on the backs between the bed and her bathroom. Whoever's on shift will need to walk on the other side of her to help. She'll need support sitting down and getting up again."

Nina rolled her eyes and threw herself backward in her chair, but she said nothing.

Neil's face took on a very serious expression. "Guys, Gram will be okay, but right now she's very sick. This is serious. If her temperature goes above one hundred and two, you come get me. If she's thrown up, come get me so we can decide what to do about medication. If she's asleep, don't wake her unless she needs medication. If she seems asleep, be sure she's breathing in a regular way, and if not then come get me. If she says she has to go to the bathroom, come get me. I've written all that down here."

He set a third sheet of paper onto the table and looked intently and each of us in turn. "Any questions?"

Neither of us spoke.

He handed Nina the phone. "Here you go. At the end of two hours, come get me for my shift. Got it?"

Nina looked like she was struggling between righteous indignation and a heavy dread about whether the world was going to continue. Neil called someplace to get take-out food for our dinner.

At first I hated my shift. I'd gone to bed early at Neil's insistence, given that I'd be up later. I had managed to get to sleep, so that when Neil woke me I was barely able to form words. Sitting in the chair Neil had placed near Gram's bed, I dozed off once or twice, but otherwise I did everything I was supposed to do. Nothing happened that meant I needed to get Neil. And when my shift was over, as I walked down the dark hallway toward Neil's door I felt older than I had felt that morning. I felt as though I had done something important, something that assured my value in my home. In my family.

The world did survive, but the news on Sunday morning, Halloween, was not great. Gram was able to hobble slowly down the stairs and into the kitchen, still in her pajamas, and even managed to drink some chicken broth Neil heated for her. But she needed help getting back upstairs.

Neil declared the need for sitting beside Gram's bed over, though he said we still needed to check on her frequently. He said he'd put a pan and a metal spoon on her bed table that she could bang on if she needed anything. Then the three of us sat listlessly around the kitchen table, half-eaten breakfasts before us, for a silent minute or two. Then Nina turned to Neil.

"You're gonna have to take me and Nathan out later. For Halloween."

Neil must have been even more exhausted than Nina and I were. His face didn't register any emotion I could detect as his eyes, only partly focused, stayed on Nina. I couldn't tell if he was thinking, or if he'd drifted off with his eyes open.

"Well?" Nina prodded. I was as interested in a response as she was.

Neil picked up Gram's phone and placed a call. We heard only his side of the conversation.

"Yeah, listen. My gram's really sick. I've got to stay with her, so I can't go out with you guys tonight." There was a bit of a pause. Then, "That's right. So I need to ask a favor. If you're not sitting down, sit down. It's a big one." He took a deep breath and let it out slowly. "I need you to take Nina and Nathan out for a bit. The guys will be going a little later, and you could probably catch up with them."

The silence lasted what seemed like a long time. Then Neil said, "I know. Really. But—see, I can't leave her. We have to keep taking her temperature, and if she tries to get up and falls...." Pause. "I owe you, man. I know this is a big one."

So that year, a very sleepy Nina and Nathan walked

around our neighborhood under the care of Jeremy Ford, who watched over us like we were his own children. And Neil didn't get to go out at all.

I don't think that even now, at my age, it would occur to me to do everything he did. I'm not sure he actually saved Gram's life, but—maybe. And he sure saved my Halloween.

CHAPTER SEVEN

After my evening of pleasure with Alden, I found that my feelings about Daniel changed. Oh, sure, he was still attractive, and fascinating, but I stopped following him around the dishroom with my eyes. I stopped hoping he'd suggest sitting down for coffee after a shift. I stopped worrying that he and Nina weren't really hitting it off. But I found myself wondering what sound Daniel made when he came. I wondered what his cock would feel like in my hand. I wondered whether he would moan, or hold his breath, or grunt. And it amazed me that I wondered about him in a way that was kind of academic, in a way that almost didn't make me hard.

I have to admit that I felt conflicted, confused. I could honestly say that my horny thoughts were for Alden, but I couldn't deny that my mind went to Daniel more than I would have expected.

And thinking about Alden, I was a little fixated on next steps. Was I supposed to wait for him, seeing as how I couldn't exactly offer him a ride, pay for a nice dinner, or provide a place to fuck? Somehow my dorm room didn't seem like a good offer, even on the weekends when El Speed went to Maine.

Alden had said he didn't always feel like cooking. Maybe I could make dinner for him? I was no chef, but I could put a meal together; Gram had made sure all us kids at least knew our way around a kitchen. Still, it seemed awkward for me to say, "So, Alden, invite me over again and I'll make dinner for you."

Speaking of El Speed, he was anxious all week, wondering what (if anything) the campus police were doing, whether Gordon was taking drugs, whether Ellie would be pissed that El Speed wasn't taking good enough care of Gordon.

Thursday night, when I came back to the dorm from the library, I could hear shouting all the way down the hall that led to my room. I picked up my pace and stepped into the room just as Gordon was about to storm out. Our inadvertent chest bump nearly knocked us both over.

Gordon grabbed the doorframe. "Fuck you, Nathan!"

"What? What did I do?"

"Don't pull that innocent shit with me. It could only have been you guys."

"Us guys?"

"They arrested our social chair!"

"For what?"

Gordon's face was red, and his breath rasped in and out of his nose like on a cartoon dragon. He stared at me another several seconds and then nearly ran out.

El Speed was looking like a real dragon, but then it was a part he could play more convincingly than Gordon. He said nothing, so I did.

"I take it this is the result of our trip across campus Tuesday?"

"Seems likely."

"Did you admit what we did?"

He slumped onto his desk chair. "Not exactly. But I couldn't hide it very well. I mean, I couldn't hide that I was glad the guy got arrested."

I sat in my chair, facing El Speed, though we didn't look at each other. Why, I wondered, was Gordon as furious as he was? I could think of only two possibilities. Either the brothers knew Gordon had revealed that the drugs were there, which would no doubt destroy his standing as a pledge, or the social chair (whatever that was) had been supplying Gordon with fentanyl even though the hazing was over, and Gordon was hooked. Alden's warnings were front-and-center in my head.

So I asked, "What do you think is going on there? I mean, do they blame him?"

"Not only do they blame him. He got rejected."

"Holy shit! But—how did anyone know he'd said anything?"

"Nathan, be real. The guy is hardly in your acting class. There was a calling-out of everyone, complete with threats if no one confessed, and they all started looking at him. He'd have given himself away even if seventeen other people had let the secret out."

"Do we know who the social chair is? Was it Byron Moreno?"

El Speed shook his head. "No, unfortunately. Some other guy."

"Um..." I wasn't sure how to bring this up, but it seemed important. "Do you think Gordon's been taking the stuff? Since he got in, that is?"

"You know, I wouldn't have thought so. But given his reaction today, I'm not so sure." We stared at each other for a few seconds before he added, "And at this point, as angry as he is, it won't be easy to figure it out. I'm not sure he'll ever talk to me again. Or you."

El Speed wasn't wrong about Gordon. A couple of times I saw him around campus, and when he saw me he'd cut me pointedly. But at least he seemed okay. I mean, he wasn't looking messy or totally out of it or anything.

Turns out Alden got kind of a kick out of fucking in my dorm room. He'd driven us to Portsmouth on Saturday to see *The Martian*. He'd already bought tickets. I didn't know whether to hold hands. No one would see. But he didn't, so I didn't. Then we'd stopped for a dinner of burgers. I'd picked up the tab for that.

On the ride back to Durham, he asked, "Is this one of

your roommate's weekends in Maine?"

"It is. Why?"

"I'd kind of like to see your room."

"Nothing much to see."

He chuckled. "Nathan, I wanna get into your pants again. Can we do it there or not?"

We did. Still didn't do anything that required condoms, but I think we did everything else. And as if I hadn't had enough, I fantasized about him that night. I wanted to dream about Alden and only Alden.

What was this feeling? Was it love? Was I falling in love? It felt—well, it made me feel like my head was floating somewhere above my body. It was an excited euphoria that made it hard for me to sleep. It made me feel like I'd landed on some secret island where I'd always belonged but hadn't known it, an island I shared with only one person. Alden.

When El Speed got back Sunday night, he was miserable. Ellie was furious with him for losing his connection with Gordon and furious with both of us for telling the campus police as much as we did.

"But we had to tell," I reminded him. "Legally. Did you tell her that?"

"I did." Then he pitched his voice a little high, I guessed to sound a little like Ellie. "So report the hazing. Why did you have to report the drugs?"

I told El Speed I thought Ellie was being unreasonable. He didn't reply. After all, she was his girlfriend, he wasn't likely to say anything against her.

Over the next couple of weeks, El Speed retreated into his meditation practice. He'd wake up early, sit cross-legged on his bed, silently, with his back against the wall. I didn't always wake up early enough to see this, but the first time I did it freaked me out. Gradually I got used to it. Hard to say whether it helped him any; he still seemed to feel guilty about

Gordon. And, it seemed, he was taking this TM stuff seriously. Up to this point, I would have strongly suspected that El Speed had gone with Gordon to the TM intro course just to keep tabs on him.

Alden invited me over for Halloween, which was on a Saturday. He wouldn't explain why I needed to be there by three, just said it was for an early dinner and then to help him with trick-or-treaters. When I got there, he was on the porch, bags and boxes around him full of Halloween decorations. He grinned as he saw me approach.

"Hey, Nathan. I need your help, here. I'd hoped to get more of this done earlier in the week, but—" He shrugged.

"No problem. What have you got?"

"First," and he lifted masses of silvery rope from a box, "here we have the foundation of my plan."

I reached out and fingered a coil. It had iridescent sparkles in it. "The foundation?"

He leered at me. "Spider webs! And over here," he reached into a large plastic bag behind him, "is one of the residents." With one hand he gripped the body of a huge, black, hairy spider with pink eyes. With his other hand he pushed something on the spider's belly, and the eyes lit up bright fuchsia.

I laughed. "Oh. My. God. How many of these do you have?"

"Probably too many."

"Did I ever tell you," I said, tiling my head and eyeing Alden conspiratorially, "that I was totally into Spiderman when I was a kid?"

"Then you should feel at home here for so many reasons." He grinned and planted a kiss on my mouth. "And if I ever get that Lamborghini Spyder I have my heart set on, I'll think of you whenever I drive it."

As we worked, I told him about the Halloween Gram

had made me the Spiderman costume. I told him how Neil had organized the care of our very sick grandmother. And I'd told him how amazed I was now, looking back, at what a little grown-up Neil had been at the ripe old age of twelve.

Alden let me finish before he said, "I like how much you talk about your brother."

I let my arms fall from my work of trying to throw a length of spider web over a nail that was sticking out from the porch roof. "What do you mean? Do I talk about him too much?"

"I wouldn't say *too* much, no. That's why I like it. That, and the sense I get that he was very good to you, and that you appreciate it."

Of course, this made me like Alden better than ever.

By the time we'd struggled (and it was a struggle) with the ropes, there were several webs hanging at different angles from all around the porch roof and strung around the wooden supports. We positioned seven spiders, different sizes and various eye colors, suspended throughout the mess. It was glorious.

The last thing left on the porch was a large, black, plastic cauldron that he set between the chairs. Alden promised to show me what would happen with that, later.

It had been a gorgeous day, sunny and crisp, but by now dusk was approaching. We stood away from the house to admire our work, and Alden declared it perfect.

"Come on upstairs. We can have something to drink, and some munchies. And then I'll describe my plan for the evening."

We did have something to drink. Eventually. As soon as we were in his apartment he wrapped himself around me, and we kissed and kissed, ending up on the floor laughing like idiots.

He sat up. "Okay, that's enough for now."

"What? Why?"

He stood and pulled me up with him. "We don't have

much time before the little monsters start threatening tricks if I don't treat them."

"Let them wait!"

He shook his head. "I love Halloween. I love sex with you, too, but for that I want any knocking and ringing to come from what we're doing to each other, not from the front door."

There were more plastic bags in the kitchen, some with candy and some with lots of black cloth. I chuckled. "Boy, you really go all out for Halloween."

"I do. It's great fun. Burgers okay for dinner? I didn't want to get too fancy with the food, given that we won't be lingering over dinner."

"Love me some burgers. So, we're greeting the candy thieves on the porch?"

"Yup."

Alden gave me a few chores for dinner prep, and even as we sat down to burgers and beers the front door bell rang.

"Shit. They're starting already! My downstairs neighbor left for the weekend to avoid this, but with all those spiders down there, we can't pretend we aren't here." Alden jumped up and grabbed a bag with candy in it. As he disappeared down the stairs he called out, "Eat fast, Nathan!"

We managed to finish eating without further interruption, and then Alden grabbed the black cloth, throwing some of it at me. "Your cloak, my dear."

I watched as Alden struggled with his own cloak, tattered black cloth enshrouding him almost completely. He tied it loosely at his neck, pulled the hood up over his forehead, and nearly disappeared. I arranged my own cloak around my body as Alden threw his hood back and picked up a jar of water.

"Grab the candy and that large orange pumpkin over there."

The pumpkin was hollow, light plastic, and I was sure we'd be putting candy into it, even though it had something else in it at the moment, something wrapped, that turned out to be black light bulbs.

On the porch, Alden had me replace the regular light bulbs on either side of the door with the black ones, which shone purple when I turned them on. Meanwhile, he had a funnel with a long, skinny spout that he used to pour a small amount of water into the cauldron.

"There's a metal dish inside," he said. "I'll have to add more later. Can you plug that cord over there into the outlet in the wall?"

Alden flicked a switch near the bottom of the cauldron, and then another one, and an eerie orange light shone from inside it.

"What's the water for?"

He grinned at me. "You'll see." He emptied the bags of candy into the now-empty pumpkin, sat in one of the chairs, and gestured for me to take the other. It was nearly dark by this time, and in the weird light the look Alden gave me sent shivers up my spine. Peering from under his eyebrows, he grinned a truly evil grin. And then he cackled.

I laughed, but it was kind of a nervous laugh even to my own ears. He was positively creepy.

But he wasn't done. Fishing under the cloak into his jeans pocket, he pulled out a short stick, removed the cap, and proceeded to blacken two or three of his teeth. He couldn't see what he was doing, but it didn't matter. He handed the stick to me.

I'd never seen this kind of thing before. "This stuff will come off again, right?"

He cackled again, and the blackened teeth were truly horrible. "Eventually."

Whatever. I blackened a few of my own teeth, wishing I could admire the effect. As I handed the stick back to Alden, I noticed a cloud of steam rising from inside the cauldron, lit ominously by the orange glow.

"Okay Nathan, now, before someone else shows up,

you need to practice."

"Practice?"

"Pretend we're in Lena's class. Let's hear you cackle."

"I—I don't think...."

"Repeat after me." He cackled again, loudly, mouth open wide to reveal the blackened teeth.

It took me a good four or five cackles until he was satisfied with my act. As I practiced, he fussed with something in the pumpkin.

"Now," he said, "we wait. And we rock." He rocked in his chair slowly, and I did the same, and pops and creaks came from the porch floorboards and from the chairs themselves. He pulled his hood over his head, and I did the same, and we waited. But not for long.

From his chair, Alden could see people approaching the house more easily than I did, and he cackled. I cackled. A group of three kids, one adult in tow, moved slowly toward the porch.

Alden's voice, pitched for maximum spookiness, startled me. "Come closer, my pretties. Come see what I have for you." He grinned broadly enough to show off his black teeth and held out the candy-filled pumpkin, the sleeves of the black cloak draping around his outstretched arm.

One of the kids laughed more nervously than I had a few minutes ago. Alden fell silent, and I grinned to show my own teeth.

The oldest kid, a boy of about ten in a Chewbacca costume, stepped boldly up onto the porch and reached toward the pumpkin.

Alden warned him, "Just one, my pretty, or you'll pay dearly."

The boy paused with his hand in the pumpkin, looked up at Alden, and grabbed something. He opened his hand and looked to see what treasure was in it, then gave a little yelp and dropped a glowing eyeball, complete with veins and a blue iris. The thing rolled toward the kid, who jumped to avoid it. Alden and I both cackled.

I decided to get in on the act. Using the creepiest voice I could produce, I said, "It's all right, child. There really is candy in there. Are you brave enough to try again?"

By the time they left, all the kids had at least two pieces of candy, and their adult chuckled until we couldn't hear it any longer.

It went on like that for the evening, with Alden replenishing the water when the steam started to thin. At one point I asked Alden where all the kids were coming from. "You're on this main road, set back behind trees, and there aren't a lot of other houses around. Where do these kids live?"

"There's a housing development just over there." He pointed north. "One road leads off the highway toward several more, with lots of houses. I was surprised last year when I got so many trick-or-treaters that I ran out of candy. This year, I wanted to be prepared."

He cackled suddenly, and I realized there was yet another group of kids, older than most of the earlier ones had been. Their response was more one of appreciation than fright, and they quizzed Alden about the cauldron. He had to knock off the cackling creepiness to answer them, and after they left Alden decided the evening was over.

"When the tricksters are as tall as me, it's time to stop."

We turned off the purple lights, left the spiders and their webs where they were, and carried everything else but the chairs back upstairs. I started to untie my cloak, but Alden grabbed my hands, smiled, and shook his head. He released my hands and made sure the cloak's tie was stable. Then, oh so slowly, he began to undress me. I reached for him, but again he shook his head. Alden took his time with my shirt buttons, teasing my lips with his tongue the whole time. He left my T-shirt in place and ran his hands slowly underneath it, fingering his way across my chest and around to my back.

I was hard long before he got my jeans undone and

pulled down around my ankles, along with my undershorts. So there I stood, clad only in a T-shirt and a tattered black cloak, dick poking out the front like some kind of obscene coat hook.

Alden pushed me gently backward until my shoulders and ass were pressed against a wall, and then he kissed me for real.

The sensations were no longer new for me, but what nearly took the top of my head off yet again was the knowledge, the deep understanding that this was how it was supposed to be. I was supposed to kiss guys. Guys were supposed to kiss me. This was right. This was perfect. I closed my eyes and reveled in the feeling it gave me to know how much Alden's male body, his male strength, was turning me on.

With one hand Alden kept me pressed against the wall. With the other he lifted my T-shirt and began kissing and licking his way down my chest. Soon—almost not soon enough—he was on his knees, caressing my balls with his fingers as my dick slid in and out of his mouth like both body parts were meant just for that. The warmth... the slight roughness of his tongue... the occasional light tease of a tooth... I couldn't imagine why I'd ever want my dick to be anywhere else.

I heard myself groan. And again. And then I heard myself cry out as I came against the back of Alden's throat.

I don't remember sliding down to the floor, but that's where I ended up, breathing ragged breaths, legs twitching with residual ecstasy.

When I finally opened my eyes, Alden was sitting cross-legged on the floor beside me, grinning. The black was almost all worn off of his teeth, and he looked comical and sexy all at once. I laughed as he leaned over to kiss me again.

"My turn," he said. "Now, I'm not expecting you to take everything in like I did, unless you want to. But you do need to know how to eat a guy."

I pushed him down onto the floor on his back, my knees on either side of his hips. I undressed him more quickly than he'd done for me, because I could tell he was already hard, and I didn't want to make him wait. Hell, I didn't want to wait, either.

His dick had a sideways curl to it, a little off to the left. I bounced it off my tongue a few times before wrapping a hand around it, and it occurred to me that I'd been so transported by what he'd done to me that I hadn't paid attention to the technique, and I wasn't sure I'd be able to do the same. So I just did what I expected he'd like. And he did seem to.

I had intended to take all of him in, to swallow as he had done. But somehow when it came time to decide I wasn't so sure. I worked him to coming with my hand in the end. Then he sat up suddenly and grabbed my hand, claiming as much cum as he could. With his other hand he pushed me sideways and then onto my belly, with both of his knees between mine. I almost told him to stop; I wasn't ready for this. But I clenched my jaw and waited.

His wet hand slid between my rear cheeks, fingers prodding gently until he found what he was looking for. He used just one finger. It was enough.

In. Out. In. Out. In, out. In out in out in out until I was groaning again. I'd played with myself like this, so it wasn't an altogether unfamiliar feeling. But—man, it's different when someone else is doing it.

When he stopped, I lay there wishing he'd go on. I felt him take hold of my undershorts, knowing he was wiping his hand on them.

"When you get back, you smell this. It will be us."

It was everything I could do not to laugh; this was so different from when El Speed had sniffed his own used undershorts.

Alden managed to get his jeans up enough to walk to the kitchen sink, where he washed his hands. I rolled onto my back, waiting for the afterglow to subside before following his lead.

He leaned against the counter watching me, smiling. "That was dessert number one. Our second dessert is ice cream."

"What, more cream?"

He chuckled. "Good one. Seriously, though, chocolate, or mint chip?"

"If I'm going to *eat* it, mint chip. Otherwise, those chips would mean trouble."

I did love the sound of that man's laugh.

He drove me home and pulled over around the corner from my dorm entrance, like last time.

"Are you avoiding the front of the dorm because you don't want to be seen, or because you think I don't?"

He shrugged. "I guess it was for you. I don't care who knows I'm gay."

I took the plunge. "Neither do I. Go ahead."

"You got it."

I think that was my final decision about coming out. Telling Neil my secret had been huge. Telling El Speed had been important. But I was a virgin no longer. I had entered manhood.

By Thanksgiving, Alden and I had been together at his apartment two more times, and on the first of those I made a point of examining his scars. He lay quietly on his stomach as I traced the lines with a finger. Neither of us spoke, but I could almost hear a teen-aged Alden crying out as the skin was ripped away, retribution for having the gall to be gay and to let it be known—justice landing painfully on him for letting a straight boy know how he felt about him. I knew it was a cliché, but I couldn't resist kissing those lines of scar tissue that protected the once-tortured flesh but would never make it safe to be gay. He lay still, so I think it was the right thing to do. And it was the first time he asked me to stay all night.

Gordon still saw El Speed and me as enemies. In other news, Daniel and Nina had been out a few more times, with Nina still insisting that he was "fine" but nothing more. I could tell Daniel thought Nina was "truly fine," which was totally different.

The Thanksgiving holiday this year was going to be a big one for me. All three of us kids were home again for the first time since the summer, and I was keenly aware that only Neil knew the truth about me. I was determined to come out to my family.

Of course, I came out over Thanksgiving dinner. It's traditional, right? In households all across the country, somewhere between "Pass the potatoes, please," and "I'd like a little more cranberry sauce," kids are telling their families, "I'm gay."

The decision had seemed easy enough. For one thing, I'd come out to two straight guys already, and neither Neil nor El Speed had had an issue with it. And now that I had some experience with Alden under my proverbial (and literal) belt, experience I'd loved and wanted to have more of, there was no way the reality of it could be denied. Even so, there were so many butterflies in my stomach I had trouble getting turkey and cranberry sauce into it.

We sat before our piled-high plates, Gram said a brief grace, Neil did something on his phone to cause mellow saxophone music to play, and the meal began for everyone but me. I pushed potatoes high around the pool of gravy and stabbed a cranberry, trying to look busy. Gram asked Nina how some class of hers was going—I forget which, as I wasn't able to focus on anything other than hiding how shaky my fork hand was. Then I heard my name.

"Nathan?" I looked up at Gram. "Sweetie, I asked how your psych course is going."

"Um, yeah. Great. Um...."

She set her fork down, no doubt hearing the tremor in my voice. "Nathan? What is it, dear?"

I gave up pretending to eat and clasped my hands in my lap. "There's something I need to tell you." All eyes were on me. I swallowed hard. "You know how a lot of people sort of figure out who they are in college?" I paused briefly, but no one said anything, so I kept going. "Well, I mean, I sort of knew this before college, but—"

Nina lost patience. "Spit it out, Nathan." No one disagreed with her.

"Fine. I'm gay."

Nina's eyes opened wide. "Oh. My. God."

I ignored her. I was much more concerned about Gram's reaction, anyway, though I'd been watching Neil out of the corner of my eye, not sure whether either of us would let on that this was old news to him.

Gram leaned back in her chair, her wrists resting on the edge of the table. She looked at me, a little sadly it seemed to me. "Oh, Nathan." I couldn't move. "Sweetie, are you sure? Sometimes young people go through a stage—"

"Gram, I'm sure. Very sure."

She didn't look happy. "But your life will be so difficult. So many people will be—unpleasant. They'll make you feel horrible about yourself."

I felt my spine straighten as I sat a little taller in the chair. "You think I wouldn't feel horrible otherwise? You think lying about who I am, hiding who I am won't feel horrible?" My tone was sharper than I had intended, and Gram looked as though she'd been stung. I softened my tone. "As long as it isn't my family making me feel that way."

Neil came to my rescue. "Nathan, if we can do anything to support you, we will. We want you to be sure, but we want you to be yourself." He looked at Nina and then Gram.

Nina shrugged unconvincingly but said nothing. Gram said, "Oh, of course! Of course." It was hard to gauge her sincerity. Then she sighed and added, "Well, I guess it's a good thing I already have my grandkids." And she gave me a forced smile.

Maybe she didn't throw a fit and tell me I needed therapy or something, but she was still struggling under antiquated ideas. "Gram, you know, I could have kids. It just wouldn't be the way Neil would do it."

"Or the way I would do it." Nina spoke under her breath; I'm not sure Gram heard her, but I did.

"I don't do anything the way you do it, Nina."

Gram let that go by without comment. "Are you all right, though, Nathan? I mean, how do you feel about it? Do you need to, you know, talk to anyone?"

There it was: the suggestion of therapy, something I'd once thought I might need for a different but related reason. In high school, I'd thought I was going crazy. Now that I was confident, she thought I needed help.

I decided to ignore that question. "I'm great with it, Gram. Really. It feels right. *I* feel right, kind of for the first time."

That left me open to a snarky comment from Nina, but she said nothing.

Gram had another question. "Are you—I mean, you young people don't 'date' these days, do you? But is there anyone... you know."

"There's someone I've seen a few times. Don't know yet how serious it is, but we have fun."

"I'll bet."

Gram heard that one, all right. "Nina! Leave your brother alone."

And that was it. Almost. Gram cornered me later.

"Nathan, this is a huge step you're taking."

"It's not a step, Gram. It's who I am."

"But it's not—" She stopped short of saying whatever she was thinking.

I offered a few options to completed the sentence for her. "Not normal? Not natural? Not moral?"

She just stared at me, looking worried, or confused, or both.

"Gram, you know, this isn't a choice. No one chooses their orientation. Hell, no one even chooses who they fall in love with, whether they're gay or straight."

She still just stared.

"How do you know you're not gay, Gram?"

"What?"

"Seriously. How do you know?"

That took her by surprise. I said nothing else until she did; whoever spoke first would lose.

"Well, I... I fell in love with your grandfather."

"But what if he'd been a woman? Would you still have fallen in love with him as a her? Would you have felt romantic about 'her?' Would you have married 'her?'"

"Nathan, that's not the question."

"Of course it is!" I hadn't meant to raise my voice, but it felt like she was being obtuse. "Sorry. But, Gram, it is the question. Because if you couldn't love a woman like that, you're straight. *I* can't love a woman that way, either."

She looked both hurt and ashamed. "I just want you to be happy, Nathan. You know that. And I don't see how that's possible if this is true."

"Trust me. It's possible. This is the only way it *is* possible."

She heaved a sigh and rubbed her face, effectively giving up any further argument. "All right. We'll see how this goes. Just tell me if you're being careful."

"If you mean condoms, Gram, I haven't needed them yet. But, yes, I'll be careful. Don't worry."

"And no drugs, Nathan? Please tell me the truth."

I heaved a sigh of my own. "Gram, being gay doesn't

121

mean you take drugs."

"But are you?"

"No. Definitely not. Don't worry."

Later, Neil knocked on the door to my room, opened the door, and leaned on the frame. He didn't come in, but he said, "That took guts, Nathan. I'm proud of you." He shut the door quietly.

El Speed's Thanksgiving didn't end as well as mine. Ellie broke up with him.

"It's all because of Gordon," he told me Sunday night, leaning against his bureau, arms crossed over his chest. "Now it seems he's kind of hooked."

"Shit. But that's your fault in what universe?"

"This one, evidently."

"Do his folks know? I mean, is he back at school, or is he in rehab or something?"

"He's in denial, that's where, according to Ellie. So, no, I'm gonna say his folks don't know."

"Jesus."

"Yeah, maybe Jesus knows. But he ain't helping."

"Do you know how bad it is?"

El Speed shook his head. "Not really. Ellie just said he always seems tweaked out."

I'd thought that expression was specific to meth users, but I decided against challenging it. "Are you okay? I mean, about Ellie?"

"No, Nathan, I'm not okay. I thought we were headed for—you know."

"Marriage?"

"Yeah. Fat chance, now."

"You never know."

"I don't want to talk about this any more. I don't want to talk about anything." He grabbed his coat. "Going for a walk."

I wasn't sure whether to offer to go with him or not, but he didn't seem like he wanted company. Maybe ten minutes after he'd left, though, I felt like I should have gone with him. Okay, so I'd gone with him to talk to campus police about the hazing, but now there was a new level of trouble. Was there something more I could do? Neither of us knew anything about addiction. Would it help if we did? Maybe, maybe not. But I knew someone who understood better than I did.

Alden's folks had flown out here from St. Louis for the holiday, but I figured they'd have left by now. I pulled out my phone and texted him.

Can you talk?

My phone rang. "You okay, Nathan?"

"Oh, yeah. I mean, I came out to my family. I'll tell you about it later. The reason I texted was... you remember my roommate's friend Gordon getting laced beers during rush?"

There was a pause. "Yeah. Why?"

"I don't remember whether I told you, but he got kicked out of the frat. They figured out it was because of him that anyone found out. The police arrested the frat's social chair—"

"Yeah, I remember all that. What else?"

I took a deep breath, knowing that I was divulging something that could reasonably be considered a confidence. "He's hooked. His friend at home said so. And it seemed like you knew something about the stuff, so—"

"Are you at your dorm?"

"Yeah."

"Meet me out front in fifteen." And he hung up.

When I got downstairs, I saw that it had started snowing lightly. I'd collected a dusting on my shoulders and hair by the time the white BMW cruised up.

Alden didn't look at me, didn't speak, nothing. So I sat quietly as we drove off. He parked near our usual pizza place, and inside he scouted around for as remote a table as possible. He ordered a ginger ale and a slice, and I did the same, and then I waited.

Alden folded his hands on the table and stared at them until the waiter came back with our order. Then he stared some more. Still, I waited, getting more anxious by the minute.

Over the recorded background music, I heard Alden's deep intake of breath. "Okay. Here goes. The reason I know something about this stuff is I was using." He lifted his glass with a shaky hand and took a couple of gulps, ignoring the straw. He still didn't look at me. "I've told you how I took a year off before college. I got hooked my senior year in high school and spent the first part of what would have been my freshman year in college at a rehab center in Canada."

I almost echoed, "Canada?" but caught myself just in time; that was hardly the salient point, here. I took a bite of pizza, hoping that would prevent my saying something stupid.

Alden took a bite of his slice and sat back in his chair to chew it. Sipping through the straw this time, he had some more ginger ale. Then, "It had its advantages, being in Canada. I got to see the northern lights. And I think I said something to you once about the polar bears in Churchill. I saw them on a field trip from the rehab center they took a few of us on, those who were doing well. I think it was meant to be a distraction. It worked, actually. It helped me see that there was cool stuff out there in the world I'd never experienced, stuff I never would experience if I didn't stay sober."

He leaned forward again. "How bad do you think it is with your friend?"

I almost corrected him for what would have been the second time, because Gordon really wasn't my friend. But it hit me that Alden didn't want to mention names where we might be overheard. And it wasn't important.

"All I have to go on is what El Speed's girlfriend—sorry, ex-girlfriend now—said. Also, his folks don't know."

"She broke up with him? Over this? What the fuck?"

"She holds him responsible, I guess. She expected him

to watch over Gor... watch over the guy."

"That's completely unreasonable. There was nothing he could have done."

"Maybe she'll come around."

"Maybe. Meanwhile, your friend needs to get help. This is not something he's likely to power his way out of alone. And he might not even want to."

We munched for a couple of minutes. "Do you think it would help," I asked quietly, "if El Speed found a good rehab place and maybe gave literature or something to the guy?" I was remembering the flyer Officer Kemper had given El Speed at the campus police station, wondering where it was now.

Another deep breath from Alden. "Probably not. But he should try, even if just so he can feel like he did something. Bottom line? And I'm sure you've heard this before. No one climbs out of that hole without really wanting to. You could try an intervention, but he's not likely to thank you for it."

We sat silently for a minute, each of us looking down at whatever was left on our plates. Then he said, "When you're in it, what you're addicted to feels like your friend. It's a place where you can at least stop whatever emotional downward slide you're on. It seems better than suicide. It's a substitute for hope in a hopeless situation. So, giving it up.... Fuck. That feels like letting go of the only thing that's keeping you alive."

As I'd watched his face, as I'd listened to his words, a question had come to me. I wasn't sure it was a question I could ask, a question I had any right to ask. But it came out anyway.

"I know how Gordon got hooked. How did it happen for you?"

He rubbed his face with his hands. The response, when it came, didn't really answer my question. Not exactly.

"Addiction to any one thing has a lot in common with addiction to any other. Being addicted to, say, sex, looks very different from addiction to fentanyl. But the thing is, if someone feels they aren't good enough, not worthy enough, and they believe—or they're made to believe—that they can acquire that worth from something external to them, then whatever gives them that feeling becomes their addiction." He leaned back, eyes on the table, one hand toying with the straw he'd lifted out of his glass. "And that's all I'm going to say."

Several heartbeats went by. "Alden?" I waited for him to look up. "I really admire you. For climbing out. I just want you to know that."

He looked up. "You understand this is a confidence, right?"

"I do. Yes. Completely."

"Do the guy's folks have money? My rehab was private and very costly. There are others."

"I don't know. I kind of doubt it. But El Speed would know."

"It's just—if anyone gives him a brochure or anything, it should be to a place he could go if he decides to. He'll grab at any excuse to avoid rehab."

"Right."

There didn't seem to be much else to say. I felt disappointed that Alden hadn't been able to offer anything more concrete by way of advice, but I guessed he was right that there really wasn't much to be done. Or, not much El Speed and I could do, at any rate.

To ease the tension, I brought up El Speed's point about the disconnect between the outside of Alden's house and the inside of his apartment.

"My folks bought the house after I got out of rehab, after I decided to come here. Mom had the upstairs redone for me. It was a wreck. The guy downstairs was already a tenant, and she didn't want to kick him out."

"But she decided not to fix the outside?"

He shook his head. "The place isn't worth it. She just wanted to know I had a nice place to live."

I was thinking, *And I know now that his family has money to burn.* It was true that she'd have the rental property after Alden graduated, but that upstairs apartment would never bring in what it deserved. Not my problem.

When Alden dropped me off back at my dorm, there wasn't the usual affectionate farewell. Perhaps he was unsure how I felt about his revelation and didn't want to test it. I didn't reach for him, either. Because that is exactly how I felt: unsure. Very unsure.

On my way up to my room, deep in thought and trying not to let emotion take over, I had to admit it had been a shock to hear that Alden was in recovery, which I think is how you refer to someone who's gotten clean. Or, that is, sober, the word Alden had used. Because from what I've heard you never really get over it. As far as I was aware, he and Gordon were the only people I'd ever met who were addicted to anything. I'd heard a lot of news items about what they were calling the "opioid epidemic," but it had never hit close to home before. If people like Alden and Gordon could get caught in it, who else might?

Jesus. What if Alden had stuff in his apartment? What if this terrific guy, a guy who'd said he couldn't stop thinking about me, had drug connections right here on campus?

Stop it, Nathan. You'd know.

Would I? Really?

I pictured Alden, alone in his lovely apartment, maybe studying or reading or something, and all of a sudden he gets hit with this nearly irresistible urge to go out and find some fentanyl. Or maybe that urge is always there, right behind whatever else is going on, ready to leap forward, block out everything else, and take over his life again. It must be hell. Maybe he'd climbed out of the hole, but could he stay out? All I knew was that if he couldn't, I wouldn't be able to help him. And maybe he'd never try to get me into that scene, but if he got back into it, I might get caught up in the churn anyway.

After making myself crazy going around in mental circles about Alden and drugs, I made a huge effort and managed to talk myself down from suspecting Alden. And when I asked myself if I still wanted to see him, the answer was a resounding Yes. And how had he felt when I hadn't kissed him before I'd gotten out of his car, which I almost certainly would have done any other time?

I texted him: *Thanks for talking to me about this. See you soon.*

His reply: *Very soon, I hope.*

I was tempted to call Gram and reassure her that I'd never, ever, not in a million years do drugs, but I knew she would just wonder what was going on. And I knew I couldn't tell her. So I just said it to myself.

INTERLUDE VI

Life with Neil: One Man's Baby Stuff....

In case there's any doubt, Neil was as active during the winter as he was at any other time of year. He didn't do a lot of winter climbing, but that was at least partly because he loved to ski. Downhill ski. Like me, he'd had some sort of job all through high school. And Gram, bless her heart, had set aside a portion of my parents' insurance payment for each of us to get something special, something we could choose any time after we were twelve. Or we could save it. Nina saved hers. Neil didn't. He bought skis.

Most of my memories of Neil are of his caring side, his loving side. Skiing is different. He was competitive to the point where Jeremy, who had started skiing when Neil did, refused to ski with him. I think part of it was that Jeremy wasn't as good at it, and Neil lorded it over him whenever Jeremy fell or couldn't quite ski well enough to get into a competition. Neil always got in, and he always did really well. I wouldn't have said he was Olympic material, but his attitude was in that general direction.

Jeremy enjoyed skiing, though, and a few times he took me. I rented boots and skis, not ready to purchase equipment with my insurance spoils, and Jeremy patiently stayed with me on the blue run slopes as I struggled through the requisite face-plants in my efforts to learn how to snowplow to slow my descent and how to do those carve turns that look so cool when skiers actually know how to transfer their weight from the right edges of their skis to the left and then back again as they bend their knees and lean forward. It was a major frustration for me that I couldn't manage this process well enough to progress to the red slopes, try though Jeremy might to help me. I finally decided downhill wasn't for me.

Neil said nothing at this announcement. It wasn't until I had tried Nordic skiing that he expressed an opinion. It was one of those rare occasions when I was allowed into Neil's room while he and Jeremy were planning some activity.

"Seriously, Nathan? That's for people who can't ski."

Jeremy came to my defense. "Neil, knock it off. Not everyone has to risk their neck on the slopes, you know. Let him have his own fun."

I stood up for myself as well. "Yeah, well at least I don't have to wait for some stupid machine to pull me up the slopes! I can get there by myself."

But it stung. It stung badly. And it motivated me to find a way to do Nordic skiing that required more skill and strength than an afternoon on a snow-covered golf course. But of course that required that I buy some equipment; renting skis is fine if you go only a few times a winter. I wanted to get *good*.

I did.

And then came the day when Neil was home for Christmas, his last year at UNH, and I challenged him.

"You know, Neil, I tried downhill. You don't know how to ski Nordic, do you?"

"Of course I do. It's baby stuff."

"Prove it."

"What?"

"Rent some skis, and come with me. *Follow* me."

This was a little bold of me, considering Neil's athleticism and the fact that he was twenty-one and I was all of sixteen.

He laughed. "You're on!"

He'd been at college, so he hadn't known how much work I'd put into my own kind of skiing. He didn't know how hard it was to carry off a sharp turn with no edges to the skis, and with only the toes of your boots attached to them. He didn't know how to herring-bone his way up a slope almost as fast as a hiker in summer, and he didn't have a lot of practice maneuvering skis around the trunks of small trees growing close together.

He suggested the walking trails in White Park, which is close to home, either because he didn't think I could handle anything tougher or because he didn't want to devote a lot of time to this child's-play, or both. But that's not what I had in mind. And when he suggested it, it was my turn to laugh.

"Oh, I don't think so." I looked right at him. "That's baby stuff."

We rented skis in town for Neil and drove the forty-five minutes to Mt. Kearsarge State Park, which has some open spaces that call to the casual Nordic skier. I said nothing as Neil chose a parking spot close to those open spaces, but as soon as we had our skis in hand I headed toward the woods.

"What are you doing?"

I half-turned back toward him. "I'm going skiing. What are *you* doing?" And I headed off, Neil following in obvious confusion.

There was a trail access point at the edge of the parking area that climbed steeply uphill through the woods, and that was my starting point. Skis on my boots, poles in hand, I charged into the woods and worked my way swiftly up the slope and around little trees and over logs and across gullies. I didn't look back until I heard Neil call out to me.

"Nathan! What in God's name?"

I stopped and turned sideways to the hill, my feet angled so that the uphill sides of the skis cut into the snow above me to hold me in place. I planted both poles on my downhill side and leaned nonchalantly on them.

Neil was way down the slope. His skiing form... well, it was non-existent. His face was red with effort, there was snow on his hat—evidence that he'd taken at least one tumble—and he was panting.

"What's the problem?"

"Where the fuck are you going?"

"Skiing. Where are *you* going?"

It was a wonderful day. A *fabulous* day. I led poor, exhausted Neil up to a point where there was a place to take a different run back down the slope, avoiding little trees but weaving around larger ones and among boulders. There were turns in odd places because it wasn't a groomed trail, and there were obstacles everywhere.

I'll say this for Neil. He kept going. But when he emerged, finally, back into the parking lot where I'd been waiting for maybe ten minutes, he was covered in snow, missing his hat, and shaking his head.

"Where did you learn to do that?"

Yup. A fabulous day.

CHAPTER EIGHT

Alden was very excited about our acting class final, which was to form teams of between two and four students, select a play, and present a short excerpt to the class. As soon as it was announced, he texted me, right in class.

Got a play all picked out. You in with me?

I chuckled quietly. *Hell yeah. What is it?*

Coffee. After class.

At a table in Zeke's, our favorite place for coffee and something, Alden confessed that he'd looked up what Lena had done in the past for a final in this class, and he told me something he'd never mentioned.

"I really liked working with you on that improv piece. You know, the bedbugs, and—whatever. You have an innocence tinged with a touch of pain and mitigated by a healthy dash of optimism that's really interesting, and it comes out in your acting."

My hand, cookie between thumb and forefinger, had stopped halfway to my mouth, and it hung there for a stunned moment while Alden sipped from his cup. I let my hand drop down to the table as I asked, "So this acting stuff. Is this something you're seriously considering? For the future, I mean?"

He grinned. "It surprises me a little, but I'm enjoying it so much that—well, let's say I haven't ruled it out. Maybe I'll even write plays. Anyway—eat your cookie—after you and I met here that first time, I started thinking we'd be good together for this final scene, as it were."

I chewed a bit of cookie and gulped some coffee while he watched me. Then I asked, "Okay, so what is this play you have in mind?"

"It's called *Eastern Standard*, written by Richard Greenberg. Shall I tell you about it?"

"By all means."

"You didn't have anything else in mind, did you?"

"Nope. Take it away."

"There are four important characters, but if we do just the beginning of scene one, we won't exceed our time limit, and that section features only two characters. The scene is from the late nineteen-eighties, in one of those chrome-black-and-white restaurants that were so trendy in Manhattan at the time. There's Stephen, who's straight and enamored of this woman who comes into the restaurant all the time, but he's never actually met her. He's talking with his friend Drew, who's gay and gets a lot of those snarky lines gay men are expected to say because we're gay."

He stopped to breathe. I asked, "Who gets which part?"

Alden reached into his pack and came up with a thin paperback in a bronze-colored cover. He handed it to me. "Why don't you take this with you and read at least the entire first scene, past where two more characters enter, so you can get a good sense of where things are going. Read the whole thing if you want, of course. Then we can argue."

"Argue?"

He lifted one side of his mouth in a snide smile. "I suspect we're both going to want to play Drew."

He was right. I definitely wanted to play Drew. As I read through the play that evening, I could easily imagine the conversation between Stephen and Drew. It would be fast-paced and leaning toward sarcasm without ever quite getting there, and it would outline the friendship between the two men in a way that was insightful and entertaining.

I said as much to Alden the next afternoon, when we met in a practice room. Alden agreed, conditionally.

"That's true, Nathan, but keep in mind that even though

you might think you know the guys by the end of what we'll do, you can't really know who they are at all. That unknowability will come through, if we do a good job."

I nodded as though I understood. "So, now we argue?"

"I don't think so. Here's what I'm thinking. I've been out for quite a while. You just came out this year. If you're brave enough to play Drew and have our audience think that maybe you're gay too, the part is yours. What do you think?"

"But—I thought you were aiming at an acting career. Wouldn't that mean—"

"Do you want to be Drew?"

"Well, yeah."

His grin was slow and sly. "Good. Because I've changed my mind. If you read the script with a critical eye, you can see that Stephen's is the more challenging part. Drew's lines are fun but obvious. If Stephen is going to be anything other than—pardon the pun—straight man to Drew, he'll have to come across as having some depth. And that depth is not in his lines."

I laughed. "So your generosity has an ulterior motive!"

"If you like. But Drew's part is still more fun."

It was. We met several times, and each of us spent time individually memorizing our parts. Twice, Alden had us reverse roles. I accused him of lusting after Drew's part despite what he'd said, but he said no, it was to make sure we could see how our own lines felt when we heard them, and maybe to get a few insights on hearing someone else interpret them.

He was really good. I mean, really, really good. He used his voice the way a master chef uses a knife: quick, short cuts here, long slices there, stabbing at something that looked like it might get away. When the character Stephen realizes that something Drew refers to as "pretty rotten" and "the worst, actually" is something other than getting a positive result on an HIV test, Alden hisses, "You asshole" at Drew. That hiss, the way Alden delivered it, contained not only relief for his friend, not only anger because Drew has drawn out the revelation deliberately, but also something unidentifiable that speaks of Stephen's deeply conflicted feelings about Drew. Sometimes I was so affected by Alden's interpretations that I was struck dumb and had to be fed my line.

By the time we had to perform, his Stephen was much richer and deeper than my Drew. Of course, you could say the playwright had meant for that to happen, but I was pretty sure it took a natural, someone like Alden, to open the part up in that way.

Alden couldn't have known this, because I'd never talked to him about Daniel, but there were so many uncomfortable references to my relationship with Daniel that I was glad of all the rehearsing we did; otherwise, I wouldn't have had time to get over the discomfort enough to carry my part. I needed to play Drew with the superficial exterior the lines called for, while revealing subtly that Drew is much more uncomfortable in his own skin than he wants anyone to know.

I was both nervous and excited when it was time for our performance—obvious, I suppose, but I'd never felt quite like that before.

During our performance, our audience was mesmerized, mostly by Alden, though most of the laughs were mine. And just as he had made me speculate about the characters' relationship, he compelled the class members to do the same: Was there ever a thing between these two, even though Stephen is straight? Alden made the audience wonder.

A little further on, Drew chides Stephen for trying to match him up with someone Drew considered so boring as to be catatonic, and again, thanks mostly to Alden, the exchange left the audience confused regarding exactly how Stephen feels about Drew.

Alden and I spent the entire weekend after that last acting class at his place. The next week was finals, and he would be done by noon Thursday and on his way home that afternoon.

Over dinner Saturday, in Alden's apartment, I told him about my infatuation with Daniel. I saw it as pretty much over, despite the ongoing fascination, so I felt safe telling Alden how uncomfortable some parts of the play had made me.

He listened without speaking until I fell silent and then shrugged as if to dismiss the whole thing. But he didn't dismiss it.

"You've seen my scars," he said. "You've kissed them. My scars are physical. Visible. They caused a good deal of physical pain when they were created."

He picked up his wine glass, filled with a ruby red beverage he must have used his illicit ID card to purchase. "Gay men who fall for straight men usually end up with scars. It's just that most of them can't be seen." He took a sip and set the glass down. "Please don't collect any of those emotional scars. You're worth so much more than that."

He held my gaze for a few seconds before picking up his fork. He had to set it down again to laugh when I said, "El Speed calls him Dishroom Daniel."

"Oh, that's rich! That's great. Just keep thinking of him like that and you'll be okay."

"And you just keep being in my life, and I'll be even better."

It was a momentous weekend for me. I needed a condom for the first time. Or, Alden did.

"Are you sure you're ready?"

I was on my back, naked, knees bent, and Alden hovered over me, propped on his elbows. His look was intense and a little scary.

I laughed nervously. "No. Yes. No." Deep breath.

"Yes."

It hurt. I won't lie. But just like our first time, he was gentle with me. He made sure I knew I was in control, and that whoever played this part should always have the control. And he made sure that before we were done, it was very clear to me why so many men like this role so very much. I know that I'll do it again, and I know that it will hurt less, and what pain there is will become part of the pleasure.

Because, truly, there is *nothing* like having your prostate massaged for your pleasure.

And in unrelated but coincidental news, although I said nothing about it to Alden, I realized those euphoric feelings I'd had about him were mellowing out in a really good way. I kind of fell in love.

Finals week was about what I expected: a combination of "That went well" and "Oh my God I hope I passed that." I kept working in the dishroom, though the job got easer as the week went on; it was finals week attrition, a combination of some students not having time for meals and others leaving campus as soon as they could get away.

Daniel had more time than I did for post-shift coffee, not having any finals himself, so although he invited me a few times I couldn't manage it until Thursday. It was a welcome distraction, actually, from knowing I wouldn't see Alden again for weeks. I asked Daniel about his plans for the break.

"I'll be staying right here," he told me. "Hoping to do some skiing. Maybe some ice climbing. The Whites have a few good places for that, and I think it's been cold enough. Maybe Mount Washington."

"Where is home for you?"

"Philly." There was something final in his voice, like a subtext that said, *Ask nothing.* So I didn't.

"I'll be in Concord," I told him. "Not doing anything

that I know of." I considered telling him about Alden (which would have meant revealing that I was gay) but decided against it for reasons I couldn't have explained.

I hadn't seen Alden again since our weekend, but we'd texted and called each other. By the time I headed home for winter break on Friday, I was pretty sure he felt the same way about me that I did about him.

It was the first time I'd been home since Thanksgiving, when I'd made my big announcement. I'd wondered how Gram would treat me, and a lot of images and possible weird moments had tortured my mind. And she was a little different, I could tell—something awkward, almost as if she were walking on eggshells, though not quite that extreme.

One evening after dinner, I was washing the dishes when she approached me, almost sideways, to lay a used serving bowl on the counter beside me. It must have been overlooked when the dishwashing items had been collected.

I paused in my actions and watched the bowl's progress as she set it down slowly, saying nothing, not looking at me. She started to back away, just as slowly, just as tentatively.

"You know, Gram, I'm not made of glass. I'm not going to shatter."

She turned away from me but didn't move. "I'm sure I don't know what you mean, Nathan."

"Yes you do. You're not sure who I am any more, and you don't know how to act around me."

I grabbed a towel and dried my hands as I turned toward her. "Look at me, Gram."

She turned her head only enough for me to see the side of her face.

"Look at me, Gram."

I waited until she'd turned completely around to face me. I'd given a lot of thought to what I would say if she acted like this, and I was ready.

"I'm the same me, Gram. No difference. It's just that instead of a colonial pine, rough-hewn, rectangular table like you've always thought of me, I'm a round, polished maple. You think some of what you knew about me has fallen off of that pine table, and now you don't know how much of it should go back onto the round one."

I set the towel onto the counter and leaned my hip against the hard surface for support. "All of it goes back. All of it. What's different is the table, but that's all. I still like the same things. The same foods, the same activities, the same music. I still love the same people in the same way."

She stared at me in a way that told me she was taking this in, but like maybe she didn't know what to do about it yet. Then she nodded, and as she moved close to give me a hug, I saw tears in her eyes.

We wrapped our arms around each other, and it hit me that I was taller than she was. This was hardly a revelation; it had been true for a while. But at that moment, it meant something more than physical height. It meant I'd come into my own in a way that both of us acknowledged.

Grown up or not, fully adult or still part little kid, I tortured myself over the next few days, unable to stop thinking about Alden, debating whether to text him, or call him, or leave him alone. Neither of us had reached out to the other since I'd left campus to come home, and that seemed odd. Wrong. Worrying. I did finally cave on Christmas Eve.

Hey. Thinking of you. Missing you.

All I got in return was, *Same*. It felt abrupt, dismissive. I decided to wait and see if he texted or called; I wouldn't take the first step again. It was a painful decision.

Daniel, however, did text me a few times while I was at home for the break. At first I thought he was just trying to keep tabs on Nina without pestering her; she hadn't outright rejected him, but she had been seeing someone else recently.

ON CHOCORUA

But then, the first full week of January we had a snowstorm that dropped about eight inches of soft, powdery stuff in Concord, and more than that had fallen in the mountains. Daniel didn't text me this time. He called.

"Nathan, didn't you tell me you had Nordic skis?"

"I did, yeah. I do. Why?"

"And you said you loved trailblazing?"

"I do."

"Great! We can't waste this snow. How about I pick you up this afternoon? We can head up to a cabin I know of around Jackson and ski our brains out until Friday."

My brain froze. My mouth didn't. "Um, sure, okay."

The whole time I was giving him instructions to my house, some corner of my brain was squirming. Should I tell him I'm gay before he spends a couple of overnights with me? And if I tell him, will he be pissed, either because the idea of being alone with a gay guy gave him the heebie-jeebies, or because he'd be insulted that I hadn't trusted him enough to have told him already? Would he ever want to talk to me again? Would I lose even his friendship?

And how would I introduce him to Gram, who might very well assume that we were a couple, and that he was the person I'd mentioned at Thanksgiving? It seemed unlikely that Nina would have talked to Gram about Daniel, so that was no protection. I could maybe get ahead of things by explaining to Gram, before Daniel got here, that he was just a friend. She wasn't home at the moment, but how much time would I have between her return and his arrival?

So in between telling Daniel to take this highway and that exit and this right and that left, my brain was like, *What should I do? What should I do?* ***What should I fucking do?***

"Nathan, bring your woolies. We'll be in a cabin with no electricity and only a wood stove for heat."

"K."

"I'll swing by at around two. That will give us plenty of time to warm the place up before we have to sleep in it."

He was about to hang up. It was now or, maybe, in a truly awkward moment in front of Gram.

"Wait!"

"Problem?"

"I need to let you know about something before you meet my grandmother."

"K. Shoot."

I stood in my room, facing the street, my eyes fixed on the big, white, New England colonial with black shutters across from our house. There was a huge, spreading tree in the front yard, its dark bones showing through white snow that had collected where branches intersected. A red Toyota Highlander stood in the driveway in front of the closed garage door. Time stood still.

Why was I more nervous about telling Daniel than I had been about telling my own grandmother? Hell, I was almost as nervous as when I'd come out to Neil.

"Nathan?"

Deep breath. Close eyes. Open eyes. Stare at the red Toyota.

"I'm upset with myself for not telling you this before now. But it's possible that Gram will say something that gives it away. And just let me say that if it means you'd rather not do this trip, then—"

"Spit it out, kid." His tone was teasing, and that seemed like something I'd lose if things went badly. "Ye gods, you'd think you were trying to tell me you're a serial killer."

"Okay, yeah. Well, the thing is—it might bother you, or it might not. It doesn't bother me, and it doesn't affect, y'know, being friends."

"Nathan?" Still teasing, though there might have been some impatience in there.

"I'm gay."

The pause was just long enough for me to register that it was a pause. Then, "And?"

"And... and I just thought you should know."

"What is it you think your grandmother might—oh!" and he laughed. It was a real laugh, not a fake one, coming from low in his body. "I get it! She knows about you, and she might think we're together, is that it?" I heard a low chuckle. "Doesn't she know I've been going out with Nina?"

"I'm not sure." Liar.

He sighed. "Yeah. I get the sense that I enjoy being with her more than she enjoys being with me. But I haven't given up! And as for you, why wouldn't you just introduce me as someone who's seeing Nina? That would solve the whole problem; I doubt that your grandmother would land automatically on the idea that I'm bi. Which I'm not, by the way, since we're being all up front about ourselves today. Now, are we on? Snow's a wastin'."

I grinned at the red car and took a couple of shaky breaths. I'd heard so many horror stories about what happens when gay people come out to family and friends that I couldn't believe how little chaos my revelations were creating in my life. It wasn't perfect, but was I lucky, or what?

Daniel drove up in a well-used Jeep Wagoneer of a muddy brown color, and I was at the front door before he powered off the engine. As he hopped out, he opened his arms wide, a huge, facetious-looking smile on his face, and called, "Nota Bene! Welcome to the mungmobile tours!"

"Okay, you have to explain that."

He gestured toward the Jeep. "Is there an uglier color anywhere? Mung. It's the best description. But she's a great old car. Reliable, and the four-wheel-drive has gotten us out of a couple of places I shouldn't have made her go into."

"And the other part? Nota Bene?"

He laughed. "N.B. Your initials. I've been thinking of you as Nota Bene ever since you told me about singing. It means to note well. Or, beautiful notes, maybe?"

I did my best to hide the secret pleasure that gave me,

143

knowing he'd been thinking about me, hearing that he'd come up with a nickname for me that might be a little silly, but that wasn't altogether unwelcome. It was a lot better than Dishroom Daniel, which he'd never hear from me.

Daniel helped me load my stuff into the back of the Jeep. "Where's this grandmother of yours? Do I get to meet her before we head out?"

"Maybe on the way home Friday. She's still out, actually. I thought she'd be back, but it was only a guess. I left her a note, and she has my cell number."

Neither of us said anything about my true confession on the drive north. It was an incredible rush that Daniel was so accepting. The truth was out, and it was okay. The old weight-off-the-shoulders cliché didn't come close to how great that felt.

The deeper we got into the White Mountains, the darker it seemed at the road level; the mountains blocked any late afternoon sunlight. The sky was noticeably lighter than the landscape by four thirty when Daniel pulled the mungmobile into what was no more than a cleared spot off the east side of Route 16, a little south of the Wildcat Mountain ski area. At least the spot had been cleared of all but a few inches of snow.

Someone had also scraped most of the snow off of the twenty-five or so steps that led up a steep incline from the car to the cabin.

Daniel set a battery-powered lantern on the only table inside the cabin on our first trip, and as I looked around he said, "Holy crap, but it's cold in here! Before we bring up another load, let's get the stove going."

He held a hand toward it and then placed his palm fully onto it. "It's been used recently, probably earlier today. Probably by whoever cleared the snow."

"You're sure the people whose cabin this is won't want

it for the next few days?"

He shrugged. "I called him. He said no. But even if someone showed up, there's plenty of room."

I'd never used a wood stove, so I just brought wood inside from a shelter on the side of the cabin and let him start the fire.

We had to make three trips each to bring everything up from the car, including some plastic gallon containers of water. The last haul included the skis, which Daniel didn't want to leave in the car.

"We'll leave them hidden behind the cabin," he told me between panted breaths on that final climb, "so they'll be the same temperature as the snow in the morning. But I don't trust leaving them in the car by the road."

By the time we'd hauled everything into the cabin, the stove had barely begun to warm things up; it was still cold enough inside that we could see our breath—barely, but it was visible. The table had six wooden chairs around it, and there were three sets of double bunks—one up, one down— installed along two walls. Daniel threw his stuff on one of the bottom bunks, and I chose another. He poured some water into a pot and set it on the stove.

"That'll take a while. Now, I don't think we want to try and cook here. You stay with the fire—shouldn't leave it alone at this stage, and it might need more wood—while I go hunting and gathering. K?"

"K." I knew how to throw a log on a fire; I figured I could handle the stove for a while.

Daniel was gone for nearly an hour, but when he got back he had take-out stuff from a pub. He also had a six-pack of beer, and I wondered if he got his ID from the same place as Alden.

As we ate, I tried to get a sense of whether there was any change in our conversation, any tension that might have come from my revelation earlier. Didn't seem like it. We chatted, we laughed, he called me Nota Bene once or twice, and the way that made me feel caused me to bring Alden's warning to mind: avoid the emotional scars I'd earn if I fell for a straight guy.

After dinner was cleaned up, Daniel pulled a bottle out of a duffle bag he'd brought.

"I had only one beer," he said, "and you did, too. Let's put our feet up and have some pretty decent Kentucky bourbon. Whadya say?"

I laughed. "I say, yeah! I've never had bourbon."

"Excellent. Do you care about glasses?"

"Not if you don't."

We pulled two of the chairs over near the wood stove. Between slugs of the fiery stuff, Daniel and I talked about our lives in a way we never could have over a table in the dining hall.

He opened. "You seeing anyone, Nathan?"

"Sort of. A guy I met in acting class." I decided to test Daniel. "We started as fuck buddies. It's kind of gone beyond that now." At least, I hoped it had; I was feeling a little isolated from Alden about now.

I'd kind of hoped to shock Daniel. But no. He said, "Had me one of those, once. Young woman at school. Jordan. Very bright. Ambitious. Competitive. She wanted nothing to do with marriage or kids, but boy did she like to fuck. And she liked to fuck me." He laughed out loud. "She was easily the most physical, sensual person I've ever known."

"Pretty?"

His hand, fingers wrapped around the bourbon bottle, halted midway between his lap and his face. He looked at me oddly. "Why do you ask?"

I'd committed some faux pas, I could tell. I just didn't know what it was. "No reason. Maybe because Nina is so different."

"Nina is no fuck buddy. And I don't say that just because she's your sister." He took a swig. "I wouldn't have said Jordan was pretty. Interesting face, rather. Heavy-set.

Very strong. Powerful, even." He shook his head, grinning as though remembering carnal pleasure that might never come again. "Wonder where she is today."

He handed me the bottle almost absentmindedly. More to deflect from my stumble than anything else, I moved into what I thought would be mundane territory. "What's your family like? Siblings?"

Suddenly there was a hole in the room. Or maybe it was a psychic cold spot. I was sure I'd stepped into another pile of shit. What the hell was wrong with me?

Daniel's voice had a ring of false nonchalance. "Not any more. My sister and my dad died when I was fifteen."

"Oh. Sorry to hear that." I was scrambling for yet another diversionary topic when Daniel decided to add a few details.

"My mom remarried two years later. I don't get along with the guy. Didn't even consider a college close to home."

He reached for the bottle, and even though I hadn't yet taken any bourbon, I gave it to him, saying, "My folks are both dead. Car crash. My grandfather was with them."

"Yeah. Nina told me when I asked her why you live with your grandmother."

Maybe that's what encouraged him to say something about his own loss? But no details, nothing about what had happened.... Whatever. I reached for the bourbon.

It seemed like anything personal between us, between Daniel and me, still hinged somehow on Nina. Was that fair? Or true? I wasn't sure it mattered any more.

I expected to have trouble falling asleep, and I might have, except that I began to hear Daniel's light snoring within a few minutes of snuggling into my own sleeping bag (which was actually an old one of Neil's), and it kind of lulled me into a pleasant state and then out like the proverbial light.

I woke early, before the cabin was fully light. No

snores. No sounds of any kind, except the occasional snapping coal in the wood stove, which made me think Daniel had probably fed it once or twice during the night. Was he awake now?

As quietly as possible, I got up onto an elbow so I could look in the direction of Daniel's bunk. It took me a couple of minutes to figure out that the hulking shape there was Daniel, sitting up, totally still. In a flash I realized he was meditating.

I lay back down and dozed on and off until I heard Daniel stir, and then I headed for the chemical toilet. I would have expected it to smell; maybe the little hallway between the main cabin and the toilet, a closed door at either end, helped let some odors escape the building. For sure it kept the toilet about as cold as the outdoors, and that would keep smells down, too.

Daniel had packed hard-boiled eggs for Saturday breakfast, and he'd made a loaf of what he called "Mrs. Cooke's Famous Cardamom Bread." It deserved to be famous. There was enough heat left in the stove to keep the water in the kettle barely hot enough for instant coffee. It was very cold in the cabin, but we didn't want to stoke the fire right before we left.

We stepped into our skis behind the cabin. Cold temperatures in the mountains had kept the snow, fresh and new yesterday, in great condition for today.

Daniel led the way, gliding with practiced, powerful strides as he headed north, across a couple of open areas—fields for summer planting?—and toward a wooded area. The trees were fairly far apart, so the way was easy-going, until Daniel headed a little more toward the east. Here the land, which had been a gentle uphill climb, dipped steeply down to a stream, partly frozen around the edges. I followed Daniel along the bank until he spotted a crossing.

A thick log, stubs where branches had once been in various places along its length, lay across the narrow gap.

Daniel didn't hesitate. Still in his skis, he turned and side-stepped across the log, as sure-footed as a mountain goat, removing most of the snow in his progress. He hopped off at the other end of the log.

"Your turn, Nota Bene."

It wouldn't be my first log crossing on skis, but this one looked especially sketchy. It was critical that I didn't look like chicken shit in front of Daniel. I stepped up onto the log and inched my way across, forcing myself to move carefully in favor of showing off with a fast crossing. Why did I feel the need to impress him? I told myself it was just two guys doing something athletic, with neither wanting to seem like he couldn't hack it.

I followed Daniel up steep slopes, around trees, up more slopes and around more trees, and when he came to a stop I was right with him. As comfortable as I was on skis, I was proud and even a little surprised that I'd been able to keep up.

Daniel stood, leaning on his poles a little as he angled them together, skis pointing a little sideways on the slope. An open space gaped directly uphill from where he stood. I maneuvered my skis between young trees and into a position beside him as best I could. The woods ended here, and the incline rose to what looked like a narrow, snowy road. It went steeply uphill to the right and around a curve, and to the left it went down just as steeply and around another curve. It was no road; there were slalom stakes on it.

Daniel craned his neck in one direction and then the other. When his head turned quickly in my direction, his face wore an eager, even conspiratorial expression.

"I don't have my telemark skis," he said as one eyebrow went up and down a couple of times, "but I can't help myself. Wait here."

I watched, with interest at first and then concern, as I realized what Daniel was going to do. He was going to ski this slope on his Nordic skis, a slope obviously set up for people who really knew what they were doing on downhill skis. Even telemark skis wouldn't be up to a professional downhill run like this, despite having edges like downhill skis and a fully-attached boot. I looked down at my own foot, secured to the ski at the toe only, and lifted my heel. No way there would be enough control. Daniel was crazy.

I clambered up the last bit of rise to be as close to the ski run as possible without being on it, and I watched as Daniel skittered out onto the run. His technique, over open fields and through trackless woods, had impressed me. I wasn't surprised to hear him say he had his own telemark skis, though that sport isn't exactly robust anymore. And I wouldn't have been surprised to learn that he was equally good at that. But on Nordic skis, with no edges to support a sharp carve turn, heels helping only a little and only if he pressed his weight down on them hard, he looked awkward and wobbly. As he rounded the downhill curve, the last thing I saw was a pole that stabbed hard into the snow at an angle. I half expected to see him herringboning his way back around the curve toward me, covered in white powder from the fall I thought he must have taken, but—nothing.

Before long, a whispering sound to my right made me look up the run. I nearly jumped as a figure in tight clothes of bright colors whisked by at a break-neck speed. Knees flexed and close together, he whisked around the slalom poles like a pro. As I watched him disappear around the curve to my left, I noticed the number on his back: sixteen.

Sixteen. Why would that skier be sixteen? I was still staring downhill when that whisper from uphill made me turn that way again, and there was number seventeen.

"Holy shit," I said to the trees around me. "Holy fucking shit."

Another skier flew past me. Number eighteen. Then number nineteen.

"Daniel is going to get slaughtered," I told the trees around me.

What I was seeing was a timed slalom run—a competitive run, either a qualifying run or even the competition itself. Having watched Neil compete in a couple of amateur events, I knew what Daniel would see at the end of the run, if he made it that far. There would be a crowd, maybe a small one, but they'd be clustered fairly close to the final gate. At that gate an automatic timer would register the run time for each skier, in the same order as they had left the top of the run. At any one time, there were multiple competitors on their way to that gate.

Daniel would come unsteadily down the final slope toward the gate. He would have very little control, he'd be going pretty fast, and he wouldn't be able to stop. He might be able to manage a gentle turn, but that would take him plowing into the crowds. He could fall, but he might be injured, and unless he could scramble out of the way quickly he would be in the path of skier sixteen. He would have little choice but to go through the gate.

We weren't very far up the side of the mountain, so we were fairly close to the end of the run. Daniel would get to the gate ahead of skier sixteen and ruin the timing of him and of every other skier who'd left the top of the run before they could be stopped.

All I could do was wait. He had his phone on him, and I had mine, so if he got arrested maybe he could text or call. If he got injured maybe he could text or call. But if he killed himself falling, or if the competition skiers killed him in a rage, I wouldn't know.

Not sure how long to wait, not willing to follow Daniel down the groomed alpine slope, I stood where I was. Anxiety made time go painfully slowly. In the near silence I heard the gentle gurgle of a tiny stream nearby, and although usually I love the soft plop as pine branches release their pads of snow, I couldn't enjoy it. At some point I realized I hadn't seen a skier for some time. The top of the run had gotten word, then, and Daniel had fucked things up.

I can't say how long I stood there, but for sure I was starting to chill; Nordic skiing is aerobic, and if you have too many warm clothes on you'll steam yourself out, so you don't wear a lot of layers while you're skiing. When you stop, you get cold. I was just considering digging something warmer out of my backpack when I saw motion at that curve just downhill from where I was.

It was Daniel. He was working hard—very hard—to get back up the slope as quickly as possible, jumping from ski to ski and flailing his poles. When he got closer he waved a pole at me.

"Into the woods!" he shouted. "Get away from the run!"

Maneuvering my skis around the trunks of saplings, I managed to turn and slide back down the way we had come. The terrain continued down and northwest, away from the run, and I took advantage of it to move as quickly as I could, Daniel close behind me.

At some point I could tell he had stopped, so I stopped and looked back. He was staring behind us, no doubt watching for pursuers. All I could hear was my own panting breaths and pounding heartbeats.

Finally he turned back toward me. "I think we're safe."

He leaned his hands on his knees and waited until his breathing settled and then said, "Do you understand what just happened?"

I nodded. "How badly did they want to kill you?"

He shook his head. "I'm lucky to be alive and a free man." He straightened up and looked at me, and I looked at him, and he started to laugh. So did I.

We laughed until we couldn't stand. First Daniel and then I fell sideways into the snow, rolling as much as our skis would allow, and we laughed some more.

My belly hurt. Honest to God.

Daniel sat up, still chuckling kind of helplessly. "I gotta take a piss."

He reached for the boot release on one ski. Too weak

from laughter to manage it, he fell back onto the snow and laughed some more.

"Maybe I can just do it from here. You won't mind, will you?"

"Not as long as you point the other way. Think I'll join you."

So we lay in the snow, dicks exposed to the cold, enough on our sides to point away from ourselves and each other, and we let loose. If you've never heard the expression, "Don't eat yellow snow," this might be a lesson for you.

Daniel managed to sit up again, and so did I. He said, "If I'd waited long enough to see a skier go by, I wouldn't have done that. I would have known. But I didn't!"

He laughed some more, but not so hysterically. I just grinned and watched him. God, but he was gorgeous. The contrast of the pure white snow and his slightly coppery skin seemed to highlight the Cherokee part of him. His eyes sparkled with humor, and his grin was infectious.

On top of all that, there's nothing more attractive to me than a man who can do something ridiculous and then truly enjoy laughing at himself about it. In my book, a good sense of humor requires a person to be able to laugh at themselves. I was working toward that. Wasn't quite there yet, still too concerned with not doing anything ridiculous, ever—or at least not to be seen doing it. But I could laugh with Daniel.

Confidence. That had a lot to do with it. Confident people are seductive without trying to be. Daniel was exceptionally seductive. I reminded myself to resist.

He seduced me again, and again unwittingly, late the next morning. We were on a much tamer trail, one that was intended for Nordic skiers and had been recently groomed. We had just come down a magnificent run through the woods, with tight turns around trees and boulders that might do you in if you were going too fast to control the turns. I let Daniel stay ahead of me by a good bit; if he fell, I needed to be able to avoid him, and this was a narrow, winding trail.

The run leveled out in an open area where the trail curved to the left just before a stand of trees. I'd managed the turn when I heard something behind me. I looked back in time to see Daniel emerging from the trees, covered in snow. One ski was still on his right foot. He held the other ski and both poles in one hand, his free hand batting snow off of himself. He was obviously unhurt.

He looked up at me, and with the most deadpan face he could manage, he said, "Absolutely nothing happened."

God, but I wanted to hear from Alden.

That night, after dinner in Conway, we headed back to the cabin to enjoy more from that bottle of bourbon. We were headed home in the morning, and maybe that was why we recounted our adventures, laughing about most of them, sitting in our usual spot where we could enjoy the heat coming from the wood stove.

At one point I handed the bottle to Daniel, and instead of taking a swig he said, "Sing me something, Nathan."

To say that I was not expecting that would be a huge understatement. "Sing?"

"Sure. It doesn't have to be Mozart, or anything. Do you know any popular songs?"

I searched my mind for two things: one was an answer to his question; the other was any excuse at all for not singing. I hit on this excuse: "Nothing that wouldn't really need to be accompanied. You know, guitar, or keyboards, that sort of thing."

"Nothing?"

I examined his face, as well as I could in the soft light the lantern and wood stove were throwing. He seemed genuine. He seemed like he really wanted to hear something. He wasn't trying to put me on the spot; he must have thought that singers like to, you know, sing. I decided to take a chance. I'd had just enough bourbon to do it, and not so much that it would hamper my ability to croon.

"Well, maybe some torch songs come to mind. I mean, any of it would benefit from some backup, but there are torch songs that can stand alone."

"Torch songs?"

"You know, songs about love and loss and heartbreak. Think Judy Garland in her heyday."

"Wow. You know some of those songs?"

I sat up a little straighter, considered my opening pitch in relation to the song's overall range, closed my eyes, and sang one of the two songs that had gone in and out of my mind just after I'd met Daniel, and especially since I'd realized that he was not for me. One of the songs was, in fact, "Not For Me." The opening line was, "They're writing songs of love, but not for me." It goes on about what a fool the singer was to act like they expected anything to happen. When I finished, I opened my eyes to see an incredulous expression on Daniel's face.

"My God, Nota Bene! You've been hiding your light under a bushel!" He leaned back a little in his chair, mouth hanging open in what looked like naked admiration. "Do you know any more?"

How could I not sing more? I went through "What Are You Doing the Rest of Your Life?" and "I Only Have Eyes For You" and "Mean to Me" and "Stormy Weather" and a few others.

Finally I told Daniel I'd end this impromptu concert with one of my favorites. What I didn't tell him was that thoughts I'd had about him earlier in the fall inspired it: "You Go to My Head."

I sang with a languid feeling, letting my voice slide between notes when that felt right. It ends with, "And though I'm certain that this heart of mine hasn't a ghost of a chance in this crazy romance, you go to my head."

There was no sound in the room but crackling noises from inside the wood stove for maybe a minute. Then Daniel said, "Thank you, Nathan. Man, if I could sing like that, I might just do that for a living."

I looked sideways at him and smiled. "Oh, I don't think so. Not unless you could give concerts on mountain tops."

He threw his head back and laughed. He knew I was right.

On the drive back the next day, it occurred to me Daniel had wanted to decide by December whether he would transfer schools, and I hadn't heard anything more. So I asked, "By the way, are you enrolling at UNH next year?"

There was a pause just long enough to make me wonder whether he'd heard me before he replied, his tone flat and lifeless. "If I go back to New Jersey next fall, my mom and stepfather will pay the tuition."

"But not here?"

"Not here. No."

It wasn't what he wanted. I knew it wasn't. And it seemed obvious he didn't have the money to pay his own way. I was sorry I'd brought it up.

It was a difficult weekend. My mind kept recreating images of Daniel, the man with the perfect body, the man who could seduce me with his confidence and his sense of humor and his compliments and—well fuck, with his attention. Attention I wasn't getting from the man I wanted it from.

When I thought of Alden, my emotions bounced around between longing and painful resentment. I remember thinking, *Come on, Alden! You're the one who told me not to let myself fall for Daniel. Dishroom Daniel. Where are you when I need you?*

At that point, it felt like he was nowhere. And it hurt.

156

INTERLUDE VII

Life with Neil: The Fist Fight

It was Neil's second year in high school, tenth grade. He was fifteen and revealing occasional embarrassment as his voice pitch tried to lower itself and often sounded like one of Gram's old vinyl records that would skip over a scratch. And there was the ridicule from Nina. I felt like the baby, still in the fifth grade, not even in middle school yet, but that didn't stop me from trying to deepen my vocal pitch artificially and getting ridiculed for it by—you guessed it. Nina.

For her part, Nina was eleven, just starting middle school, and although I knew how to do the math, it annoyed me that she would always be ahead of me. And she had her own growing pains to deal with, though I was thoroughly and upon-pain-of-death excluded from knowing anything about it and from snooping around to try and understand it better. All I knew was that it had to do with blood. It was totally mysterious. She did her best to distract any curiosity I might express by pointing out that she was precocious, being ahead of almost all her girlfriends in this rite of passage on her way to womanhood.

I have to say, it didn't seem like any fun. Not only did she have to deal with blood, but also she would sometimes roll on her bed, arms wrapped around her belly, and groan softly. I wasn't even sure that the pain and the blood went together, but it seemed likely.

I learned more about it one day in late October. The weather had been chilly—mid-fifties on a sunny day, down to thirty-something at night. Then right before Halloween there was a really warm Thursday, all the way into the seventies.

Nina had had a fight with her best girlfriend earlier in the week. Wednesday, they didn't walk home together. Nina wanted to avoid her friend altogether, so she had walked past the high school on her way home and had waited for Neil, and he'd walked with her the rest of the way.

On that warm Thursday, Nina must have decided to repeat her Wednesday journey, but when she got to the high school she didn't see Neil right away. In her typical impatience, she didn't settle someplace, send him a text, and wait. She did sit on a bench to send him a text, but then she paced, back and forth in front of the driveway into the high school.

The rest of this story is a little sketchy. I wasn't there when it happened, so I'm recreating the scene from the bits and pieces I heard through Nina's weeping and Neil's angry words as they told Gram about it.

Evidently, at one point in her pacing, Nina happened to turn her back toward two eleventh-grade boys who immediately exploded in whooping laughter. They closed the distance between Nina and themselves quickly, and while one of them stood behind her, the other blocked her forward progress.

"What's the matter, little girl?" the one in front taunted her. "What's wrong?"

Nina says she snorted at them—a bravery I almost buy, considering it was Nina—and told them nothing was wrong and to get out of her way.

At which point the boy behind her, using a tone of voice dripping ridicule, said, "Oh, something's wrong, all right. I think maybe you need to go home and talk to your mommy about why girls have to bleed."

In my mind, I imagine Nina whirling to face the boy behind her but immediately realizing that would leave her red-stained back side exposed, so she took refuge on the bench, sitting on the offending body part and hiding it in the process.

"Go away! Leave me alone!"

Nina says she wasn't crying yet at this point, and maybe I believe her. But the boys weren't through. They bantered back and forth, taunting the mortified Nina, dancing toward her and away, toward her and away as they threw their barbs.

"I know! Let's go to the little girls' room and get one of those tampon things."

"And then we'll need to get some stain remover. And some laundry detergent."

"Hey, little girl, come to the laundromat with us. We can shove you into the washing machine. Might remove all kinds of stains!"

When Neil ran full tilt into one of the two boys, I'm sure Nina was bleeding emotionally from several wounds. Neil's tackle knocked one boy into to the other, and they both hit the sidewalk. He stood over them, fists clenching, breath hissing.

"You assholes! You leave my sister the fuck alone!"

One of them got up and started swinging, and he and Neil went at it. Nina kept her eyes on the other boy, and when it looked like he was going to join his friend she got up and reamed him from behind with her book bag.

By the time a pair of teachers came running and put a stop to the melee, both Neil and his opponent had damaged each other's faces enough to need cold packs.

At home, I didn't understand about the stain, but I relished the story thoroughly while Gram seemed torn between chastising Neil for starting a fight and wanting to hug him for coming to Nina's rescue.

Later I knocked on Neil's door. I wanted to know what the stain was. He told me. That was the first I heard about the start of a girl becoming a woman.

CHAPTER NINE

Winter break ended, and the next semester got underway the second Wednesday in January. Back in the dorm on Tuesday night, El Speed had some good news; Ellie had—well, maybe not quite forgiven him, but was at least his girlfriend again. And Gordon was in rehab. El Speed didn't say where, but I'd have been willing to bet it wouldn't have been as luxurious as I was sure Alden's had been.

Speaking of Alden, I was conflicted. I was angry with him, but I was also really looking forward to seeing him again. No more acting class meant we were unlikely to have any classes in common, and we'd made no specific plans when we'd left campus a few weeks ago. He'd told me he wasn't looking forward to St. Louis, but he didn't say why. I'd tried to get him to elaborate, but he'd changed the subject pointedly. Did he not get along with his folks? They seemed to have accepted that he was gay; was that acceptance not as complete as he'd made it sound?

In my more generous moments, I told myself I didn't want to pressure him or make him feel penned in. But when I hadn't heard from him by Thursday night I texted him.

Hey, guy. Just checking in. You back yet?
Nothing.
Friday afternoon I sent another message.
Nothing.
Saturday evening I was alone in the room, what with El Speed and Ellie being back together, and I was unable to stop myself from calling Alden. All I heard was his outgoing message: "It's Alden. You know what to do and when to do it."

I did my best to make my voice sound breezy. "Hey

Alden. Nathan here. Um, just checking in to see what Santa brought you for Christmas. I'm not telling you what I got till I hear from you, so there."

I needed El Speed. Scratch that; I needed anything to distract myself from fixating on Alden's silence. Maybe if El Speed hadn't gone back to Maine already, having just spent time with his fucking girlfriend for weeks....

Down, Nathan. This isn't Ellie's fault. It isn't El Speed's fault. But if he'd been there, maybe he and I could have gone somewhere, done something, to distract me. Hell, maybe he'd have let me borrow his car so I could drive myself to Dover and confront that *ex*-boyfriend of mine and make him account for himself!

Well... I could get to Dover without El Speed's car, couldn't I? I could take the bus! So I did. But first I pulled out my phone to check one more time, in case I'd missed a tone of one kind or another. There was nothing from Alden. No phone call, no text, no email, nothing.

Fuck.

The white BMW was parked beside Alden's house. Near it was a battered Chevy truck of an indiscriminate color, which I had learned belonged to the downstairs neighbor, and in front of the house was a large, black Lincoln.

I stood in the trees, unsure what to do. Lights shone from Alden's windows, which pissed me off; if he was home, why the fuck was he avoiding me? I called his number one last time and got the same recorded message.

Shivering, watching the windows, I saw a figure moving around behind the blinds. It didn't look like Alden. I could have sworn it was a woman. So—what, had Alden left school? Had he gone home to St. Louis and just decided not to come back, not to let me know? If so, why was his car here? And whose Lincoln was that? Did it belong to someone else he was seeing? But—hadn't that been a woman's silhouette at the window?

I had to know. I rang the doorbell and heard it chime from inside.

Nothing happened. I waited a full ninety seconds. I rang the bell again, twice.

Maybe a minute later I heard someone on the stairs, and a woman opened the door. She was tall, light-haired, and maybe approaching sixty years old. She didn't speak.

I did. "Sorry to bother you, but I was hoping Alden was here."

I half expected her to ask who Alden was, but instead she stared at me. Seconds passed, maybe ten of them, before she said, "Who are you?"

Who was I? Seriously? I didn't know what to tell her other than, "Nathan Bartlett."

She nodded. "You'd better come in."

My chest felt tight as I climbed the stairs. What the hell was going on? Something was wrong, that was certain.

The apartment was in total disarray, boxes everywhere, things being packed. I stood at a spot between the living room and the kitchen, not clear what to do next.

"Please," the woman said, "sit down."

Half the couch was clear of boxes, as was the chair beside it. I took the chair.

"I'm Diane Armstrong, Alden's mother," she said as she settled onto the front edge of the couch cushion. She took a shaky breath. "Alden mentioned you. I know you were very close."

Were? "Um, where is Alden?"

Her eyes closed for just a second, and she took a deep breath. "Alden is in Canada."

There was no sound in the room, but my ears reverberated with a dull thrumming. Canada. The word made no sense. Other words flew through my brain, unspoken and equally meaningless: *What? Why? What the fuck?* And then it hit me.

I barely heard my own voice say, "Rehab?" I looked around the room, eyes searching for the tall figure who had to be here. He *had* to be.

Mrs. Armstrong cleared her throat, and the sound brought my attention back to her. She seemed haggard, even through her composure. "So you knew about his addiction?"

I tried to get a sense of whether she was probing to see if I'd been involved with drugs, if I could be implicated in some way. "He told me. But he wasn't using any more. At least, as far as I know."

"He had a relapse over the holidays. It's not uncommon for that to happen to people in recovery. And he must have—" Her voice broke off. She closed her eyes and held her face as still as she could, then took another shaky breath. "He must have gotten a bad batch. One that was far too potent. And maybe his tolerance was down because he'd been sober for a year. He—" And she had to pause again to collect herself. "He nearly died. He was in a coma for three days."

I had to clear my throat. "Fentanyl?"

She nodded, pulled a tissue from somewhere, and blew her nose. Then, "I'm not sure why, but he decided not to keep anything from this apartment. I suspect it has to do with making a clean break, because part of his process relies on that. So I decided to come here, to do this myself. It's not an easy task, but I felt I had to do it. Is there anything you'd like? From his things, I mean."

Alden. I wanted Alden. A clean break? From everything? *Including me?!?* How was this *my* fault? And was there any way his connection with me had made him start using again?

I shook my head. My eyes burned, and a few tears escaped down my face.

"Take a few minutes, Nathan. I need to keep busy." She didn't add, "or I'll fall apart," but I listened between the lines.

I sat there, tears running down my face, listening to the sounds of things being lifted, wrapped, tucked away. Boxes scraped across the floor. Time passed. Not enough time. There would never be enough time.

I stood and paced the room, wanting to scream and yell but not wanting to upset Mrs. Armstrong. How could he do this to me? How could he just desert me, how could he exclude me not just from his recovery but *from his whole fucking life?*

I hated him. I loved him. I was furious with him! And I pitied him.

Christ!

I went into the bathroom to find some tissues and blew my nose thoroughly. I splashed cold water onto my face and wiped it with another tissue. I looked at myself in the vanity mirror.

Alden. Gone. Might as well be dead.

I should leave. I should let Mrs. Armstrong do what she needed to do. But if I left, it would be to go back to that dorm room where I'd be alone. I could walk the halls and see who else was around, but that seemed almost worse. How could I talk to anyone and be civil? How could I open my mouth without screaming? The fact was that Mrs. Armstrong, this person I didn't even know, was the only person I could talk to right now.

Several deep breaths later I went to find her. "What can I do to help? I guess I need to keep busy, too."

She put me to work stripping the bed, packing the sheets and pillows. I wondered whether she knew how poignant a task that would be for me; together, Alden and I had made good use of the bed clothes. Then I packed kitchen items—pots, pans, utensils, dishes—that Mrs. Armstrong said would be picked up by some charity tomorrow, along with all the furniture.

When I'd finished that, I found her in the bedroom, kneeling on the floor and packing books. "Mrs. Armstrong?" She looked up from her chore. "Have you found a couple of black, hooded, cape-like things?"

She stood, obviously an effort for her, and walked over to an open wardrobe box. "I was wondering what these were for."

"Alden and I did Halloween. We dressed in these, and blackened our teeth. We sat on the porch on those rocking chairs with a steaming cauldron and scared the willies out of trick-or-treaters. It was—it was kind of a special event for him. Do you mind if I have one of the capes?"

Her smile was tender. "You may have both of them." She reached into the wardrobe and pulled them out. As she held them toward me, something clicked. We wrapped our arms around each other and sobbed like little kids.

Wiping her face, she said, "I found something else while you were in the kitchen. Something else you might like." She went to the bureau and lifted a notebook off of it. "It looks like his notes from that scene the two of you did in your acting class."

Eastern Standard. Alden, the natural actor, who had schooled me in life and relationships. Alden, so rich in understanding and insight. Alden, gone. *How could this happen?*

I watched my hand take it from hers, imagining the conversation he'd had with her about the play, feeling sure it spoke of a close relationship between them. "Yes. Thank you."

"It's getting late, Nathan. You should probably go back to campus."

"I don't mind staying, if you could use some more help."

She thought for a minute and then said, "I am having a very hard time throwing out things that really should be thrown out. Things like his razor, and other personal things that I can't give away and I can't keep and I can't bring myself to discard."

I nodded and headed for the bathroom with a trash bag. It seemed to me that probably everything in here should go.

And mostly, it did. The only thing I didn't toss was a bottle of scent. I couldn't remember Alden wearing any, and yet it was half gone.

I carried it into the bedroom. "Before I toss this," I said, "I wanted to make sure it isn't important to you."

She reached for the bottle, eyes shining with tears. "This is mine. He must have brought it with him last fall. I couldn't image where it had got to."

"He didn't use it, though. At least, not that I know of."

She shook her head. "I think it reminded him of me."

I felt as though I'd been punched in the chest. If she was right, and it seemed likely that she was, she must have a very large, very special place in Alden's life. Why hadn't he told me more about her than the little I'd heard?

Stop it, Nathan. This is not about you.

Mrs. Armstrong uncapped the bottle and sprayed just a little onto her wrist. A woody fragrance, barely softened with something almost floral, floated to my nose. It didn't strike me as a woman's fragrance or, particularly, as a man's. The bottle itself was stylish but androgynous-looking. Even through my self-pity, it dawned on me that Alden's mother was a woman of strength and power as much as she was tender and loving. He must adore her.

I felt a profound sadness that had nothing to do with Alden. I'd never known my own mother.

Alden's mother lifted her eyes from the bottle to my face. "Did he ever talk to you about his addiction?"

"A little. Mostly what he said had to do with someone else I know who's been struggling with fentanyl. He mentioned his rehab center in Canada and going to see the Churchill polar bears."

"I just wondered... he never was able to articulate what had made him start using. My husband and I have tortured ourselves with the possibility that we were at fault somehow."

I didn't want to repeat what he'd said to me: *If someone feels they aren't good enough, not worthy enough, and they believe—or they're made to believe—that they can acquire that worth from something external to them, then whatever gives them that feeling becomes their addiction.*

What I told her was true as far as it went. "I never got that impression. The only things he said about you were good."

"Thank you." She started to get up, and I reached out to help her. "You're a good person, Nathan. And it's time you went back. Did you drive?"

"No. I took the bus."

"Will you go back that way?"

I shook my head. "I got here on the last run for today."

"It was that important to you to get here?"

"I—Alden—I'd left messages and called and didn't hear anything. And I guess I was worried. So I took a chance."

"There might have been no one here!"

"Yeah. It was a risk I was willing to take. I can hitch back."

She regarded me for a few seconds. Then, "It has helped me in ways you can't know for you to be here this evening. Will you do me one last favor?"

"Of course." More boxes? Carry stuff outside? Clean the sink?

"I can't bear to think of anything bad happening to you. I'm going to call a cab for you, and you are going to let me pay for it."

She didn't wait for an answer. I followed her into the living room where she scoured the room with her eyes until she located her cell phone. I wanted to tell her not to call anyone, that I could certainly get back on my own, but I wasn't entirely sure that wouldn't mean walking all the way.

So I let her do this favor for me. While we waited for the cab, I found myself staring at the tapestry by Sarah Warren that I'd noticed on my first visit here, and I realized that without any conscious intent, I had admired it each time

I'd been here.

"Mrs. Armstrong? Um, there is one other thing I'd like, if it's all right with you."

"Name it."

I pointed. "Alden really loved that tapestry. And I love it, too."

I watched her face, determined that if I saw the slightest hesitation I would withdraw the request.

She smiled. "It's yours. Other than belonging to my son, it has no special meaning for me."

I set down the black capes and the notebook, and lifted the beautiful thing from the wall. The edges of the work had been wrapped around a wooden frame, so that from five sides—front, and all four edges—all you saw was color.

"If he decides, you know, that he'd like it after all, just let me know."

The cab arrived, and I was about to head down the stairs. Mrs. Armstrong stood in the doorway. Already fairly sure what her answer would be, I asked, "Is it okay I contact him? Can you tell me where he is?"

She shook her head. "I'm sorry, Nathan. My husband and I can't even contact him. Not yet. And a clean break—"

"Yeah. Okay. Once you can talk to him, if it's all right to mention me," I nearly choked on the words, "please tell him I hope he'll be okay." I turned away quickly so she wouldn't see the tears pooling in my eyes.

On the drive back to Durham—my fists clutching the black fabric of Alden's capes, Alden's notebook pressed against my chest, the Warren tapestry propped against the side of my leg from its position on the floor—something changed in me. It felt as though I was turning into someone else, or at least into a different version of myself. All these things of Alden's surrounded me like a snug cocoon, and inside it I was morphing.

ON CHOCORUA

That mantra shot into my head again: *College is where you're supposed to do this*. But I had imagined that to "do this" would mean to do things like come out as gay. Or to see who you are when you're not with people who've known you since you were young and unformed. But this felt like another level. Reality had dawned, and any safety nets I'd relied on in the past were not going to save me from this pain, this confusion, this feeling of hopelessness. Because if this could happen to Alden, it could happen to anyone.

Gram.... Neil.... They'd been my surrogate mother and father.

They couldn't help me now.

So what could help me? Daniel was useless, at least for this. Nina—no way. El Speed?

El Speed had tried so hard to be Gordon's safety net. Images of Gordon in a room full of frat brothers and pledges tumbled together with my feelings about what had happened to Alden. The way Alden had described this substance, fentanyl, had made it seem evil. Malevolent. I knew it had good, medical uses, but also it seemed to have a will of its own, a will to entrap and even kill. It had nearly killed Alden. It might do so yet.

Once on television I'd seen an interview with a Muslim cleric who'd described evil as a force that was outside of life and outside of Allah. He'd made it sound like a wolf at the door, a wolf that could not come in unless someone opened that door.

Mrs. Armstrong had been as confused as I was as to why Alden had started using, confused about why Alden had opened that door. So it couldn't have been that he'd been on a prescription of some kind, and he'd gotten hooked that way, because she would have known that. When he'd told me he was in recovery, he'd said something about the drug stopping you from an emotional downward slide. What was there in Alden's life that would have sent him on that slide? It was infuriating that now, now that Alden was essentially dead to me, I couldn't ask him. This must have been the tiniest sliver of what haunted Mrs. Armstrong.

Why? Why would he do it? He had a good life. His family had money, his parents loved him and even accepted that he was gay. He was attractive, personally appealing, generous, and intelligent. He had a sense of humor and of decency. There was nothing wrong with his life.

I keep hearing that we should stop treating drug addicts like criminals. I agree that there are good reasons to stop that, to find a better way. But the fact remains that if someone starts taking recreational, illegal drugs, not something prescribed by a doctor, they *know* it's illegal. They *know* they're committing a criminal act. Do they think they won't get caught? Do they think they won't get hooked? Do they think they're immortal?

Do I think I'm immune? I'm pretty sure I wouldn't be immune to the drug, to the addiction. But am I immune to the influences that tempt smart, gifted people like Alden to start down that road of no return?

Why had he opened that door?

Sitting there surrounded by Alden's things, it seemed like I'd been inside a cocoon all my life. I mean, sure, bad things had happened, and I'd been anxious about a lot of things. But now I was aware of that cocoon. I knew I'd been in some kind of soft, protected space, and I knew the cocoon was disappearing. Hell, it had disappeared already, right here in the back of this cab.

Back in my dorm room, alone, with El Speed far away in Maine, it felt impossible to be still. I knew I wouldn't sleep, so I didn't try. And it wasn't long before I knew I had to get out of that room. Where I would go, I had no idea. I just had to get out.

As I stepped out of the dorm, the cold night air hit me harder than I would have expected. In my mind, I saw Alden's white BMW waiting by the curb, about to take us away from town to watch the lunar eclipse. The car's top had been down, and driving like that had felt very cold. He'd said it made him feel alive. What did fentanyl make him feel?

I shuddered and pulled my arms closer to my body.

Wandering around the dark campus in the cold wasn't much better than being in my room, so I headed for town. I wanted so much to get something to drink, something alcoholic, but I didn't have a fake ID or enough genuine years to my name. Even so, I went into a late night place that served pizza and soda and beer, not even knowing whether I wanted to order anything. It was noisy and crowded, and there was no place for me to sit, so I just paced slowly around, feeling alone, confused, hurt, angry.

A couple of people got up and left a table, and I noticed they hadn't finished their pitcher of beer. There was even some beer left in one of the glasses. I poured the pitcher's contents into the thick, heavy beer glass and chugged.

It felt good to do that. Satisfying, like I'd pulled one over on—on someone? Something? It didn't matter. I strolled around the room looking for similar opportunities and was amazed at how many there were. I don't think I was drinking a lot, but I was drinking fast, and I hadn't been able to eat much of my dining hall dinner, hours earlier. I began to feel a sense of invincibility, as though I was not going to get caught. And even if I did, what's the worst that could happen? I'd get kicked out of the place, right?

I had just started to chug from yet another glass when someone pushed me from behind. Some of the beer went up my nose, and some went onto my clothes.

I heard, "What the fuck do you think you're doing?"

I wheeled around and stared directly into the eyes of Byron Moreno.

"You!" he said.

"You!" I echoed.

"You're the rat who got our house into trouble."

"You're the asshole who got Gordon hooked!" Byron wasn't alone, of course, but I neither took this in nor cared, so I went on. "You're a bunch of sick bastards. You should be arrested and thrown into a bottomless pit!"

He shoved me again, from the front this time, and I noticed a couple of his companions, no doubt frat brothers, circling around behind me.

Byron nearly growled, "Go back to China or wherever you came from, you ugly immigrant."

I had no idea how to respond to that; all I could do was ignore it.

"You're a pack of wolves!" I shouted at them. "You attack people who can't fight back! Well, you've made a mistake with me!"

The heavy beer glass in my hand became a weapon. I swung it hard at Byron's head and heard a gratifying thunk as it connected hard with his jaw. Someone tried to grab me from behind, but I managed to swing the glass down hard onto his kneecap. I heard a yowl of pain from him as I felt someone's hands grab my clothing.

Immediately I was on the floor, the handle of the glass clenched in my fist and my arm swinging to keep attackers at bay, but it was no protection against the feet that kicked and kicked until my ribs were in agony and my face was a bloody pulp.

I was semi-conscious in the back of the ambulance as it wailed through dark streets. Nothing existed but pain and the siren. And maybe the knowledge that yes, I was now definitely a different version of myself.

Evidently there was some arrangement between the Durham police and the campus police, so no one got arrested. Probably it helped that the events of that fight were unclear enough that witnesses disagreed on what they saw.

There was a campus hearing before a disciplinary

panel, the Friday after the fight, where I got to tell my side of the story, and where El Speed would testify to my heretofore impeccable character. I laid it on thick about the fentanyl and its connection to Byron's frat, describing how Byron had led an anonymous friend into his trap, a friend who was now in rehab because of the hazing. I was going to mention Alden, but that felt so raw that I didn't trust my voice to remain steady. And it wasn't entirely relevant.

I was half-way through my tale when I noticed that Officer Kemper was there. His chair was right behind where El Speed was sitting, and when I'd finished my account the panel chair called on him.

"You know this witness?"

"I do," he said. "He was one of the individuals who reported hazing being perpetrated at Nu Lambda Psi."

"And that hazing involved fentanyl, is that correct?"

"It is."

Face all bruised, I must have looked like some kind of combat victim, or maybe a poster for stopping domestic violence, and as I'd made my way to and from the front of the room I'd moved slowly and carefully due to two badly bruised ribs. That, and maybe Kemper's and El Speed's testimonies, must have weighed more in the end than the minor injuries and complaints of Byron and one of his cohorts. I remember thinking that although I kind of wished I had broken Byron's jaw, I knew it would have made him more of a sympathetic character.

In the end, the panel wasn't sure what punishment to give anyone. So all those involved were put on a kind of probation where we had to report three times a week for a month to a designated panel member. The panel also required that the random drug testing that all members of Nu Lambda Psi had been required to submit to after El Speed and I had ratted on them be extended through the rest of the semester.

All in all it was the best outcome I could have hoped for.

I managed to get to my classes the week before the hearing, but there was no way I could work in the dishroom. This meant I didn't see Daniel there. But he came to me. He visited me two evenings, coming to my dorm room and chatting comfortably with El Speed and me. He didn't criticize my stupidity at starting that fight; instead, I sensed an undertone that told me he was impressed and maybe even a little proud of me.

El Speed made no secret of his position. He was thrilled at what I had done, and maybe four or five times told me, "That took guts, man."

I didn't talk about Alden. And he didn't ask.

Friday afternoon, Gram came and took me home for the weekend. She wanted me to see my regular doctor on Monday, and I knew she wanted to alternately baby me and chastise me. She gasped when she saw me; my bruises had taken on nearly all the colors of the LGBTQ flag.

I had plenty of time that weekend to do something that had been on my mind since my conversation with Alden's mother. Or, really, since my own struggles to understand why he'd been addicted at all. So what I wanted to do was research. I'd thought it might be hard. No way.

There was so much stuff out there about fentanyl it was hard to know what to read first. You know, I'd heard about this problem. Who hadn't? But—man.

Alden had said it hooked you really fast. I saw that sort of comment everywhere. But one site in particular gave me some insight that helped me understand what Alden had gone through. It said fentanyl, which is something like fifty times stronger than heroin, creates an elevated pleasure experience, and it's so high that nothing else can reach it. Nothing else could ever feel so great. This drug actually raises the pleasure threshold in your brain, and that means ordinary pleasurable experiences feel like nothing—at least, in comparison to taking fentanyl.

So maybe I'd never know why Alden started taking the stuff. But I got a lot closer to understanding why he might go back to it.

Gram certainly did not approve of my attack on Byron, but her dressing-down was nothing compared to Neil's phone call.

"What were you thinking, Nathan? *Were* you thinking?"

"Look, that asshole's getting people addicted to fentanyl! Do you know what that shit does to you?"

"Gram told me you and your roommate put a stop to that."

"Like that's going to stop him. He's probably selling the stuff to feed his own habit!"

"Starting fights isn't going to help, and you know it."

Unfair! "What about you? I seem to remember you crashing into two other boys and then smashing one of their faces in!"

"Are you talking about the time I rescued your sister from a couple of juvenile terrorists? Were you rescuing someone in that bar?"

"I was standing up for anyone who's being taken advantage of! I'm standing up for anyone who's addicted to that shit!"

There was a pause, and I was feeling self-righteous enough to smell success. I was wrong.

"Nathan, what's the real reason you were so angry?"

My turn to pause. And then a kind of lame, "I told you."

"Does it have anything to do with being gay?"

"What?"

"Were you trying to prove something?"

Where was that coming from? Where did he get that

idea? But he had hit on a connection, even if it wasn't the reason I'd gone ballistic. "I was not. For your information, I personally know two people who are addicted to fentanyl. They're both gay. So yeah, maybe it is because I'm gay. You sure hit that nail on the head."

"Two? I heard about the friend who was pledging. There's another one?"

My throat closed in an attempt to hold emotion in, so there was a silence before I could answer. "As a matter of fact, my boyfriend was in recovery. He went home for Christmas and didn't come back. He's hooked again."

"Oh, Nathan. I'm so sorry."

Here it comes, I thought; *he'll ask me if I'm using.*

He didn't. Instead, "Look, I get it. You were beyond pissed. You were in pain. But, kid, fighting isn't a good way out of it. And I'll bet it didn't help."

It hadn't. He was right.

Meanwhile, I spent some time that weekend—kind of a break from the heavy addiction research and being yelled at by various relatives—learning a song made famous by Edith Pilaf: "Je Ne Regrette Rien." I regret nothing. And despite what Neil had said, it was true.

CHAPTER TEN

I managed to report for dishroom duty that week, although because of my painful ribs I had to avoid the Hobart. And the amount of swishing and slogging with rags and squeegees necessary for clean-up proved too much for me, so after I finished dish removal duty for the shift, Daniel sent me away.

It took me a few weeks to feel like I was pretty much myself, in terms of healing. And even then, every once in a while I'd move in a certain way, or exert myself without thinking, and the ribs would scream.

El Speed was embarrassingly solicitous. The first time we ate together at the dining hall, he asked, "Want me to bring you a tray while you find us a table?"

"What? No, thanks. I can handle the tray." It was almost impossible, though, to stifle completely the grunt I made when I picked up the full tray at the end of the serving line.

Or, when he saw me removing sheets from my bed to do laundry, "Want me to help?"

I turned him down with a slight edge to my voice, but when the sheets were clean and dry and I was struggling to pull the fitted sheet around, I decided to give in. "I wonder if I could ask you to help me with this."

He got up from his desk and stood watching me a minute. "You sure?"

"Yeah. Sorry if I've been a turd. You know."

He nodded. "I do know."

At one point during our joint effort, which (to be honest) was mostly El Speed's effort, his foot bumped into a bundle under the bed. It was Alden's possessions, wrapped in one of the black capes and pushed into a heap. "What's this?"

I stood up straight with a sudden motion that made me gasp in pain. "Man. I hate this." But complaining about my ribs was just a distraction, an attempt to avoid describing what he'd bumped. "That's, um, that's some stuff of Alden's."

He looked at me and, I think, was about to say *Alden's?* as if puzzled by why it would be here.

I heaved a sigh and sat on the half-made bed. "I never told you this. It was kind of confidential. But Alden had been in rehab before I knew him." I raised my eyes to El Speed's face. "Fentanyl."

"Jesus." He sat down on the other side of the bed.

"And over the break, he—" I almost couldn't say it. I swallowed hard. "He's back in rehab."

El Speed lifted his chin in acknowledgement as if to say that no further explanation was needed, then stood up and went back to his task.

Once the bed was fully made, he did his best to lighten the mood. Pretending to hide a grin, he said, "If you like, tomorrow I can carry your books for you."

I punched the side of his arm and then winced as my ribs yelled at me.

He headed back to his desk. "You know, Ellie had a really hard time hiding how she felt about what you did."

"Oh?"

"Yeah. She's against violence. Made a big point of that." Another grin. "But she also said she was really proud of you, and really glad you were standing up for Gordon."

"So you've got two people in your life who are contradicting themselves."

"Pardon?"

"Ellie hates violence but loves what I did. I don't want to admit I need help, and then I ask for it."

He laughed. "Yeah. Clearly I'm the only sane one."

Life on campus since Alden had disappeared into the wilds of the north and out of my life forever weighed on me heavily. I'd spent so much time with him, or so much time thinking about him, that I'd kind of isolated myself from any other social scene I might have been a part of. El Speed was there for me, making sure I didn't eat meals alone. And although neither of us said anything about it, he stayed on campus every weekend except Valentine's Day. And he was apologetic about leaving even then.

"Uh, Nathan," he opened toward the end of dinner the Monday before that famous lovers' celebration, "I gotta go home this weekend. Just so you know."

I was clueless. "Look, I know you've been hanging out here more than usual. You don't have to do that. Not for me. So go." I grinned at him by way of thanking him without making either of us feel self-conscious. "Is this a special weekend?"

He looked like he didn't want to say. He nearly whispered, "Yeah. Valentine's Day. I gotta spend it with Ellie."

And it hit me; he figured it would have been important for Alden and me. He was probably right. Quickly, before I had enough time to feel as sorry for myself as it seemed he felt for me, I said, "Of course." I smiled and stood. "Gotta get to the library. See you later." And I headed out, but not to the library.

I had nothing specific to do at the library. I had nothing specific to do at all. All right, there was always classwork, but I was in no mood to concentrate on psychology terms or famous experiments or Freud or Jung (though the last two might have done me some good). I wandered toward Candy Bar, the ice cream shop where Alden and I had met for that walk, and retraced our steps. Then I wandered over to Mill Pond and nearly fell trying to find my way in the dark over snowy ground. If I'd had a car I might have driven out to where we'd watched the eclipse.

Alden was gone. I felt profoundly alone.

By the end of February I was able to heft the heavy trays full of china and flatware onto and off of the Hobart again, and the last Friday of the month, Daniel took me out for pizza to celebrate my recovery, or so he said. We went to the same place where Alden had told me about his addiction. The same table was open, but I steered Daniel away from it.

He treated me to a couple of pizza slices and some ginger ale, and we talked about all kinds of things: his disappointment at having to return to New Jersey; his disappointment that Nina wasn't accepting his invitations any longer; my brave idiocy at attacking Byron et all with a beer mug; Neil's hiking expeditions.

With just a little of his ginger ale left, Daniel said, "And are you aware that they're having a talent competition here tonight?"

I'd noticed the sign about it as we'd entered earlier. "Yeah. Karaoke? I don't think so."

He sat back a little in his chair. "Too bad. Because I entered you."

"You what?"

"They're about to start."

"Forget it!"

"Why?"

"Well… if for no other reason, they won't know what to make of my vocal range—an alto voice coming from me. And my face is still all purpley. No; I'm leaving."

"First prize is two hundred dollars."

I froze half-way out of my chair. "For real?"

"For real."

I sat back down. That might be worth some embarrassment. "And did you also happen to tell them what I'm going to sing?"

"Nope. You're supposed to use this app to select what you want." He pulled out his phone, opened an app, and handed the phone to me.

"How long have you been planning this?"

He just grinned, so I bent over the screen and scrolled through. Most of the songs were rock or pop, but I wanted something more unusual. Then a title caught my eye, something Ella Fitzgerald had sung, but I'd also heard it by an old rock group Gram liked from the sixties, The Mamas And The Papas. Neil used to play it on his guitar while I sang, and Gram would close her eyes and sway every time.

Daniel and I sat through quite a few—um, I'll call them attempts by people who'd entered the contest. Some were okay, but I didn't think anyone stood out as competition for me. Then one girl, Linda something, tore through the Indigo Girls' "Let It Be Me" so amazingly that I wished I'd backed out. But after her, a few more duds struggled through predictable songs.

"And next, Nathan Bartlett, with 'Dream A Little Dream Of Me.' Nathan?"

The announcer on stage looked around the room. Daniel kicked my foot under the table, and I stood, reluctant once more.

I'd seen Linda take the mike off the stand and hold it while she sang, and somehow that had made her look more comfortable on stage, more professional. I took a second to figure out how to get it off and then nodded to the announcer.

I let the familiar guitar opening wash over me. Eyes closed at first like I was dreaming, I swayed gently back and forth until I began to sing. Imitating Mama Cass Elliot, I started out soft, easy, lilting—crooning, really, repeating the performances that had moved Gram so much, not caring whether the audience was shocked that I was singing the same range as Ella and Cass.

The first time I sang the bridge section, I was still quiet. Then I built up during the third verse, and I belted the repeat of the bridge. And when I sang the final verse, I got quieter all the way through to the last double bar.

At the end of Linda's performance, the crowd had exploded into applause. When I ended mine, trailing off in a quiet hum of the main tune, the applause seemed slow to start. I was sure I had lost to Linda, and I steeled myself for the embarrassment I'd predicted. But the applause got louder, and louder, and it went on and on.

I don't think I'm exaggerating when I say it was nearly half a minute before I felt like I could leave the stage.

Daniel had his own take on that. Grinning broadly at me as I sat down, still clapping, he nearly had to shout, "I knew it! You love that applause. You're a natural."

I won. Two hundred fucking dollars. It felt great. Hell, it felt fantastic! If this kind of courage—and, of course, reward—was the result of the change in myself I'd been feeling lately, I was all for it. And I owed this one to Daniel. Maybe he hadn't played the guitar for me, but he'd orchestrated this win.

INTERLUDE VIII

Life with Neil: That First Hike

It was the first time I remember Neil yelling at me. He must have yelled before, but this is the one that stays in my mind.

For Neil's sixteenth birthday, in August, Gram had taken him out to get what would be his birthday and Christmas presents for that year and the next. He and his best friend, Jeremy Ford, had decided their favorite thing to do in the world was hiking. So Neil wanted hiking equipment. He wanted "real" boots, as he referred to them. He wanted a good pack, and wicking clothing, and several pairs of socks and sock liners, and new water bottles, and a new Swiss army knife—the list was quite long. And it was expensive, at least for our family's budget.

In previous years Neil and Jeremy had been on various short hikes and overnight camping trips with their boy scout troop, but they'd been frustrated by the puny hills the leaders had chosen. They wanted real peaks. Mountain peaks. They felt driven to press their boot-shod feet onto the metal geodetic survey markers, embedded into granite, that prove the achievement of these peaks and declare their official height.

So they'd chosen Mount Monadnock, in south-western New Hampshire, with a summit at the respectable height of three thousand, one hundred and sixty-six official feet above sea level, for their first unsupervised adventure. In summer weather, it was a mountain that could very reasonably be scaled and descended in one day.

They couldn't get there on their own, so Mrs. Ford and a friend agreed to drive them, then cruise around the area for some antiquing and sight-seeing, and pick them up later for the ride home.

The hike was to be toward the end of August, just before school started for the fall, but the conversations and planning had begun weeks before that. Neil's excitement must have been contagious, because I found myself listening in rapt attention whenever he and Jeremy talked about it.

I think it was about a week ahead of the trip when I sat in the hall outside Neil's bedroom, my back to the wall beside the closed door, straining with my eleven-year-old ears to catch every word they were saying.

Neil had done his homework. "If we go up White Dot, and descend on White Cross, we'll get a variety of great views from a lot of the upper parts of the trails."

Jeremy's deep voice responded, "And both trailheads are at the park headquarters in Jaffrey. That would be a good place for my mom to wait if she comes to get us before we're all the way down."

"Good point."

"You should stay at my house the night before. That way we can have breakfast with no one around other than my mom, and then head out as soon as we're ready."

"Yeah. It can get a little crazed here in the mornings. Gram has to fight with Nina to eat anything, and Nathan is the fussiest eater. You wouldn't believe it."

Fussiest! How could he *say* that?!? It was everything I could do not to give away my presence by telling them Nina and I weren't likely to be up for breakfast at the ungodly hour they'd need to eat, anyway. I listened quietly as they talked about what food they'd pack, how many water bottles, whether extra socks would be a good idea. They discussed details about the trails they'd take—how long they were and how steep they were and how fucking amazing the view from the summit would be.

I scrambled up and dashed into my own room when Neil and Jeremy started making noises about heading downstairs, and once they were gone I tip-toed into Neil's room. He'd been storing his new gear in the back of his closet, but today he'd left some of it out. I picked up a clear, blue water bottle and set it down. I picked up a compass and tilted it to watch the magnetic pointer shake and turn. I unfolded and examined a trail map, struggling for a couple of minutes to refold it along the same folds it had been in.

When I picked up a pair of socks, something outside of me took over. I kicked off my sneakers, peeled off my own socks, and wriggled my feet into the tweedy-brown hiking socks that Neil would wear over silk liners (which I didn't see nearby, or I would have put those on as well). Then I picked up one of his new boots.

The boots didn't look as new as when he'd brought them home a few weeks ago. He'd been wearing them everywhere to break them in, to make sure that the boots and his feet were well enough acquainted with each other that blisters on the trail would be less likely. But they were still new. The thick, black sole was deeply ridged in a herringbone pattern. Above that on the boot itself, a bright navy band of something like cloth was wrapped all around the boot above the sole. That gave way to a darker blue material that felt like sueded leather, which formed the top of the boot and was cut into a zig-zag pattern as it rose up toward the ankle. The name "MERRELL" appeared on one of the zigs near the top. The laces, a navy and beige weave, threaded their way up the boot through tabs that allowed for quick tightening.

Holding one boot in my hand, I pinched the thick, padded material at the tops of the sides. I couldn't pinch the toe; it felt like there was metal in there.

My favorite part was this long tab of very tough material, again blue and beige, that was securely attached to the back of the boot. It rose to a flat loop that extended less than an inch higher than the back of the boot. I thought at first it was merely decorative. And then I took the next step. I put the boot on.

Obviously, it was far too large for me, but almost automatically my fingers grabbed that flat loop to pull the back of boot onto my foot. I tugged on the laces to get them as tight as possible and then reached for the other boot.

I didn't exactly walk right out of the boots when I stood and took a few steps, but it was close. Despite the large size, as I moved around the room something about the boots made me feel powerful. Strong. Invulnerable.

"What the fuck, Nathan?"

I froze, startled, and stared at Neil where he stood in the doorway. I didn't know what to say, so I said nothing.

"Get the hell out of my boots! Take them off, right now!"

He didn't wait for me to decide whether to sit at his desk chair, or on the side of the bed, or on the floor to do as he told me. He pushed me onto my backside and nearly tore at the laces as though removing sacred objects from the filth of blasphemy, to get them away from my unholy feet. Then he stared at those feet.

"Socks, too?" He was nearly yelling. "These are *my* things, Nathan! *Mine!* Do you understand?"

I didn't understand, no. I didn't understand what was so horrible about my feet, or about me, that would have brought sacrilege down onto these divine objects. Glaring at him, doing my best not to cry, I nearly ripped the socks off and threw them at him.

He watched as I retrieved my own socks and sneakers and carried them out, slamming the door behind me. I slammed the door to my own room after I had stomped, as loudly as possible in bare feet, down the hall. I threw first one sneaker and then the other, leaving marks where they hit the sky-blue wall, and then I threw myself onto my bed, still fighting tears but not giving in. Never giving in.

I didn't respond to the knock on my door, so Gram opened it.

"What's going on up here?"

"Ask Neil! He's an asshole!"

"Nathan! Language! Now, I need more than that."

I managed to tell her my tale of woe without breaking down, and when my sulky voice fell silent she went to a shelf beside my closet and picked up a model airplane. It was German Messerschmitt, light gray with a mottled effect that was probably to help make it hard to see in the clouds. The cockpit canopy was divided, and it opened to reveal a very detailed interior, complete with instrument panel. The three propeller blades extended out from a green and white spiral pattern on the nose, and they moved when you touched them. There were other details that made it an amazingly realistic replica.

Gram held it gently, carefully, and looked at it as she asked, "Where did you get this?"

I had a feeling where this was going, and I didn't like it. It wasn't relevant. It wasn't fair. "Neil."

"But he didn't buy it for you, did he?"

I let a few beats go by. "No."

"He saved up his money. This was not a cheap model. He bought it for himself, and then he put it together." She set it back onto the shelf. "He worked so hard on that thing. He loved it."

She turned to me. "Do you remember why he gave it to you?"

I shook my head. I did remember, though.

"You were always going into his room and playing with it." She pointed to one of the propeller blades. "And one day, you broke this off."

She came and sat on the edge of my bed. "You might not know this, Nathan, but your brother cried over that broken propeller. He fixed it. And then, on your birthday that year, he gave you the plane."

I crossed my arms over my chest; I didn't want to hear this.

"And where did you get the baseball glove you use

when you play ball with your friends?"

More beats. "Neil. But it was a hand-me-down!"

"It was not a hand-me-down. You kept taking it. He gave it to you. Not even as a birthday present. He just gave it to you. And where did you get Panda-Boo?"

I'd put the black-and-white panda bear with golden glass eyes and a head that swiveled all the way around into the back of my closet a couple of years ago. "I don't even play with that any more."

"But where did you get it?"

I let out a breath I'd intended to sound annoyed, but it had too much shake in it for the effect I wanted. My voice barely above a whisper, I said, "Neil."

"It had been his. And you kept taking it. What I'm trying to get you to see, Nathan, is that you ended up with a number of things that your brother loved, things that belonged to him and that he gave you before he was ready to give them up, because you wanted them. You never asked, but you— let's say you more or less took them over."

"Okay, but—"

"No. No 'but.' This hike Neil and Jeremy are going on is huge for him. Those boots are the most important item I bought for him, and he's given up other gifts for two years to get them. Maybe there's no danger of you 'borrowing' the boots. They don't fit you. But seeing you in them might have brought back the feeling of having to give away something he wanted."

"What about what *I* want?"

She pulled her head back a little, surprised. "What is it you want?"

"Maybe I want to go hiking! Maybe I want Neil to take me, too!"

And there it was. My outburst, or the reason for it, pulled at my gut.

After Monadnock, Neil asked me to join him for some shorter hikes. But every time I considered it, I thought of the repaired propeller on the Messerschmitt, and I decided to let Neil keep hiking for himself.

CHAPTER ELEVEN

On St. Patrick's Day, with shiny green cardboard décorations everywhere, and green carnations appearing at odd times, and shiny green cardboard hats on people who were anything but Irish, and with announcements every few feet about a green beer keg party somewhere over the coming weekend, Daniel and I sat across from each other after a shift, coffee mugs between us. He looked around and shook his head.

"I've about had it with all this crap." I agreed, and then he looked directly at me. "Nota Bene, I think you should learn to hike."

I couldn't have said why, but it was as though Neil were speaking to me. Neil had never told me I *should* hike, but he'd made it clear many times that something was missing from my life because I didn't.

"Oh? And what do you recommend I do about it?"

He leaned forward, elbows on the table. "There's a mountain that seems perfect for a first hike. Chocorua. It's not a four-thousand footer, but there are no other mountains close to it, and it has a bald peak, so it stands out. It looks impressive, and from the summit you should be able to see for miles. I've never hiked it, and I'd like to. What do you say?"

I shrugged, hands wrapped around my barely-warm mug, and feigned misunderstanding. "To what?"

He leaned back again, grinning. "Let's hike Chocorua. And," he looked around, taking in all the green paraphernalia with the sweep of an arm, "let's go this weekend. Let's get out of here, away from all this ridiculous fuss."

In one way, this was kind of like having Neil ask me to go hiking with him. In another, it wasn't; Neil had never just come out and said, *You're doing this.*

Last semester, when Daniel had asked why I'd never hiked, I hadn't told him the truth. Or, maybe only part of the truth. Another part of the truth crashed into my brain as I sat there warming the now-cold coffee mug with my hands. I wanted to impress Neil. I didn't want to look like an idiot in front of Neil. If I hiked with Neil, I wanted to know what I was doing. And I wanted him to see that. So I had to start somewhere else. That is, not with him. I would make use of Daniel, at his own invitation.

"Okay."

Daniel looked almost surprised, like it had been too easy. But he recovered. "Great! Let's talk about gear."

"Gear?"

"You know, the right clothes, boots, a frame pack, water bottles, that sort of thing. We'll need to bring food and water. I have a white kerosene stove that's saved my life a couple of times, and I have a supply of freeze-dried things we can cook."

He was starting to get excited. "One thing about hiking when there's snow on the ground is you don't need to carry quite as much water. It takes a lot of snow to make a cup of water, but in a pinch I can boil snow on my stove. And there's a cabin near the summit, where we can spend the night. I'm told it has a wood stove in it. We'll need sleeping bags, but we won't be out in the snow. So, what gear have you got?"

There wasn't much. My boots weren't hiking boots, just work boots, and not waterproof. I could use the same old sleeping bag of Neil's I'd taken for the ski trip—serviceable but not especially effective against real cold. I could wear my ski clothing under warmer layers, and I had a couple of water bottles, but I had no frame pack.

"You'll need one," Daniel assured me. "Anyone you can borrow from?"

I pulled out my phone and texted El Speed, who replied that sure, I could borrow his.

"We're set!" Daniel declared. It didn't quite feel like that to me, but he was the expert here. He was going to be Neil this weekend.

Daniel picked me up at around six thirty Saturday morning. I set my pack in the cargo area of the Mungmobile alongside Daniel's, which was not black with rainbow trimmings as I'd pictured it in my imagination. It was bright red. El Speed's navy one looked dull next to it. Like Neil, El Speed had a cross of white tape on the pocket where the first aid stuff was, and Daniel had done the same to one of his pack pockets.

Daniel seemed cheerful enough as we started our trip north. I did my best to respond, but as we traveled up Route 108 toward Dover, Alden was heavy on my mind.

Staring out of the side window, acutely aware of the chill coming off of the glass, I noticed every house along the east side of the road. I'd traveled this route on the bus enough times that I should have been familiar with the houses on the way to Alden's, but somehow, today, they looked different.

I noticed every lit window, picturing kitchen scenes, imagining people with cereal or coffee or e-readers or whatever in front of them. I imagined I could smell bacon and buttered toast and hear the thud of a coffee mug set a little too hard onto a wooden surface by the hand of someone still groggy with sleep. I could almost hear the clink of flatware on dishes. I noticed where smoke floated out of chimneys.

"You okay, Nota Bene?"

"Sure." I'd barely heard him; we'd just passed Alden's house. The white BMW was gone.

"You seem kind of distant."

I turned toward him. "Did I ever tell you what happened to that guy I was seeing? The one I mentioned during that skiing weekend?"

"No. Is he all right?"

I faced the road ahead. "No. He's in rehab. In Canada."

I didn't want to elaborate.

Daniel took a few seconds. "Nathan, I'm really sorry to hear that." Another pause. "Do you want to talk about it?"

"Not really, no. We just passed the place where he lived while he was at UNH. That's the only reason I brought it up."

From the corner of my eye, I could see him nod. "And maybe why you're quiet."

"Yeah."

We were both quiet for a while after that. In fact, we said little until we were approaching Rochester, when Daniel said, "Traffic's picking up a little. Surprising, this early on a Saturday."

After that it got easier to talk about nothing in particular, though there were still long silences between chatty moments.

We'd been driving for just under ninety minutes when Daniel turned off to the left onto what appeared to be a narrow lane and then turned the car to face a snow-covered expanse to the north. Across that, at a distance that was hard to determine, was a mountain.

"Chocorua Lake," Daniel told me; evidently the expanse was a frozen lake. "And, of course, Mount Chocorua."

Daniel had said that the mountain would stand out because of not having any other peaks close to it. He was right. It stood out.

From the right, a line of bumpy, hilly terrain led up and up. It was covered in dark evergreen trees and white snow that gave way suddenly to a pile of rock: the summit. The slope on the other side of the peak was steeper. It looked impressive and scary. Perhaps in sunny weather, across the blue lake in early fall with reflected color from deciduous trees, it would look friendlier. But today, there was so much snow on the lake I didn't know it was a lake. And with only the dark green of pine trees adding color to the mountainside, and with the dark gray sky hovering over the darker mountain, the overall effect went all the way to ominous.

"It's named for Chief Chocorua of the Pequawket tribe," Daniel told me as we gazed through the windshield. "Early eighteenth century. Somehow the chief's young son wandered into a settlement of pale-faces. There are conflicting stories about what happened next, with the most common one saying the kid got into the poison that a fellow named Cornelius Campbell had used to kill foxes. The kid made it home, but then he died."

I was thinking we might die before we made it home. But Daniel wasn't done.

"Anyway, it seems the chief blamed the Campbell family, and when Mrs. Campbell and the assorted little Campbells were found slaughtered, the settlers blamed Chief Chocorua. Several of them chased him up the mountain. They surrounded him at the summit, with him hurling horrible curses at them, and then either he threw himself off or they shot him."

I blinked hard and swallowed. "Um, did you leave word with anyone? Does anyone know where we are and what we're doing?"

He shrugged as he shook his head. "It's a good day to die."

I remember thinking, *Yeah, that could happen.* What I said was, "Something you want to tell me?"

Daniel laughed. "It's a line from the film *Little Big Man.* Don't know why, but I've always liked it."

The words *Maybe this isn't such a good idea* were forming in my brain when Daniel backed the car away from the lake and turned onto the road north.

"Onward!" he said, grinning at me.

On the road again, I was thinking I should have let someone know. I would have told Alden. I could have told Gram. I'd actually thought of calling Neil, but I hadn't wanted to listen to him tell me all the things he thought I'd need to know. And I kind of wanted to tell him about it *after*

I'd conquered this peak. I could have told El Speed. There were a couple of guys on the floor I could have told. But until now, it hadn't occurred to me that it might be a good idea. Daniel wasn't worried, despite his movie quote, so why should I be? He was the expert.

Around quarter past eight, Daniel pulled into a parking lot that hadn't been plowed since the last snow-storm, but evidently people used it as a turnaround, or a meeting place, or whatever, and we had no trouble in the mungmobile.

As Daniel opened the back of the car he said, "Hope it's okay if I check your pack for efficiency." He glanced at me. I shrugged, and he proceeded to dump everything out of it.

"Always put the heavier stuff near the top, unless it's something you know you're going to need quick access to," he told me as he re-packed. He checked the first aid pocket, which had El Speed's idea of necessary supplies in it, and made no comment. He checked the straps holding the sleeping bag in place. Then he picked the whole frame up.

"This is a little large for you, isn't it?"

"El Speed is taller than me."

"Ah. Right."

He checked the integrity of straps and buckles, and I was thinking, *You're doing this now? Neil would have done this the day before at the latest.*

With everything more or less to Daniel's satisfaction, he opened his own pack and handed me a plastic bag. "Bet you didn't get any breakfast in your dorm room, and the dining halls weren't serving yet when we left."

I took the bag, which contained two hard-boiled eggs, and accepted the roll he handed me next. He'd brought the same for himself, and we ate standing there—a mungmobile tailgate. We drank some water, donned our gloves and hats, hefted our packs onto our shoulders, and Daniel declared us ready.

"Onward!" He grinned, turned, and led the way.

The first thing we encountered after leaving the parking lot was a flat, open area we had to cross to get to the trail head. The snow was maybe four inches deep through there, and although the sky was thick with clouds, it must have been sunny in the past few days, melting a little snow that refroze overnight. This had left an icy crust almost an inch thick that I had to break through with every step. The constant lifting of my legs out of the snow and pushing my feet through that crust was not fun, and it felt like we'd never get to the trees.

There were no footprints ahead of me except Daniel's. Despite his cavalier attitude, it was weighing on my mind how very alone we were out here, and how very helpless we'd be if something happened. I let Daniel get farther ahead before I shrugged out of my pack and dug into it for my cell phone. El Speed was in Maine with Ellie (of course) for the weekend, but even so I texted him.

Hiking Chocorua Piper Trail. If I'm not back by Sunday night send St. Bernards.

"Nathan?" Daniel had figured out I wasn't behind him.

I hefted the pack, settled it in place, and moved forward.

Before long, I started to hear slight slapping noises as little frozen pellets struck the shoulders and sleeves of my nylon anorak. There weren't a lot of them, and they melted immediately. Even so, it was frozen rain. It was a warning.

I looked at the red pack on Daniel's back, wondering if he'd stop and say something like, *Gee, maybe we shouldn't do this today.* But he didn't stop. He didn't turn around. He just reached behind his neck, found the edges to his jacket hood, and flipped it over his navy wool hat. I did the same, though my hat was orange.

I was glad when the Piper Trail reached the woods. I didn't yet know that trees would offer their own challenges to my progress.

Almost as soon as Daniel and I left that snow-crusted field behind, I planted my right foot in the usual way, the way that would have worked as I'd crossed that field. Only this time: surprise! My foot kept going, and going, until I was in snow up to the middle of my thigh.

I fell forward and, again in the usual way, threw my arms out in front of me to brace myself. My left hand found solid ground under about three inches of snow. My right arm kept going, and going. Before I knew it, I was on my right side with that arm deep in snow. I nearly cried out, more in surprise than pain.

As I struggled to free myself from the malignant white stuff, I thought, *Neil thinks this is fun?*

So I started planting my feet more carefully, but that led to another problem that I discovered when I planted a foot slowly to test for depth. I touched a level that felt solid and shifted my weight onto that foot, which caused the false bottom to give way to more snow beneath, sending me sprawling yet again.

"Fine," I said quietly through gritted teeth, and I decided the best way forward was to send each foot down hard enough to break through any layers of false solidity. That worked for about twenty steps. That's when my boot hit the side of a large, hidden stone only a few inches below the surface. My foot slipped sideways, wrenching my ankle and forcing me to catch myself with my other leg and making that knee scream.

I lost track of how many times I hissed, "Fuck!" under my breath, not wanting Daniel—way ahead of me—to know how much trouble I was having.

Daniel and I were still on the lower part of the Piper Trail, still under the trees and plunging unpredictably either into snow up to our knees or up to our ankles, when the trail grew suddenly, if briefly, very steep. Daniel had to work to get up the slope, but at least his equipment didn't thwart him. El Speed's ill-fitting pack made things awkward, and my wafflestomper work boots had very little traction. Also, they were sueded leather, so not only were they not especially warm, but also they were getting wet.

Watching Daniel struggle ahead of me, I stared at his gaiters—those zip-on coverings Nordic skiers wear to keep snow out of their boots. Gaiters hook onto your boot laces, then zip up several inches of snow-shedding material to a tie, or to velcro, that you can tighten just below your knee. I had gaiters; most Nordic skiers did. Daniel knew this. But had he suggested to me that I bring them? He had not. Had he taken into account that I might not realize how useful they'd be hiking through all this snow? He had not.

And, by the way, why *were* we hiking through all this snow, exactly? Was Daniel trying to prove a point? Was I?

Maybe it was partly the frustration of working my way through the confounding snow depths and partly being pissed at Daniel for neglecting to tell me to bring my gaiters that made me lose my footing on the steep incline. I grabbed desperately at the skinny branches of a young tree, to no avail. Daniel turned just as I began to slide backward and downward.

One of my boots lodged against a hidden rock, and that was enough to send me tumbling down, rolling through snow as I went. My body came to a rest at the bottom of the incline, spread-eagle in the snow.

I could barely understand what Daniel called out to me, he was laughing so hard. All I could make out was, "You okay?"

Flat on my back, I waved a hand in the air, torn between yelling at him and laughing with him at how absurd I must look. I took my time getting onto my feet, a process that was complicated by the too-large frame pack. I had to extricate myself from that so I could stand.

Daniel watched, hands on hips, chuckling, as I struggled up the slippery incline, hauling myself up by gripping branches and the trunks of small trees until I reached him, out of breath and ready for a break.

"Onward?" he asked. So, no break. I just waved again.

I didn't notice when the slapping noises of the frozen rain stopped. But at some point I became aware of flakes of snow. They made a sound, too, but it was subtle. Tiny clicks now, which I could hear only if I stood still and held my breath. Not many of them, but they were now flakes, not pellets.

The snow wasn't heavy at first, just a few flakes floating down through the trees. The incline here was only moderately steep, and the snow depth was more predictable for reasons I couldn't have explained. So I was staring down at my feet, focused only on the effort of walking uphill through snow, the sounds of my own labored breathing almost all I could hear, and I nearly bumped into Daniel, who'd stopped ahead of me on the trail.

We hadn't talked much; the conditions took a lot of focus, and the climbing took a lot of breath. Between pants, I managed, "What?"

"This isn't great. I was going to suggest we sit and have lunch. But the weather's turning." Clouds of breath fog swirled with his words as he spoke.

At the mention of lunch, I realized I was hungry. I mean, *hungry*. And I wanted to see if all the snow in my boots had melted, or if I could knock some of it out. "It's just a few flakes."

"Are you kidding?" He made a wide sweep overhead with one arm. "Look at those clouds!"

"It's been cloudy since we started."

"Those are snow clouds."

Snow clouds. Was this surprising? "Didn't you check the forecast before we left?"

"Of course I did. But the mountains make their own weather."

I guessed that phrase hadn't originated with Neil. "So?"

"So we don't have time for lunch." He sloughed out of his pack and dug a couple of power bars out of a pocket, handing me one. While we munched, he told me, "More snow means harder hiking, difficulty following the trail, lower visibility... all that can make things end very badly. No, we have to keep going if we're going to make the cabin. And we have to make the cabin."

Pack in place again, he turned without waiting for my agreement. I was on the verge of saying maybe the direction we should go in was down. He didn't give me a chance, and something about his attitude left me with the impression that turning around would be cowardly.

I took a deep, shaky breath and hitched my pack up a little before trudging after him.

Head down, struggling constantly uphill through deeper and deeper snow, I almost didn't see the sign that pointed to my right for the Nickerson Ledge Trail. Daniel had already passed it, and I was glad; I couldn't imagine that being anywhere near a ledge right now would be a good idea.

I was also feeling profoundly frustrated. My feet were wet, my shoulders hurt from the ill-fitting pack, and this snow... this SNOW! Christ, but I was tired of fighting my way through it! Even following in Daniel's footprints didn't help much. More than once I avoided the spot where he'd gone in up to his thighs only to find myself up to my hips. How many times had I already had to take my pack off so I could scramble out of the stuff? Fifteen? Eighty?

And why the fuck did Neil keep going?

Neil.

Neil! I meant Daniel.

Daniel was slamming each foot down hard, harder than would have been necessary if all he wanted was to be sure he found something solid before shifting his weight. And I realized he was angry. No; he was furious. It looked like the snow was his worst enemy, and he was going to kill it if it didn't kill him first.

This furious approach was apparently helping him make progress. I decided it might work for me.

It didn't. Over the next hundred yards or so, it became obvious that the more furiously I attacked the mountain, the more it fought back, and the more often I found myself backward or sideways or face down, nearly buried in snow. The stuff got up my sleeves, down my back, and I could even feel it melting around my waist. It was in my hair and my nose and all the way into the fingers of my gloves.

Pulling myself out of a snow pit yet again, I opened my mouth wide for a silent scream. I had to let something out, but I didn't want Daniel to hear me yell. I was near tears of pure frustration by the time I hefted that pack again.

I watched Daniel nearly disappear around a bend before he looked back to make sure I was behind him. We stared at each other for a second, across maybe a hundred feet and through the falling snow, and something happened inside me.

I'd say something snapped, but it was more of a thud. Suddenly I was empty. Empty of frustration, empty of fury, empty of resentment for Daniel's evidently inept leadership. I was a zombie. A snow zombie. I put one foot in front of me, felt for stability, shifted weight, moved my other foot and planted it in front of the first, felt for stability, shifted weight, moved the first foot... and there was nothing else. Nothing existed in the world except moving uphill through the snow.

Lift. Place. Stabilize. Shift. Repeat....

I followed Daniel. In my zombie state, all I did was follow, and follow and follow. I didn't watch him, though occasionally I glanced up to be sure he was still ahead of me. I might have been cold. I might have been hot. One of my arms might have fallen off. I wouldn't have known. All I did was put one foot in front of the other, shift weight, wait to see how far in that foot sank, pull it out, and repeat. Over. And over. And over. And over.

I noticed nothing until the light around me brightened radically. I stopped, looked up, and saw Daniel watching me. Behind him was open rock face sloping upward. The occasional dark spot of low-growing evergreens, whose roots had somehow found purchase there, was visible through the snow, which was now falling heavily. The wind was blowing enough that Daniel, maybe fifteen feet away, had to raise his voice so I could hear him.

"Stay here while I check out where the trail goes. I'm going to find the cabin and come back. There's less wind in the trees, so stay here where it's more protected. Back soon."

Again, without waiting for my agreement, he turned and moved off to my left, a dark form moving across the rock. My zombie state was lifting, and I realized I was cold and wet. I wasn't shivering yet, but if I stayed still it wouldn't be long before that started.

I watched the dark form that was Daniel disappear around a rock ledge, and I waited. And waited. And waited. The wind would blow, and then stop, and then whip around. When it wasn't blowing, I could hear the tiny ice crystals land softly on the snow piled around me. The sound was almost a musical tinkling.

Finally the dark form reappeared as Daniel worked his way toward me. I heard him shout, "Fuck!"

As he got closer, he shouted, "This is the first time in my life I've ever been sorry to see the summit of a mountain!"

"What does that mean?"

Daniel came closer so he didn't have to shout. "I could have sworn the cabin should be between where we are and the summit, but I didn't see it. The only thing I think we can do at this point is follow the trail, which goes around the rock face to the right, and hope we see it."

"*Hope* we see it?"

"It has to be there. Come on."

ON CHOCORUA

I will say this for trudging around Chocorua's bald pate in a snowstorm: It was easier than struggling up the trail through the woods. That is, except for the ice.

The smooth granite was exposed to the sun when there was any sun, which meant that any snow that didn't blow away landed in crevices and melted. The water had oozed out across the rock when it was warm, and had then frozen in a thin layer, some of it hidden under newer snow. I had to be extremely careful where I put every step; it was all too easy to put a boot on what looked like snow on the rock only to find out the hard way that it was snow over ice on the rock.

Daniel found the occasional trail marker, which boosted my mood and my energy. But at one point, without warning, my right foot went out from under me. Snow over ice on rock. I landed hard, and my left boot got wedged in a corner formed by two granite outcroppings very low to the ground. My knee yelled. Or that's what it felt like.

I loosened the pack straps as far as possible so I could get the thing off my back, and with both hands I tried pulling on my left calf. No good; the boot was stuck.

Daniel stood over me. "Let me help." But he couldn't; the boot wouldn't budge. He stood again, looking thoughtful, and a burst of snowy wind sent him back two steps.

"You'll have to take your foot out."

Daniel bent over and began undoing the laces. I managed to pull my cold, wet foot out of the boot, and I took off my gloves and cradled the foot in my hands while Daniel pounded and pulled on the boot. By the time he'd managed to free it from the granite, my hands were almost as cold as my foot, and I could barely tie the laces.

Before long the trail descended slightly back into the woods. It seemed to me like we were not quite on the complete opposite side of the mountain from where we'd come out onto the rock, but it was hard to tell. And kind of irrelevant.

What was relevant was that it was getting dark.

"Daniel?" He didn't stop or turn; must not have heard me. I called three times before he did. He waited while I approached him. "Do we have a plan?"

"Not a good one, unfortunately. What we'll need to do is find a place to make shelter."

I blinked a few snowflakes away. "What did you say?"

"We're not going to find the cabin in the dark. I'm looking for the right configuration—a tree, a tree and a rock, something at an angle—so we can use your sleeping bag as a roof." He waited while I digested this information.

It wouldn't digest, though. I just stared at him until he gave up waiting for a response and headed out again, into the woods.

The snow had almost stopped, and it was nearly dark by the time Daniel found what he was looking for. I had been considering mutiny, but then what? We would still have been exactly where we were, in a snowstorm, on a mountaintop, without shelter, and with no help coming. I'd sent El Speed the name of our trail, but we weren't on it any more. If we died up here, would anyone find our bodies? The thought seemed almost academic; I wasn't aware of feeling any particular way about dying. Was it a good day to die? The mountain wouldn't care. Neil had taught me that.

"There!" Daniel shouted, pointing at nothing that made sense to me.

He made his way to where a birch tree had fallen in an uphill direction and had landed on a large boulder. The boulder was far enough from the tree's roots so that there was a space of a few feet beneath the tree trunk on the uphill end. Daniel shrugged out of his pack.

"Come on, Nathan. Help me get this ready."

Imitating his actions, I scooped snow with my hands and arms away from the ground beneath that fallen birch until he said it was clear enough. He unstrapped my sleeping bag and opened it all the way. Daniel draped the toe section onto the tree's stump end, and together we settled the rest of it up the trunk of the tree, forming a protected area beneath.

Daniel broke a couple of smaller branches off of the birch and pushed them through the ties near the bag's head end, stabbing them into the snow so that the sides angled out enough for us to get under it. Then he unstrapped his own bag and positioned it under the shelter formed by mine.

"We'll both have to get into my bag."

"Why is it my bag we're using as a roof?"

"Mine is higher rated. For cold, I mean. Come on."

Daniel crawled under my bag, took his boots off, and stretched his legs into his sleeping bag. He looked at me expectantly.

In other circumstances, I would have loved this invitation. I glanced around as though for other ideas, or in hopes of seeing help arriving, or maybe of waking up from this nightmare. What could I do but continue to follow his lead? The only good news was that the snow seemed to have stopped completely.

I looked at my watch out of something like morbid curiosity. It said three twenty-eight. That made no sense, so I looked closer. The second hand wasn't moving.

My watch was frozen.

"We won't starve, anyway," Daniel assured me once we were both tucked into his bag. "We have bread, oranges, luncheon meat, and a couple of freeze-dried meals for each of us. And if we run out of water, we can melt snow."

"How would we do that, exactly?" I was beginning to shiver; my feet had gotten quite wet, and although I still had socks on, the cold was setting in. The snow that had found its way into all kinds of crevices on my body was now sapping heat away from me.

Daniel shifted so that he could lean on his elbows, and he fished around in his pack. "White kerosene stove."

Feeling dull and a little numb, I tried to imagine how

the stove situation was going to work. "And tell me again, why aren't we in the cabin?"

"Couldn't find the fucking thing. Maybe it's not on the Piper Trail. It's not on the summit, I can tell you that."

"There are other trails?"

"Must be."

"'Must be?' You don't know?" Was it unreasonable of me to have expected Daniel to, you know, know what the hell he was doing before leading me into the wilderness?

"Look, I didn't check it out, okay? I just asked someone about hiking Chocorua, and he said the Piper Trail was the least steep. And he said there was a cabin below the summit. He didn't give me any more insight than that."

Insight? I'd have settled for information. I tried to come up with a rejoinder, but my brain wasn't working well, and I couldn't even work up any anger. I wasn't in the zombie state any longer, but something else, more sinister for being mysterious, was settling in.

Somehow, despite being crammed into a sleeping bag along with me and propping himself up on one elbow, Daniel managed to get kerosene into the tiny metal thing he called a stove and light it without setting anything else on fire. He'd worked the base of the stove into packed snow maybe a foot uphill from where our heads were.

We'd had no real lunch, but somehow I didn't feel hungry any longer.

"You have to eat, Nathan. Your body's already beginning to digest muscle and fat, and it's in panic mode. So it's not trying to make you stop the flight it thinks you're in, even to eat."

I was tempted to argue, but something told me that if I kept talking, I wouldn't be able to avoid saying something nasty, something I'd regret. So I waited for him to finish whatever he was doing, which seemed to be boiling water.

Perhaps my silence was getting to him. He kept a steady stream of words going, describing everything he was doing. I didn't pay much attention, though it was evident he was making chicken stroganoff from a package of it that had been freeze-dried. At one point before it was ready, he handed me a water bottle.

"You need water in your system to digest protein," he said. "Besides, dehydration isn't just something that happens in the desert."

He watched while I took a few obedient mouthfuls and then drank some himself. It was cold, the water, and I could feel my stomach shiver in response. The shivering spread until my whole mid-section trembled.

I said nothing, but Daniel must have noticed. "Yeah, it's a natural reaction. Part cold, part fight-or-flight." He reached up to stir our dinner. "This will help."

He was right. The warm liquid of the sauce, and the small but meaty chunks of chicken went down very easily. I was tempted to take more than my portion of what was in the metal container we were sharing.

He told me, "The carbohydrates in the noodles will give your body something to burn immediately, and the protein will kick in later." I couldn't say how he did it, but he managed to wash out the container and refill it with snow. "Next is hot lemonade. I don't think we should drink any more cold water."

By the time the lemonade was ready, my belly was trembling again. Badly. And again, the hot liquid helped to relax the shivering.

I didn't yet realize how bad it was going to get.

CHAPTER TWELVE

Being inside Daniel's bag with him in the dark felt surreal in the extreme. I wanted to pull myself into fetal position. I wanted to cradle my feet, which—despite the painful, prickly feeling in them—seemed to be less and less attached to me. But there was no way the bag would allow that much movement.

Every time we finished eating or drinking something hot, Daniel turned the stove off. "I've got lots of matches," he said the first time, "and I don't want to waste fuel."

With the stove off—it sounds silly to say this, but it felt huge—there was no light. I could see the white of snow outside our makeshift shelter, but the darkness moved in on me with an intensity that surprised me. *What does Neil do, I wondered, when he's hiking, and it's nighttime, and it's dark?* Whatever Neil did, I was sure it wasn't what I was doing: shivering.

"There's a flashlight in my pack," I said, barely able to keep my teeth from chattering so badly that my words would be indistinguishable.

"I have one too, but in this cold, the batteries—" He stopped short and reached for his pack. He didn't explain what he was doing, and I couldn't see very well.

"What—?"

"Gotta keep them warm. Putting them into an inner pocket. You should do that."

I should do that. I should do what? What was it I should do? Oh; batteries. Right. Keep them warm. A line from the film *Star Trek IV: The Voyage Home* came to me: Brain is not firing on all thrusters.

Struggling against my shaking body, I craned my neck

to locate my pack, but I couldn't see it. I pulled an arm out from the cocoon of Daniel's sleeping bag so I could reach for the pack, but the shivering made me move very slowly and not exactly accurately.

Daniel must have figured out what was going on. "I'll get it. What pocket is it in?"

"Don't know."

"Fuck."

"You packed it." And he had. I had to stop myself saying something aloud: *You were so god-damned fussy about organizing my pack, but you didn't know where the hell you were going?*

There was a long pause. "Right." And he reached for my pack and pulled it closer. I could tell he wasn't shivering nearly as badly as I was, but even so maybe his brain wasn't working much better than mine. Still, he managed to find the flashlight.

"Here."

"Can't. Can't hold it." As badly as I was shivering, I couldn't hold my hands still, and I could barely understand my own words.

Without speaking, Daniel opened El Speed's flashlight, removed the batteries, and reached down to distribute them between my front pants pockets. In another situation it would have been a very intimate move. I started to giggle. Not chuckle, not laugh. Giggle. It sounded very odd, made static by intense shivering.

Daniel ignored me.

Every so often, Daniel would pull something out of our food supply for us, even if it wasn't something he'd heat. At one point he handed me a roll. A fucking roll. But something in my body cried, *YES!* and I gobbled it down as fast as my wildly shaking arms and hands would let me. In less than a minute, the shaking subsided noticeably. I was still shaking, but it was less violent.

It didn't take long, however, for the violence to reassert

itself. By now, my feet were icy cold. And they hurt.

Daniel made hot lemonade a few times, and we had some freeze-dried beef dish, the name of which escaped me; I was unable to focus on anything, and I don't even know now whether I could have formed words at that point.

With each serving of whatever we consumed, the shaking grew less before it got bad again. I don't remember Daniel declaring that we needed to save some food for the morning, but he must have said something like that.

I do remember that he commented on how badly I was shivering. "You probably got wetter than I did."

I also remember that, several times over the course of the night, he said, "Don't fall asleep."

Time didn't exist. At some point I realized I could no longer feel my feet. It was about then that I realized I wasn't afraid. *Why wasn't I afraid?* Why wasn't I imagining dying up here, getting colder and colder until my brain stopped firing altogether? Why wasn't I panicking?

Looking back on it, I think it might have been that fear requires energy. It requires a certain focus, or it causes one's brain to focus. I had almost no energy. And focusing my mind on anything took almost more energy than I had.

I tried to keep my brain firing on something by asking myself why I was here. It's true that I'd expected Daniel to have been better prepared than he was. It's true he should have checked the weather, researched the trail, learned the location of that fucking cabin from a safe distance. But that was blame. Useless, at this point.

What was my role? Had I felt the need to prove something? Why hadn't I insisted on turning back? There had been so many points at which that was the only sensible thing to do, and yet I had kept going. I'd kept following Neil. I mean, Daniel.

That I can hike? Was that what I wanted to prove?

That I can keep up with Neil?

That I'm strong, and I'm a guy, even though I'm gay?

Woah! Where did *that* come from? Do I really think that gay men are somehow not quite men? No; I was sure that wasn't it. That kind of thinking had been put onto me by homophobic bigots.

Fuck it. Didn't matter why I was here. Sometimes a mistake is just a mistake. Right? And boy, was this one huge mistake.

"Don't fall asleep."

My stomach hurt. Why? Was I about to be sick?

No. Didn't feel sick. So—what?

Pain. Pain in my belly, pain in my legs, pain in my upper chest, pain in my upper arms. But mostly, pain in my belly.

Shivering. Violent shivering. Violent shivering that didn't stop.

"Don't fall asleep."

Shivering. Pain. Shivering.

"Don't fall asleep."

At some point, light happened. I couldn't have said where it came from, what it was, or what it meant to me. I wasn't shivering. That had to be a good thing.

Right?

"Nathan. Move."

"Nathan! Move!"

Something shoved me, rocked me back and forth, slapped my face. "Nathan! Wake up!"

I wasn't asleep; couldn't he see that? "Stop." I barely managed the word.

"Then move. We need to move. I'm getting out of the bag. You too."

As he worked his way out, moving almost in slow motion, a rush of colder air hit me, colder than in the bag, and I nearly gasped. I felt something pulling on my shoulders, and after a short eternity I realized it was Daniel trying to get me out of the bag and onto my feet.

My feet! Oh, my feet. I was surprised to see them. I was surprised they were still there. They didn't feel like a part of me. They didn't feel like anything.

Later, Daniel (whose watch hadn't frozen) told me that the process of getting out of the bag, putting on our boots, eating a roll with some turkey in it, rolling his bag and folding mine (it was frozen in its tent-like shape) into a manageable bundle—that activity, which should have been done in maybe twenty or thirty minutes, took an hour and a half.

I don't remember much about those ninety minutes, just the bright blue of the sky, the bright white of the snow, and the effort of trying to get those feet that weren't really mine back into my now-frozen boots. Daniel tried to help me; he loosened the laces as much as possible and worked first one foot and then the other into a boot. But my toes wouldn't reach all the way in, and between the bottoms of my heels and the boot footbeds was maybe half an inch of empty space.

I was aware of so little that this problem barely registered. I looked at Daniel, puzzled but not anxious. He knew what had happened. He knew my feet were frostbitten and had swelled to a size the boots couldn't accommodate. But he didn't say anything.

With the feet (they still weren't really mine) riding too high in my boots, I stood mute and numb as Daniel placed El Speed's pack onto my back. He shrugged into his.

"We need to find the cabin. We need to get the stove lit. Let's go."

"Onward?" I could barely speak.

"What?"

I shook my head and followed Daniel.

We trudged in the same direction we'd been going the night before. I was barely able to follow Daniel's words as he explained that the cabin, which hadn't been on the summit, must therefore be just below the summit, and if we kept going around the tree line we'd run into it.

After another eternity in which I lifted first one leg and then the other, with the dismembered feet somehow doing what they needed to do, Daniel was proven right. He nearly danced forward when he saw the small, wooden structure, sitting primly atop a foundation of cut granite slabs. It was definitely above the tree line. And it was definitely not on the summit.

Daniel was busy inside examining the wood stove by the time I entered. The promise of heat suddenly began to affect me, and I nearly cried at the sight of the hulking black thing. I sloughed off the pack and fell to the floor, my back against a wall. My eyes closed. Time passed. When I opened my eyes, I expected to see flames inside the small black beast, flames giving off heat that would make it possible for me to go on.

What I saw was the look on Daniel's face. It was not a good look.

"There's not enough wood here. And it would take too long for the place to get warm, anyway."

I blinked. I blinked again. "Any fire would be good. Anything warm would be good."

"It's almost noon already, Nathan. We don't have time."

I nearly cried. Daniel had let me down again. Even his precious cabin was a failure.

My hands hurt.

I hadn't realized I'd said that aloud until Daniel said,

"You have an extra pair of wool socks. They would be better than gloves, because they'll keep your fingers together."

I just looked at him.

"Here." He dug around in El Speed's pack and handed the socks to me. Obediently, submissively, I removed my gloves and pulled the socks over my painfully tingling fingers while he packed the gloves away.

Daniel dug into his own pack and came up with a couple of sandwich rolls. We devoured them. He used the last of his white kerosene to heat water and make hot lemonade.

As he handed me a hot cup, he said, "If you can, leave the socks on your hands when you hold this. If your fingers are frostnipped, you shouldn't touch anything hot with them. Let them warm up a little first."

"Frostnipped?"

"The first stage of frostbite."

"What's the second stage?"

He paused before answering. "There are two stages of frostbite after frostnip. Let's hope your feet have only reached the first."

"Why aren't you feeling the cold as much as I am?

"Like I said earlier, you got wetter."

"Because you have better clothing. And boots. And equipment."

"Yeah." He looked almost ashamed. I decided he should be.

I managed to drink from the hot cup with my woolen-socked hands, and the warmth made my hands feel better. Daniel finished his drink first, and then he unfastened his gaiters. I watched, not curious, not caring what he was doing. Then he handed them to me.

"What?" I asked.

"You should wear these now."

I could have asked why. I could have said *Fuck you, Daniel*. But he was right. So I took them.

Daniel pulled two chocolate bars from his pack, and we

devoured them. Then he dug out two oranges, handing me one and dropping one for himself into a jacket pocket. "Let's go."

The sky was still that brilliant blue it had been when we'd struggled to get up earlier, and the sun shone blindingly on the snow underfoot, which was maybe two inches deep. I paused long enough to look around. As promised, there were no other mountain peaks nearby, and the day was beautiful and clear. I could see for miles.

I followed Daniel, of course, out of the cabin and down a short distance over exposed granite. He'd found some trail markings, and he was looking for more, walking in their direction as they appeared.

Maybe it was the hot lemonade, maybe it was Daniel's look of chagrin; whatever, I felt a surge of energy. It was small, but it was noticeable. I took the orange from my anorak pocket and stuffed the socks in. I peeled the fruit, dropping bits as I walked. At one point I turned, and my eyes followed the brilliant spots of orange peel back toward the cabin. The bits that had landed on the pure white snow stood out like beacons. Behind and to the left of the cabin was the summit. I stared at it.

"How unfair," I said quietly to the mountain, "that I have suffered so much here without ever getting all the way up." I sighed and tore open the sections of my orange, eating them as I walked toward Daniel.

Putting my socks back on my hands as I walked, I followed Daniel, who seemed to be still finding trail markings, because he was moving with purpose down and to the right.

Something was wrong. I knew something was wrong. At first I couldn't tell what it was. I don't think I'd ever wracked my brain so hard, or for such an important reason.

I stopped moving, and it came to me. We'd come up the Piper Trail, and while I'd waited in the trees, Daniel had gone ahead of me, up and to the left, where he'd found the summit.

Then we had turned to the right to follow the tree line around the top of the mountain, and we had descended just a little into the trees to camp overnight. Then we had kept going in the same direction.

The Piper Trail had not led Daniel to the cabin. It had led him to the summit, but not to the cabin. That meant that no trail markers leading down from the cabin would belong to the Piper Trail, and since we left the cabin we had not come across any of Daniel's footprints from yesterday, or any other footprints. The Piper Trail had to be to our left. The mungmobile was at the base of the Piper Trail. We had to follow that trail, and no other, back down, or we'd end up nowhere near the car.

"Daniel!" I waited for him to turn. I shook my head. "No."

"What?"

"Not that way."

"What are you doing? Come on, or we'll never make it by nightfall."

Maybe my energy was a little better, but I had to save every scrap of it; I couldn't waste it arguing with him. Instead, I turned to my left and headed downhill at an angle, knowing that the only way down for us was to bushwhack until we ran into the Piper Trail. I didn't turn to see if Daniel was following me.

I heard footsteps behind me, and then he grabbed my arm. "What the hell are you doing?"

I pointed down and to the left. "The car is that way."

"What?" He was shouting now. "What the fuck are you taking about?"

I tore a small branch off one of the dwarfed pine trees that peppered this part of the mountain. Dragging it through the snow, I did my best to create an image of the mountain peak. I drew a line showing the direction we'd come from, made a dotted line where we had gone around the other side of the peak to make camp, and picked up with a solid line where we'd approached the cabin this morning. It was painfully obvious to me that I was right. I stared at Daniel.

He stared back silently for maybe ten seconds and then raised both arms out to his sides and let them fall back against his body.

"Fine. I've fucked everything up royally for this whole trip. I'll follow you for a while."

I wasn't sure he was convinced, but tough shit. I nodded, turned, and led us both down into the trees.

The terrain was not familiar; we were not on a trail that I could see, and there were no footprints in the snow from our journey up yesterday, but I knew—I *knew*—that I was going in the right direction.

Before long we found ourselves crossing a large open area. Perhaps it was an alpine meadow? But no; once we were well into it, all evidence pointed toward its having been a small section of woods, mostly of young trees and saplings, that must have burned. The trees had fallen onto bare ground, last fall or five years ago—who could tell—and they lay unpredictably criss-crossed, hidden by a couple of feet of snow.

Even if my brain had been functioning at peak efficiency, I couldn't have counted how many times a step would land one of my feet deep in the snow, boot held annoyingly between two slender branches, or a trunk and a branch, or whatever the hell was down there. More than once I had to take off my pack, then find leverage somehow to pull my foot up and out of the boot—which couldn't be fastened very well onto the swollen foot—and then fish around under the snow to extricate the boot. And then, of course, I had to put the boot back on, still too small to accommodate the foot, still with my heel riding half an inch above the boot's footbed. Daniel's gaiters would have been more helpful if my boots hadn't kept coming off. And in fact, they were more hindrance than help. I took them off and handed them back to him.

Daniel was having similar problems, though I don't recall that either of his boots ever came off. But he had serious boots, boots that fit. At one point I sat still on the snow, waiting for the energy to fish for a boot the dead trees had captured, and I watched Daniel. He had reverted to the technique of being angry at the mountain and, I hoped, angry at himself, and he was using that anger to help himself keep going. I already knew that approach wouldn't work for me, so I just reached for the boot, knocked as much snow out of it as I could, put it back on as well as I could, struggled to my feet, shrugged back into El Speed's pack, and kept going. There was no other option.

By the time we made it to the other side of that hellhole of a clearing, Daniel had resumed his lead position.

"Did you see a trail marker?" I asked, hoping against hope.

"No. But I realized you're right about our direction."

I guessed I wasn't going to get an actual apology. Not about leading us in the wrong direction. Not about his ignorance of the trail system. Not about the madness of climbing in yesterday's weather. Not about his lack of advice on clothing and boots and gaiters. Not about nearly getting me killed. Not about anything.

I kept expecting we'd run into the Piper, and so did Daniel, but he had decided the cabin must be nearly on the opposite side of the mountain from that trail, and we'd just have to keep going.

We'd crossed a couple of small streams on the way up, I vaguely remembered, so we were not expecting to come across a deep ravine with running water rushing downhill. I say deep; it was perhaps fifteen feet down to where the icy water bounced raucously over boulders and bits of fallen tree.

We stood there staring into the depths until Daniel looked downstream. "Maybe there's another way across."

A way other than climbing down into the ravine, if we

could even do that, and praying we could make it through the water, was what I knew he meant. I looked upstream.

"There." I pointed with a finger in the toe of my grey tweed sock at a white pine that had fallen across the ravine.

We trudged uphill to the tree, a new puzzle to stare blankly at. The tree was thick and would no doubt be strong enough to support our weight, but the trunk was riddled with branches, big ones and little ones and tiny bumps that stuck up from the trunk just enough to trip us and send us tumbling into the ravine.

I heard Daniel say, "We have no choice."

Silently I turned and climbed onto the tree, painfully aware that my sleeping bag was woefully unbalanced and was not going to be my friend during this crossing. It had been frozen into the shape of our makeshift roof overnight, and although Daniel and I had done what we could to scrunch it enough to fasten it into place on my pack, it was hardly in an efficient roll.

We have no choice.

The rough bark of the white pine was coated here and there with a layer of ice. I reached for the first branch high enough to be helpful to me, and as I inched past it the sock on my hand caught on it, and my hand came loose from the sock suddenly. I nearly fell.

"Nathan! I'll grab the sock. If you can take the other one off, you should do that."

Hanging onto one branch and then another, shifting my ill-shod feet on the slippery trunk, I managed to pull the other sock off with my teeth. It hung from my mouth as I continued across.

You always hear, "Don't look down." I didn't. But I didn't need to; I'd already seen what it looked like down there. All my attention was on placing my boots around branches and not on little stubby bits where branches had broken off, finding hand-holds on the irregularly placed branches within reach, shifting weight gingerly to be sure the foot ahead of me wouldn't slide off the tree, and looking ahead to plan the next step.

Against all odds, I made it across and climbed shakily off the tree and onto snow-covered ground, Daniel behind me. He handed me my other sock, and as I put both socks back onto my hands, I realized my hands were painfully cold again. I tried gripping one fist inside the other hand, but that didn't help. I started to rub the back of one hand with the other, but Daniel stopped me.

"If there's frostbite coming on, you shouldn't rub the skin. Take the socks off for a minute."

I stared at him; he must be crazy. He took his gloves off and then removed the socks from my hands. Unzipping his jacket, he lifted his polar fleece and the turtleneck beneath—no doubt made of a wicking fabric—and pulled me close to him, leading my hands into positions against the bare skin under his arms. He gasped as my cold flesh touched his warmth.

We didn't actually hug, but we were close enough to lean our foreheads together, so we did that. I looked down at our respective boots, taken aback yet again at the difference between his pair and mine. I closed my eyes.

And then it came.

"Nathan, I am so sorry. I'm so sorry I got us into this. I have made so many mistakes. If you had more experience, I know you would have stopped me at several points. But you couldn't know."

I could have said, *That's all right.* I could have said, *I should have stopped you anyway.* I could have said any number of things to make him feel better. But what I wanted to do was list all the other things he should be sorry for. This was supposed to have been my fun introduction to hiking. Instead I'd nearly frozen to death, and now I had frostbite, the effects of which would last the rest of my life. So I said nothing.

ON CHOCORUA

It was nearly dark when we found the Piper Trail. And we came to the parking lot not long after that. So we'd bushwhacked most of the way down Chocorua. In the winter. Hungry. Frostbitten. Exhausted. And yet the sight of that ugly brown Jeep made us both yell with delight.

We threw our packs into the back seat. Daniel turned the engine on, and he showed me where the switch was for my seat heater. As soon as there was enough engine warmth to run the heater Daniel turned the temperature and the fan to high, and we huddled as close to the vents as we could get, teeth chattering, for maybe ten minutes.

Gradually, Daniel relaxed back into the driver's seat, and even more gradually, I sat back as well. I still couldn't feel my feet; I wasn't sure what I was going to have to do for them.

I looked at Daniel. "Onward?"

"Onward." He threw the car into gear.

I don't remember the trip back to campus, other than a stop we made, I think in Ossipee, at a fast-food place. By that time, my feet felt like they were in a slow burn.

Getting out of the car was ridiculous. We were both so stiff, and had so little energy, that we couldn't straighten up. We hobbled like mountain trolls across the parking area, just managing to straighten up before going into the restaurant.

There weren't many people in the place, but by the time Daniel and I stood at the order counter, all eyes were on us. It wasn't until we sat down with our food, across a booth table from each other, that I figured out what had attracted so much attention.

Despite how starving I was, one look at Daniel, fully exposed to indoor lighting, and I laughed. And laughed. He looked puzzled, although he shouldn't have been, because I must have looked just as absurd.

His navy wool hat was stuck full of forest detritus. Bits of twigs, fragments of dried leaves, the occasional spear of an evergreen needle had all taken up residence on Daniel's hat and, I was sure, on my own orange one. If that wasn't enough, where his turtleneck showed above his jacket was similarly decorated.

I pointed at his hat, then at mine, and managed to say, "I think we're scaring people."

We practically inhaled burgers, fries, and hot coffee each, barely rejected the idea of more, and got up. Or tried to get up. We did, of course, but sitting had made us stiff again, and getting out of that booth was harder than climbing out of the car had been.

The rest of the ride home did not register in my brain.

CHAPTER THIRTEEN

Daniel dropped me off in front of Hunter. Uncurling myself from the car seat was painful and awkward, but not as painful as the burning sensation in my feet, which had grown worse after we'd stopped for burgers. I stepped out of the car and nearly fell over.

"Nathan? You okay?"

"Yeah. Fine. Feet hurt, is all."

"Stay there." I hung onto the side of the car as Daniel shuffled around and then hauled my pack out of the back seat. He hefted it onto one shoulder and paused. "Look, I'd better take you to the infirmary."

I pushed on his chest, partly to steady myself, partly to refuse. "No. I'm good. I just have to get upstairs."

"Nathan—"

"No!" I shouted at him. "No. Not going."

He exhaled impatiently. "Fine. Lead the way to your room. I'll carry your pack."

The pain was already less, more of a hot pins-and-needles feeling. "That's okay. I can take it."

I wanted him to leave. We'd driven back mostly in silence, and my snow-addled brain had finally managed to put a few things together. This man had nearly gotten me killed. He'd done only so much to help me be prepared for the climb. He'd forged ahead when, so many times, he should have turned around. (Never mind that I could have called a halt; he knew better than I did what it would be like to climb in a snowstorm.) He'd nearly led us down in a totally wrong direction that would have left us stranded, in the cold, again. In my head, I was yelling, *Go away!*

"You sure?"

"Yeah." He slid the pack to the sidewalk, and I fished through a pocket to retrieve my keys. My fingers had recovered, I realized, and I could feel everything.

"Nathan, I don't like leaving you here."

"I'm fine. Go home."

He stood there and watched as I hefted the pack and limped to the front door. I deliberately didn't turn to wave.

El Speed, back from Maine, looked up from his tablet, propped on his elbows as he lay on his bed. And he started to laugh.

It was funny. I knew it was funny. *I* had laughed, when I'd seen how comical Daniel had looked in the restaurant. But I wasn't in the mood.

As soon as El Speed saw how awkwardly I was moving, he stopped laughing. "You okay?"

I knew there was something wrong with my feet, every muscle in my body ached, and I had a splitting headache. I stripped everything off my body, cringing anytime I had to shift weight onto one foot or the other, and grabbed my bathrobe and bathroom bucket. I slid my feet into loose slippers. El Speed had said something; I had not responded.

"Nathan, what the fuck?"

I looked up at him, door to the hallway half open, bucket dangling from one hand. "What?"

"Are you all right?"

I opened my mouth and closed it once or twice. Words wouldn't come. I finally managed, "I will be." And I shuffled painfully down the hall to the common bathroom.

No one else was in the shower area at—whatever time it was—eight? Nine? I stood on the tiles, considering what a shower would mean: standing. There was one bathtub. I scuffed my way over to it.

I sat on the side and ran the water as full as I dared. I remembered Daniel's warning about putting my hands onto the hot mug at the cabin. Testing the water with my fingers, I realized I didn't have quite as much feeling back in them as

I'd thought. So I plunged the lower part of my arm in, decided it was too warm, drained some, and ran cold water until I was convinced I wouldn't do more damage.

And then I sat there on the side of the tub.

Put a foot in, Nathan, I said to myself. *You can do it.*

And still I sat. Maybe five minutes went by before I could get up the nerve, or summon the energy—I don't know which—to swing just one leg over and dip a foot in.

The increased pain in my foot told me the water needed to be colder still. I replaced more warm water with cold and finally, gingerly, painstakingly lowered myself into the water that felt tepid to every part of me except my hands and feet. I lay back and closed my eyes, wondering how long it would take for the aching in my hands and feet to stop,

"Nathan!"

My eyes flew open. Where was I? Who yelled? "What?"

It was El Speed. "Don't you know you're not supposed to fall asleep in the tub? People drown that way, you know."

I sat upright. "Didn't realize I had." I released the plug to drain the water.

"I'm gonna ask this again. Are you okay?"

"Not really." As I climbed painfully out of the tub and shrugged into my robe I gave him a thumbnail sketch of my weekend. He didn't interrupt until I got to the part about not being able to get my feet properly into my boots.

"Holy shit, Nathan! That's not good."

We both stared at my feet, which didn't look like my feet.

"They're badly swollen," he said. "You hiked all the way down with them like that?"

"Well... I don't think they were this swollen until a little while ago."

"Stay here."

"What?"

He ignored me. He was back in minutes with a clean set of my clothes, a jacket, a pair of cotton socks, and a pair of his shoes.

"We need to keep you off your feet as much as possible. Get dressed. My shoes might be big enough to fit. Then I'm driving you to the infirmary."

I wanted to protest. I probably looked like I was going to, because El Speed raised his voice. "Shut up. No argument. Do you want to lose a foot?"

Could it be that bad? I didn't know. While I was dressing, he left and came back with a guy who lived down the hall, whose name—ironically—was Dan. Daniel. Between them, they more or less lifted me downstairs and out to El Speed's car, which was parked but running in front of the dorm.

My feet. My feet would never be the same.

They kept me in the infirmary for three days, feet alternately elevated and not elevated, applying gradually warmer cloths, sponges, lotions, all kinds of things to my feet and hands while feeding me ibuprofen.

El Speed stopped in a few times, on his first visit bringing a ziplock bag full of rice.

"Here," he said, setting it on the table beside the bed. "Keep your phone in here whenever you're not using it."

"What? Why?"

"Your watch froze, right? It wouldn't do that if water hadn't gotten into it."

"My phone wasn't on my wrist. It was in my pack."

"You willing to risk it rather than take this one simple step?" He held the bag open, and I dropped my phone in. He gave me an arch look. "Now, just be careful about answering it when it's in here. You get rice all over the floor, the nurses will make your life miserable."

ON CHOCORUA

Gram came to visit and read to me, and she brought me food, which was better than what the infirmary served. Neil called every day, promising that next time he was home we'd go over the trails on Chocorua so I could make sense out of what had happened. It impressed me that he refrained from saying anything about Daniel—or about my own stupidity—though I'm sure he was mad as hell. Even Nina visited once, stayed half an hour, and didn't respond to more than a few messages on her phone.

Daniel also visited me once, the third day, after I finally responded to one of his text messages, which had grown more frantic as I had continued to ignore them. I was trying to decide what level of fury I felt toward him, and how much of it I wanted to heap onto his head. When he showed up, even though I had no other visitors at the time, I found that I couldn't yell at him, but I wasn't feeling friendly.

At first he tried to go the cheery route. "Nota Bene! How are you doing?"

I wracked my brain for some cutting rejoinder, but the look on his gorgeous face tripped me up. "Time will tell." My voice sounded flat. Not angry, not casual. Flat.

"How are the feet?" He was more sober now.

I lifted one shoulder and dropped it. "Can't see my ankle bones. Can't walk. That about says it all."

He pulled a chair over to the side of my bed. "Nathan, I am so sorry I led you into that. I did everything wrong." He waited for me to say something, but I didn't. "I hope someday you'll be able to forgive me."

"I might. Neil won't." That was cruel. I didn't intend to be cruel, but the words fell out of me.

Daniel's voice was very low. "I don't blame him."

He sat there, hands clasped between his knees, in the same pose Neil had assumed when I'd told him I was gay. Man, what a difference. These two people weren't anything alike. How had I confused them, even for a second?

I still said nothing. Daniel looked up from gazing at his

hands. "I don't know whether this will make any difference, but I'll say it anyway. What you went through—that horrible hike, your first ever, with all the wrong equipment, with an incompetent guide, in conditions no novice should have to face—" He paused, shook his head, and then sat back. "Christ, Nathan. You are the strongest person I know. I'm not talking about sheer strength, though you proved you've got that. I'm talking about backbone. I'm talking about guts and tenacity and courage and—shit, Nathan. You've got *balls*."

I looked back at his dark eyes, and I realized that I was able to appreciate his beauty without responding to it. How had that happened? Was it because he'd made so many mistakes on this hike? Was it that before that hike I'd seen him as somehow infallible, and he'd disappointed me?

He wasn't done. "I don't know how long we'd have been up there if you hadn't led us down. Y'know, I've looked up images of trails on that mountain. Should have done it before we left, of course. Figured that out too late. Anyway...."

He unfolded a paper map he pulled from a pocket. "From the cabin, I was heading down the Liberty Trail. If you'd followed me, and if we'd just happened by chance to take the left fork at the Hammond Trail, we would eventually have ended up at the car. But in those conditions—and with us in bad shape—it would almost certainly have meant another night on the mountain. Without food or water, and with no kerosene, we might not have survived. Or if we hadn't taken that fork, we would have ended up at the head of the Liberty Trail, which is kind of in the middle of nowhere, and I'm not sure how we would have gotten back to the car."

I didn't know what to say, so I stayed silent.

He folded the map and stuffed it back into his pocket. "It sounds like you've described this fiasco to Neil."

"Yeah."

"And I suppose he said terrible things about me."

"He said nothing about you, actually."

Daniel nodded, though I didn't know what that meant. "If you need anything, here or when they let you leave the infirmary, I'm available. I can run errands, bring you food, help get you to a doctor appointment, whatever."

"Thanks. El Speed is taking good care of me."

He nodded again. "Well, if I can help, please let me know."

"Sure."

He stood by the side of the bed and we regarded each other for a moment. "Okay, then. See you."

I watched him walk away, which once would have given me pleasure. This time was different. I felt nothing much at all.

By the time they let me go back to the dorm, I'd had lots of time to think. A few connections had come to me that I wasn't sure I could make sense out of. Had I really thought Daniel was infallible? Of course that was ridiculous. No one was.

I recalled how many times, during the climb, when my brain was particularly numb and semi-functional, that I'd thought the name Neil when I'd meant Daniel. Okay, so they were both mountain men. They both had dark hair and a nice build. They both took an interest in me, and never in a romantic or sexual way. They both wanted me to hike with them. But otherwise....

Wait—did I expect *Neil* to be infallible?

You're a psych major, Nathan; what do you think?

Neil had been a father to me, in so many ways. Children think their parents are infallible, or at least that they should be. And when the truth hits, kids rebel.

Daniel was fallible. Neil....

It surprised me how reluctant my mind was to finish that sentence. It hurt me to know that one day, I would have to finish it.

The doctor released me, on crutches, on condition that I had enough support from the people around me so that I could stay off my feet for at least the rest of the week. It wasn't a hard promise to make; I still couldn't see my ankle bones, and for sure my tortured feet didn't want me putting weight onto them. The next week was spring break, and I knew Gram would take good care of me.

El Speed earned my undying gratitude, not only because he'd made me get medical attention, but also because of all the other things he did for me that week. First, he got someone from the dean's office to let my instructors know what had happened and to get assignments to me. Then, once I was back at the dorm, he wanted to be sure I wouldn't have to hobble around on the icy pavement for meals. He went to Eva (not to Daniel, he insisted) to arrange for meals to be packed for me. El Speed conscripted a couple of guys on the floor to help him bring the meals to me, working in shifts.

So maybe I was going stir crazy, but I got all choked up a number of times with all the help everyone was giving me. It felt as though I had found some kind of niche for the first time in my life—a place where I was accepted, where I belonged, where people wanted me around. Outside of my family, I'd never felt like that before. Ever.

Neil flew home over the weekend to see me, a hugely welcome improvement to being at home with only Gram (Nina was off someplace with a couple of friends). Mind you, I appreciated Gram's attentions, but after a while.... Plus my bedroom was upstairs, and my feet were still badly swollen and painful to step on. So Gram made me stay in the living room during the day, hobbling upstairs where I could have some privacy only at bedtime.

Neil hadn't told anyone he was coming, so late on Saturday afternoon when I heard a car drive up and then away I didn't know who was going to come through the door and see me draped along the couch, still in pajamas.

"Oh my god! Neil!" I tried to get up, but I couldn't move quickly. He got to me just as Gram appeared from the kitchen, drying her hands on a towel.

Neil kneeled (sounds weird, I know) and took my hands in his. "You knucklehead! I don't know whether to hug you or hit you. What the heck were you thinking?"

I couldn't stop grinning. "The answer is I wasn't. Thinking. Or if I was, it was just how to get through it."

"So who is this asshole—sorry, Gram—this idiot who nearly got you killed?"

"For what it's worth, he feels real bad about it."

"What was his damage? Are his feet frostbitten, too?"

I shook my head. "The only boots I had were waffle-stompers. Suede."

Neil sat down hard onto the floor. "And he let you hike in them? In the *snow*?"

"Plus, you know, it blizzarded. My watch froze." I felt like I was twelve again, unable to tell my tale in a cohesive way, spitting out bits and pieces as Neil peppered me with questions. Until he gave me a better opening.

He leaned against the side of the couch. "At least he got you out again."

"Well… actually, he didn't. I did." It felt so good— so *fucking* good—to be able to tell Neil the story of how I was the one who led the way out of the mess Daniel had gotten us into. I didn't put it that way, though; my feelings about Daniel had thawed a little more with each new person who called him names and heaped blame on his head.

After dinner, the three of us sat in the living room (well, I *lay* in the living room) with no TV on. Neil fetched his *White Mountain Guide* and pulled out the map of Chocorua. It looked pretty much exactly like the one Daniel had shown me, and Neil's take on the route we'd followed was just as Daniel had described it. The Piper Trail led up the east side of the mountain, and from the cabin, the Liberty descended more or less southwest.

Neil also told me about his favorite trail, Champney Falls. On the map, it came up the north side of the mountain. Neil was sure I had crossed it at some point between the campsite and the cabin.

As Neil folded the map, he looked over at Gram and chuckled. "She's nodded off."

He set the guidebook aside. "Nathan, what possessed you? Seriously. You never wanted to go hiking when I asked you, but this guy leads you into a blizzard and you follow. Is that it? You like him?"

"Almost. Not quite. I mean, he's straight."

"But you're attracted to him. Okay, fine, but why didn't you ever hike with me?"

The strangest thing came into my head at that moment, something I didn't say aloud but that shouted inside my brain: *You never had a cute nickname for me.*

Was that lame, or was that lame? And why had it never dawned on me before how much it meant to me that Daniel called me Nota Bene? Further, *why* did it mean so much?

I gave Neil some mangled combination of the excuses I'd made for myself and for Daniel, none of which was completely true, and none of which satisfied Neil. But I had no better explanation to give him. Somehow I couldn't say, *I'd taken so much from you. Hiking was the one thing I wouldn't force you to share with me.*

I lay awake later, puzzling about the nickname issue until I realized that the feeling it gave me to hear Daniel say it was very much like the feeling I'd had last week, with El Speed and other guys being so wonderful to me.

That feeling was belonging.

"Why didn't I know all this stuff was down here?"

We spent part of Sunday afternoon in the basement (I'd essentially descended one step at a time on my ass) going through hiking gear that Neil had either outgrown or replaced with something better. There was, of course, a frame pack in the basement that would have fit me much better than El Speed's; Neil is only an inch or so taller than I am. And we wear the same size shoe, so even though his old boots were scuffed up and had a knot or two where the laces and broken, wearing them might have prevented the frostbite.

Neil chuckled. "Yeah. You could have used some of it on your near-death adventure. But—didn't you say you used an old sleeping bag of mine? Wasn't that down here?"

"That was in your room, under the bed."

He gave me a teasing, sideways glance. "Oh? What else did you find in there?"

I'm sure I blushed, though I couldn't have said why. "Well... there were a few, um, magazines...."

Neil laughed. "I should really get rid of those. I don't expect you'd want them, eh?"

He didn't need an answer.

As we rummaged through stuff, Neil told me about a girl he was seeing pretty seriously at school, in Colorado. When he told me her name, I laughed out loud and then regretted it.

"Cotton Hazard? Are you kidding me?"

"Nathan, she can't help her name. Doesn't anyone ever make fun of you because you and both your siblings have names beginning with N?"

"Sorry. No, they don't. Um, what's she like?"

Neil had had girlfriends in the past. Of course he had; he was handsome and confident and sweet. But I'd never seen him go all dreamy before. His eyes got soft, and he looked down a lot in a shy kind of way as he talked about Cotton.

"She laughs a lot. Not that fake kind of laugh some people do out of nervousness or social discomfort. It's a genuine laugh. Very musical. I can't hear enough of it. She's getting her MA at Boulder, too. Communication."

"She's smarter than you, right?"

He laughed. "Actually, I think she is." He tossed an old pair of socks aside. "She loves hiking, too. And downhill skiing. But she also loves Nordic. Maybe you'll go skiing with her someday."

"Photo?"

He dug into his wallet and pulled out a picture of a young woman with long, very dark hair, eyebrows so perfect I wondered if she'd had them microbladed, a sweet smile, and dark, laughing eyes that sparkled right through the photo.

"She looks like a pixie."

"Shit, how did you know? That's want I call her."

So, no nickname for me, but Cotton gets Pixie. There was a spark of jealousy, but I put it aside. "Does she know about me?"

"What about you? She knows you exist. What—oh, you mean being gay? No. I wouldn't have outed you to anyone."

"It's okay if you want to. I'm pretty much out at school."

He smiled. "I'm glad, Nathan. I want you to be the best version of yourself you can be, and you can't do that if you're hiding."

We gave that some space, and then I asked, "Do you see much of Jeremy?"

"It's hard, you know, with him all the way out at Evergreen on the northwest coast." Then his face brightened. "But we're hiking part of the Appalachian in June. The Priest Wilderness. Doesn't that sound great?" He grinned at me. "Jeremy knows some people who have a cabin so remote we'll need a satellite phone if we want to communicate with the outside world."

"Sounds like a great trip. A little too far for me, of course." I grinned back.

"So d'you think you'll ever hike again?"

"We'll see. Maybe in warm weather."

"Actually, that's no joke, Nathan. You'll probably be okay skiing, because the activity level of the Nordic style will keep your blood moving through your feet and they'll stay warm. But you shouldn't be outside overnight or do anything that isn't active in the winter. You might find your feet hate winter, actually."

"So maybe I'll hike in the summer."

"Autumn's the best time, in my book. Not too hot, bugs are gone, tourists are gone. If Jeremy were closer, we'd hike then. But early June will have to do this year." He sat back and regarded me for a minute. "You should really plan something for the fall. Will that jerk Daniel still be around?"

"No. He's going back to school next year, in New Jersey. But my roommate hikes."

"You guys rooming together again next year?"

My mind went blank. It hadn't occurred to me to wonder. "Don't know. I'd like to. Guess I'll have to ask him."

"Guess you will."

Gram drove Neil and me to the bus station early on Monday so Neil could get to Logan Airport for his flight to Denver. He hugged each of us before he climbed on board. I think he hugged me a little longer, and then he looked into my eyes and patted the side of my face.

"See you this summer, little brother."

Back at school, it was another week or so before I could stand on my damaged feet long enough to work in the dishroom. Daniel assured me my job would be waiting when I was ready; even so, I considered not going back at all. But it was my only source of income.

One day as I was drying off after a shower, the nail fell off of my right little toe. I took that as a sign, and I went back to work.

My very first day back, Daniel had me at that metal counter where the conveyer belt moves trays in one direction and the water in the sluiceway goes the opposite. I was used to that by now.

I had the spot at the left end of the counter where the trays appear magically from behind the wall. In that position, I had direct access to the switch for the belt and also for the disposal, which I'd learned how to use by now.

Daniel came over a few times, I figured to check on me if nothing else.

At one point I had stopped the belt because of overload, and everyone along the counter worked like mad to clear stuff off to keep the belt from being stacked three trays high when it started up again. Daniel came over to help, working across from me. I wasn't watching him, just moving quickly to clear things, when I noticed that the water was beginning to back up at the drain. What I didn't notice was that Daniel had dropped a metal spoon into the disposal. I flipped the switch on.

"Aaaaaah!"

I saw Daniel jump back and I realized that his hand had been in the disposal. I flipped the switch off again, not that it mattered by now, and gaped at him. His face was as white as the tile walls, and he held his right wrist in his left hand as he stared at it.

I stared at it. I saw nothing bad. No blood, no gaps where fingers had once been.

Daniel waved his right hand. "I'm okay. Everyone, stand clear. Nathan? Turn it back on."

I looked around this time, making sure everyone was in no danger from the disposal blades, and turned it on long enough to clear the drain. Daniel waited, and when I turned it off he continued to help us clear things away. He didn't leave until the pace was manageable once more.

After the shift, I approached Daniel. I couldn't read the

expression on his face.

I said, "Look, I just want to apologize—"

He shook his head. "It was my fault as much as yours. The rule is that anyone reaching into the disposal calls out what they're doing so that doesn't happen."

"Still, I'm sorry. That could have been really bad."

"I guess we both learned a lesson, eh?" He half-smiled and then turned away. I couldn't help thinking something between us had died. Or maybe it was finally resolved. In either case, I figured that was the end of "Nota Bene."

CHAPTER FOURTEEN

Finals were hell. That is all.

El Speed and I helped each other study, even though we didn't have any of the same classes. I decided that one of my electives in the fall would be a class he'd enjoyed: Human Reproductive Biology. I figured, you know, one day I might want to father a kid with a surrogate, so I should know a little something about the process.

My last conversation with Daniel was pretty unremarkable. Truth be told, although he had accepted the blame for leading sweet, innocent, lil-ole-me into the snowy wilderness, I had admitted to myself that some of the blame was mine. It wasn't entirely his fault that I'd let him get away with something I could have put the brakes on, myself.

So Daniel and I said goodbye and wished each other well. I felt a little sorry for him, having to go back to a school where he might be doing something he believed was important instead of moving to a school where he would be doing something he loved. Pragmatism over joy. I swore I'd never get trapped in that trade-off.

I headed home toward the end of May. El Speed and I had agreed to room together again next year, and he'd suggested we get together once or twice over the summer; he wanted me to meet Ellie, and he assured me I'd love his family's cabin on a tiny little pond in the middle of nowhere. He thought it was a riot that it was called Concord Pond.

"We're just full of coincidences, aren't we?" he said. "You decided to call me something that sounds like Ellie's name, and our cabin is on a pond with the same name as your home town."

I wasn't sure I'd love the cabin as much as he said;

there was no electricity, and the water had to be carried in from a well. But I figured it wouldn't be any worse than the cabin Daniel and I had stayed in for a few days in the freezing cold. Plus, I'd always wanted to learn to kayak, and El Speed had promised to teach me.

Gram had disappointing news for me when I got home. We'd known Neil's classes would go on longer than mine; even so, I'd been expecting him to visit us before he headed out for his June hike in the Priest Wilderness. But Gram said no.

"It seems," she told me, "that Cotton wants him to meet her folks. So he's going out to California, to San Diego, to visit with them, and he won't have time to come home before he and Jeremy head out. The cabin in Virginia is theirs for a specific time."

I wanted to protest. I wanted to say that he'd need to come home first to get his hiking gear, but I knew that was futile; one of the reasons he'd decided on Colorado was to hike while he was there, and he'd taken all his best gear with him.

Jeremy, however, did come home to Concord from his graduate school in Washington State. So I went to visit him over Memorial Day weekend.

"What can you tell me about this Cotton person?" I tried to keep the jealousy out of my tone, but she was keeping my brother away, and I didn't like her already.

"I can tell you he's head over heels," Jeremy said. "I think they're headed for you-know-what."

I sighed. "Do you like her?"

"I haven't met her. I like what Neil says about her."

"So you guys didn't get together much?"

He shook his head and grinned a lopsided grin at me. "Nope. He spent pretty much all his spare time with her. And, you know, it's not exactly a hop, skip, and a jump from Evergreen to Colorado. The states are all much bigger out there than around here."

"Tell me about the Priest."

Jeremy told me they'd be staying in this rudimentary cabin—sounded rather like El Speed's—in the middle of nowhere, for two weeks. He talked about some of the trails he and Neil had researched, and they sounded like they were far deeper in the wilderness than I'd ever want to go.

"Oh, and I have something for you, Nathan. You know Neil and I bought a satellite phone for this trip, yeah?"

I nodded. "Yeah. You can call us on our regular phones from that, right?"

"We can, and you can call us, though it's not cheap. Let me give you the number. You'll want to put it into your phone; it's a long one."

I pulled my phone out and stored the number as he read it to me. "Wow. That is a lot of numbers."

"Be sure you give it to your grandmother as well."

And then he changed the subject. "Neil told me something about you. Something personal. I hope that was okay."

I looked closely at his face; I was pretty sure I knew what that something was. "I hope it's okay that he told me about you, too."

He grinned. "More than okay. How are you doing at school? Any issues?"

"No, actually. I get along great with my roommate. We're rooming again next year."

"I hope you know you can call me any time." Then he grinned. "Any boyfriends?"

I shook my head. "Almost. I was seeing a guy for a while. It's over." I didn't want to go into details about Alden. I still had dreams about him, some good and some so sad I'd wake up in tears.

"Neil said you got yourself into trouble on Chocorua. How the fuck did you do that? It's a tiny mountain."

"Ha! Try climbing it in a blizzard."

He chuckled. "Yeah, well, that was stupid. Is the guy who led you on that disaster the one you aren't seeing any more?"

"No. Though I won't be seeing that guy any more, either."

"You should climb it again. Not in the winter this time, but it's kind of like getting back on a horse after you've been thrown."

I shrugged. "I don't know whether hiking is going to be my thing."

"Honey, I ain't talkin' about hiking. I'm talkin' about self respect. I'm talkin' about self worth. Look, you'll do it or not, but I highly recommend it. And if I were you, I'd do it alone."

"Why?"

"You're the only one you need to prove something to."

I'd always liked Jeremy, but suddenly I began to see why Neil spent so much time with him. Or used to. Before Cotton.

Neil flew from San Diego to Washington, D.C., where he was to meet up with Jeremy. He called from the airport.

"Hey, little brother." I decided that would be my nickname; it wasn't the first time Neil had said it.

I did my best to sound supportive. "Hey! You all set for your trip?"

"Think so. I'm just waiting for Jeremy's plane to land. He gave you our sat phone number, right?"

"Yeah."

"We have it only for emergencies. It costs a lot to use it, so if you need to call, fine, but don't do it just to chat."

We talked for a little while longer, and then I gave Gram the phone. I was waiting for her to give it back to me so I could say goodbye, but she hung up.

"Gram!"

"Oh, sorry, Nathan. You can call him back."

"Never mind."

Neil called a couple of times the first week he was away, just to let Gram know he was okay; he didn't talk long, and I got to speak to him only once, but it sounded like he and Jeremy were having a great time.

Meanwhile, El Speed convinced me to visit his cabin for a few days during the second week of Neil's wilderness trek.

"The spring bugs are almost over already this year, and the mosquitoes haven't got all their planes in the air yet. It won't be this good again until September. So can you get yourself to Conway? I can pick you up from there."

We decided I'd take the bus. Otherwise, Gram would have had to drive both ways, twice, and that would mean three hours on the road for her each time.

I did not want to get caught out in the woods unprepared for the second time this year, so I kind of over packed. Almost forgot swim trunks and had to stuff them in at the last minute.

El Speed's beat-up, black Forester was waiting for me when I descended from the bus, and he wasn't the only one standing beside it. The slender girl beside him was nearly as tall as El Speed, and she was dressed for the woods: jeans, hiking boots, a green-and-black flannel shirt with rolled-up sleeves. Her long, strawberry-blond hair was in a ponytail high on the back of her head, a dark blue hair elastic holding it in place, and as she moved around it swung in counterbalance to the rest of her.

I dropped my bag to shake Ellie's hand, but she wrapped her arms around me.

"Nathan, thank you so much for caring about Gordie.

Part of me loves that you beat that asshole Byron up."

You're welcome didn't seem like the best response, and neither did *Oh, I did that more because of Alden*. Besides, it could hardly be said that I'd beaten Byron up. Damaged him, yes, but that was all. So I smiled and said nothing.

El Speed threw my bag into the cargo area and I moved toward the back seat.

"Oh, Nathan, no; you sit in front," Ellie said. "You and Larry can catch up on things."

El Speed nosed the car onto the road. "This will be so cool, Nathan. I love this place. Been going there all my life. It belonged to my grandparents originally."

I was keenly aware of Ellie in the back seat. "Are we going right there?"

"Yup. Ellie and I have the place all ready for company. We've been there since yesterday morning."

That was the answer to my real question: *Will Ellie be there with us?* It hadn't occurred to me to ask this ahead of time, and El Speed hadn't said anything one way or another. I guess he'd assumed that I'd assume she'd be with him.

Ellie laughed. "Company? Nathan, don't pay any attention to him. The place is way too rustic to be called worthy of 'company.'"

"How big is it?" I hoped that was indirect enough that it wouldn't be obvious I wanted to know if I'd have a separate room, or if it would be bunks like Daniel's friend's place had been.

El Speed filled me in. "There's one big room that's the kitchen, dining area, and living room all in one. There's a wood stove in the kitchen part. Then there's actually three bedrooms. Two of them have fireplaces. The third is challenging in the winter, but we've used it. I should say, *I've* used it."

So I was sure to be alone, and I had no doubt one bedroom would remain unused.

"How far is it from here?"

"About an hour and a half."

I settled in for the ride.

Ellie might have been in the back seat, but that didn't prevent conversation. She didn't chatter, but she asked me questions, and I asked her a few, and by the time El Speed announced that we were almost there I'd decided I liked her.

It didn't last.

I know that sometimes gay men get labeled as "high maintenance," which I think can mean anything from spending too much money on products and too much time using then, to demanding a lot of attention in general. I don't think I fall into that category. Even so, I found the challenge of being in that cabin with very limited amenities greater than when I'd stayed in Daniel's cabin. Maybe it was that Daniel and I had spent so much time out of the cabin. Maybe it was that without refrigeration at El Speed's cabin, all the meals were vegetarian (though eggs and cheddar cheese were allowed), and every meal left me feeling hungry. Plus there were only so many times I could hear Ellie pronounce that some herb—oregano, lemon thyme, chives, whatever—came "fresh from my garden at home!" before it started to wear on me.

Or maybe it was that there had been no bugs in January.

Here, I found it difficult to sleep through the whine of mosquitoes. Ignoring them just didn't work; I knew they were waiting for me to lie still in the dark so they could land on me, suck my blood, and leave an ugly welt that I would make uglier by scratching it raw.

How many times did I get up, light the lantern, and try to hunt them down? I'd hear one near my ear and step away to try and see it. Eyes frantically flicking through the gloom, I'd move around with my hands held in front of me and ready to slap. Suddenly I'd see the pest on the side of the wooden headboard or on the rough-hewn log wall or on the leg of the bed table, but before I could get to it the thing would disappear, and the whine would start again. They were visible only when they were silent, after landing on something. And then—poof! They'd disappear, but their whine proved they were still hunting me. They were devils!

Ellie was, I decided, even lower maintenance than I was. When I said something about the bugs at the first breakfast, she just laughed.

"What's a little blood? You won't miss it."

Kind of not the point, I wanted to say, but I didn't.

And the close proximity of the bedrooms, and the lack of any soundproofing (or even any sound resistance) didn't stop her from enjoying El Speed's attentions at night. As I lay in my room, the whine of the mosquitoes doing nothing to dull the sounds of Ellie's enjoyment, I felt thrown back to my high school days when my straight classmates thought nothing of flaunting their sexual attraction for each other, and I'd felt sure they would have been horrified if another boy and I had done the same.

Tuesday was mixed. It rained most of the day, so we didn't spend much time outdoors. Ellie tried to distract us with games, and El Speed did his best to be enthusiastic. He also kept music playing from his phone, made possible by a battery-powered charger they used at the cabin. There was one folk singer he seemed especially fond of, David Wilcox. I'd ever heard of him, but it would have been fine if El Speed hadn't played so much of his stuff.

The only good part of that day for me was dinner, when we traveled half an hour each way to Rumford for some pizza. El Speed and I each got a whole pizza with as much meat on it as the place could offer.

I wasn't sleeping much, and there wasn't enough to do. When it wasn't raining, kayaking was fun, but there were bugs out there. The rainy Tuesday had been mostly a bust, and Ellie had laughed at my bug distress (or that's how it had felt, anyway). So over yet another vegetarian meal on Wednesday night, when I said something about Cotton insisting that Neil spend his short break between classes and hiking with her and her parents instead of coming home, it hit me all wrong when Ellie stood up for Cotton.

"But, Nathan, how many chances are there for Neil to meet her folks? And if they're getting serious—"

"Lots of chances. He could have gone there after he got back from hiking, or he could go there before classes start again in the fall."

"Okay, but he could spend that time at home, too."

I didn't care that that was reasonable. I was cranky, and Ellie was getting on my nerves. "Look, I've had a really tough year. A really good friend—"

"Oh, pish-posh. Don't sulk."

I glared at her and added more edge to my voice. "Someone really important to me lost his addiction battle, and another friend led me into the wilderness in a blizzard and nearly got me killed. My feet will never be the same."

"Your friend died?"

I was feeling cruel. I didn't tell her the whole truth. "Fentanyl. And he wasn't a *friend*. He was my boyfriend." I knew that would get her.

There was enough silence in the room that I'm sure I would have heard the whine of a mosquito if one had come near me. El Speed's eyes were on his plate, and they stayed there. Ellie's shocked eyes were on me, and I glared back at her

"And," I finished, "it does me a lot of good to spend time with Neil."

Finally Ellie spoke. "Oh, Nathan. I'm so sorry that happened."

I decided to stop myself saying anything else; as it was, I was terrified that I'd already jeopardized my relationship with El Speed. *He* knew Alden hadn't died.

The rest of the evening felt strained. Everyone seemed to be walking on eggshells to try not to offend anyone else. I heard mosquitoes that night, but I didn't hear any activity coming from the next room.

After breakfast Thursday, El Speed and I headed back to Conway without Ellie. He tried to make light of her absence.

"Yeah, she likes to kayak on her own sometimes. Doesn't always want me around."

I let that hang in the air for a few miles. Then, "Look, man, I just want to say I'm sorry about last night. I didn't mean to get everything all tense."

"No worries."

I wasn't done. "You guys seem really good together."

"Yeah. I'm thinking we might take the next step, maybe by Christmas."

"You mean get engaged?"

His laugh sounded a little nervous. "If I can get up the nerve. And if she says yes."

"I'll be rooting for you." In point of fact, I couldn't imagine being ready even to consider that kind of commitment anytime soon for myself. If I met the man of my dreams in September, I didn't think that would be enough to make me want to commit to anything or anyone for a long time.

I cheered up a little at the start of the bus ride, odd as that sounds. For one thing, there were no mosquitoes, and the air conditioning made the bites I already had itch less. I spent the time contemplating what Ellie had said and how I'd reacted to it.

Neil had already told us he'd come home for a few days after The Priest, though he'd added that he had to go back to Colorado for a short internship before classes started back up. He'd be in Concord for at least as much time as if he'd come home before the hiking trip. So why was I so pissed off about the time Cotton had made him spend in San Diego? If that hadn't been before the hike, it would have been after. My feelings weren't rational. And even though I knew that, they remained.

Thinking about Ellie led to thinking about Gordon which led to thinking about Alden and addiction. And then it hit me suddenly—and so hard I sat up straight and startled the lady in the seat beside me—that there was at least a little something of the addict in me. Not for fentanyl, which I would stay away from like the plague. No. I was addicted to Neil.

Addiction, as I understand it, is something you do or need repeatedly, something you can't get enough of or can't do often enough, something you can't stop wanting, something that to some extent becomes the focus of your life, and something that's not good for you.

Did that apply to me? Was I really addicted to Neil? Was that even possible?

Okay, psych major, I said to myself so as not to trouble my seat mate further, *puzzle this out.*

I tried.

I decided to dismiss the "something that's not good for you" aspect. The only downside I could see to wanting to be with Neil was along the lines of being annoyed with Cotton.

I wanted to be with Neil repeatedly, true. Was time with him something I couldn't get enough of? Not as clear, but then there was my irrational reaction to the reasonable trip to San Diego. So... maybe?

Was I unable to stop wanting to have Neil around? No. For example, I didn't expect to spend every minute with him even when we both happened to be in the same town. And maybe it wasn't unreasonable to want to be around someone you love, someone who loves you and cares about you. And all the time I was at school, at UNH, he'd been at college for four years before that. It wasn't like I'd been jonesin' for him daily all year.

Another voice in my head didn't want me to get away with that. *What about Daniel?* it asked. *Wasn't he a Neil surrogate? And now that you aren't going to see Daniel again, how much do you feel Neil's absence?*

Methadone. Daniel had been methadone. Neil was where my true addiction lay, and Daniel had been a temporary substitute. Now the methadone was gone, and I was in some kind of withdrawal.

Why? What was it Neil gave me that I needed so badly?

I leaned my head back against the seat rest, closed my eyes, and thought about Neil, about how being with him made me feel. The words that came into my head were of warmth, and belonging, and security, and love.

Love was obvious. No psych degree was needed to understand that. Security... really? Did he owe me that? Not in any reasonable world. But did I look to him to fill that need because of not having a father growing up?

I must. I already knew I'd been looking to Neil to be my father, to be infallible, to relieve me from worry about the big, bad world, to assure me that I belonged in his house, his family, his life. I'd known all that on some level for a long time. But if my father had lived, would I have felt about him the way I felt about Neil? It seemed unlikely. So—what the fuck?

My eyes flew open. So Neil was also methadone. A substitute. My father would have been the real thing, and I'd missed out on that. So I couldn't get enough methadone.

There's a great line from one of the David Wilcox songs El Speed had played in the cabin: "You can get what's second best, but it's hard to get enough."

Something in my mind slipped sideways. Something prevented me from examining my relationship with Neil in that light, from looking directly at it, from facing it. I tried to bring it back, but—nope. It was like trying to catch a large bar of soap with one hand in a tub of warm water.

When I got home, Gram was nervous. "There are a couple of forest fires in Virginia near where the boys are hiking."

"Did you look online? Can you see where the fires

are?"

"I didn't think of that."

Neil had shown me on Google Earth roughly where the cabin was. I fired up my laptop and zeroed in on the spot. Then I did a search on the fires and came up with a day-old map of them. It didn't look like they were close to the cabin at all.

"Gram, I think they'll be fine. Neil said they weren't planning any long-distance hikes, maybe just one overnight. So they'll be at the cabin most nights. Did you call?"

"I did. He said they could smell the smoke, but it seemed far away. He also said they had—what was it, he said? A fire shelter? The boys called the park service and they recommended this shelter thing. It was expensive! I had to give Neil my credit card information so they could buy one they could both fit into."

"They should be all right then."

"Oh, Nathan, I hope so. I pray so. I said they should come home, but Neil said there was no reason. I'm so worried."

I looked up what a fire shelter was. Apparently it's a silvery oblong bag, kind of like a fully-enclosed sleeping bag, made of aluminum and silica and fiberglass, depending on which style you have. Ideally it reflects heat and protects you without suffocating you inside.

My mind flashed back to lying on the snowy mountainside, crowded into Daniel's sleeping bag with him. Gram had indicated that Neil and Jeremy would both use the same shelter. Daniel and I had been trying to stay alive by keeping warm. The fire shelter would keep you alive by not letting you burn.

CHAPTER FIFTEEN

I didn't sleep well that night. My dreams were full of air thick with something that was hard to see through, and when I tried to walk through it I kept getting tangled in it. Once I woke up with the sheet wrapped around my ankles.

In the morning, I slept in. I barely heard Gram leave the house, probably for groceries or something. I had another dream, a kind of dozing dream, where something was trying to get through the thick air. It was a sound.

My phone.

I nearly fell out of bed in my rush to get to it. It might be Neil.

It was! "Neil?"

"Nathan!" I could barely make out his words for the noise around him. "I have to tell you—"

"What? You have to tell me what? What's that noise?" I could have sworn he was between two very long, speeding trains going opposite directions.

"Fire."

"What?"

"Fire. I—we tried to outrun it. Couldn't. Too fast, and then another fire...."

"Neil! Are you in a fire? Are you in the shelter?"

"Yes. No time. Listen. Call Jeremy's mom. Tell her...." I couldn't distinguish his words. "Neil! Tell her what?"

"He loves her."

Tell her he loves her? What the fuck was happening?

"Neil!"

"Nathan, tell Gram I love her. Tell Cotton. And Nathan—"

Then the screaming began. Horrible screaming. I press-

251

ed the phone so hard against the side of my head that my arm hurt, and I pressed some more, praying I'd hear words. I called Neil's name, and again, and again.

The line went dead.

My hands shook violently as I searched through my contacts for the sat line number. It just rang and rang and rang and rang and rang until I couldn't hear it any more through my own wrenching sobs.

I'd just listened to the sound of my brother burning to death.

I was still in my room, phone in my hand and still ringing impotently, when I heard Gram come home. I had to tell her. Somehow, I had to tell her. I tried to get up off the floor where I'd collapsed at some point I hadn't been aware of, but I couldn't stand. I crawled across the floor toward the door to my room and barely managed to pull myself up holding onto the frame.

"Nathan? Time you got up, lazybones."

I tried to call out to her, but all I could do was sob.

She must have heard something. "Nathan?" Her voice was closer now; she was on the stairs. "Nathan, what on earth?"

Holding onto the door frame, I called out a strangled sound that I intended to be "Gram!"

As she climbed higher on the stairs I saw the fluffy gray hair on the top of her head, and then her face appeared. She saw me. And she froze.

Her voice barely a whisper, she said, "Nathan?"

Pain. Pain like I'd never felt before. Pain like you read about. It hurt so fucking bad! I moaned.

"Nathan!"

I held my breath in an effort to get it under control. Finally I managed, "Neil."

"Nathan! Please! What is it?"

"He's gone."

She was nearly shrieking now. "Gone?"

"Burned." *Burned.* Was that better than the word "dead?"

"What? Nathan, talk to me!"

How do you say that you've just heard your brother burn to death? What words do you use? Somehow I managed to find enough words to get Gram to understand.

"Neil! No! No! Oh my God, no!" Her hands reached up to cover her face. "We have to call! We have to find out!"

"I called, Gram. I called and called."

"Try again!"

So I ended the last call and started a new one, handing her my phone so she could hear the empty sound of a phone no one would answer.

She thrust the phone at me. "Come with me."

I followed her down the stairs as she hung onto the railing with both hands, placing first one and then the other foot on each step before moving down to the next. I followed just as carefully.

Gram hobbled into the kitchen, leaning on the counter where she'd left a note for me earlier to say she'd gone shopping, stumbling past the bags of groceries that sat untended on the floor. She fumbled with some papers until she found what she was looking for.

I barely recognized her voice. "We have to tell the park service where they are."

"Gram? They're dead." My voice was barely a squeak.

"I won't believe that."

I just shook my head. She hadn't heard the terrible roar of the fire. She hadn't heard the screams. And I hadn't told her about either of those things.

She handed me a folded paper. "Read me the number."

I opened it and saw that it was a list of dates and locations, the places where Neil and Jeremy would be hiking, with a few cross-outs and changes in Gram's hand that he must have told her over the phone. There were trail names, and a few distances, and maybe it was an odd moment for this, but I recalled Daniel's cavalier attitude toward leaving any record of where he and I would be going on our fateful hike. "It's a good day to die," he had said.

He didn't have a fucking clue.

At the bottom of the paper was the park service number. Gram picked up the hand set to our land line, still in that old-fashioned place on the kitchen wall. I called out the numbers and Gram told them who she was and why she was calling, but she didn't get very far before she broke down. I had to take over, and I was about to give them the information about where Neil and Jeremy had been hiking, but the ranger said they had the location. So Neil must have been as thorough with them as he'd been with Gram.

The ranger asked what had happened, so I told him I'd been speaking to my brother as the fire approached, and the line had gone silent. There was a long pause before he said they didn't know how soon they could get into that area but that they'd call as soon as they did.

I'd been repeating to Gram everything they had said. Before I could hang up, she shrieked, "Is that all they can do? Is that *all?*"

I held the phone so we could both hear the ranger say, "I'm sorry, ma'am. We have no choice but to wait until the fire subsides. We'll inform the firefighters about the boys' position, and they'll get to them as soon as possible. But, ma'am," and even he sounded like he had to keep his voice from breaking, "I wouldn't hold out much hope."

I don't know how long Gram and I sat across from each other at the kitchen table, staring at the placemats in front of us, before I heard her say, "Tell me what he said." Her voice was flat, featureless, emotionless.

I took a shuddering breath and tried in vain to speak. I took another breath. "He called my cell. He said the fire was overtaking them, and that they were in the fire shelter, but that it wasn't going to be enough."

"He knew?" She looked up at me, new tears welling in her eyes. "He knew he was going to die?"

I took a long, shaky breath and said, "He said to tell you he loves you. He said to tell Cotton. He said to tell Jeremy's mom Jeremy loves her. Then the line dropped." Maybe he'd been about to tell me he loved me, and Nina, but instead he'd screamed.

Gram called Nina, who'd gone to stay with a girlfriend in New York City for a week or so, and again I had to take over. Nina had to put the phone down. I wondered whether she'd let me know she was crying. When she picked the phone up again, all she said was she'd get home as quickly as she could.

Then Gram and I drove over to see Mrs. Ford. Never again do I want to have to be the one to tell anyone that someone they love is dead.

Gram clamped her hand over her face to stifle her sobs as I did my best to get the words out so Mrs. Ford would know what had happened. As with Gram, I stopped short of describing the screams. I just told her the line had gone silent, and that no one had picked up when I'd called back repeatedly. I relayed what the park ranger had said.

Mrs. Ford brushed tears from her face and jumped up and went to where the phone to a land line sat on a table.

"Tell me the number!" she shouted at me.

I called out the number from my contacts list as Mrs. Ford's shaking fingers pushed the buttons. Gram and I both looked away as Mrs. Ford listened and listened helplessly to that mechanical ringing sound. When I finally looked at her face, I barely recognized her. She knew no one would answer.

Gram was stoic as she drove back to our house. I wondered if we were both cried out, at least for a while, but the horror wouldn't leave.

Half-way to the house Gram's body stiffened suddenly. "Oh!"

"What?"

She pulled over to the side of the road. I stared at her. She stared forward. "Cotton."

"Cotton?"

"We have to tell Cotton."

Silence. Maybe twenty seconds of it.

Finally I said, "How?"

Gram looked in my direction, her eyes unfocused. "I don't know. I don't know how to reach her."

So Neil hadn't given anyone her contact info, because I sure didn't have it. "How many Hazards d'you suppose there are in San Diego?"

"Nathan, we have to look it up. We have to."

"Yeah. Okay. I'll try."

Back at the house, Gram looking over my shoulder, I used my laptop to search. Very quickly, I discovered there were more than thirty entries for the last name Hazard in San Diego.

"Do you know her parents' names?"

Gram shook her head. "I don't. Isn't that horrible of me?" She seemed genuinely distressed, as though this was somehow a betrayal of what was important in Neil's life.

Without any real hope that I'd find anything, I went into Neil's room and poked around. It hurt. Everything I saw drew fresh tears to my eyes. I was sure that any information about Cotton would have been easy to find, not something hidden in a drawer or in the back of the closet, so I didn't dig into anything.

I wondered what he'd done with his laptop; he must have had it at school, because it wasn't here. Probably it was in his apartment in Colorado, which he'd shared with a couple of other guys I didn't know. That's when it hit me how many hurdles Gram and I, and Nina once she got here, would have to get over in order to bring closure to Neil's life.

I sat down hard on the floor. The funeral, closed casket (if any) of course, would be just the beginning. If they even found anything to bury.

My brain wouldn't work. I don't know how long I sat there before Gram came to look for me. She sat on the floor with me and waited for me to speak.

"There's so much, Gram. So much. His things here. His apartment in Boulder. His school. Telling everyone." My head was shaking slowly back and forth.

Gram took a shaky breath. "He had a life insurance policy."

I looked at her. "What?"

"He knew something could happen to him. He took it out a couple of years ago."

One more thing. One more thing to deal with. They'd require a death certificate, made by a doctor who declared that a blackened pile of bones and teeth and melted plastic bits of what used to be phone parts was Neil's corpse.

I couldn't breathe. I don't think I drew another full breath for days.

After a meager dinner that we didn't eat, Gram and Nina and I sat at the kitchen table, mostly silent except for occasional sobs, a notebook in the center where we'd been writing down things we knew we'd have to do. Every so often Nina would pick up her phone and call the sat phone's number. I knew it was futile. But I'd done it. Gram had done it. Mrs. Ford had done it. No one told Nina it was useless. And we all wished Neil would pick up.

I think it was just before eleven o'clock when she put her phone down firmly. "I know how we can reach Cotton." Gram and I stared at her. "We have to contact Neil's school anyway. She's a student there. Maybe they won't give us her contact information, but we can get the news to her through them."

We were letting this sink in when Gram's cell phone rang. She practically threw it across the room in her haste to see if it was Neil. It wasn't, of course.

It was Cotton.

Gram put the phone on speaker. This would be the first time any of us had heard Cotton's voice.

"Um, hi, I hope this isn't awkward. I'm sorry it's so late there. I'm in California. But you know that already. Anyway, Neil was going to call me when they got back to the cabin today, but I haven't heard from him."

She stopped, and we all looked at each other, wondering what we would say and who would say it.

Cotton must have wondered why no one responded. I could hear the tension in her voice now. "Um, so, I don't want to worry anyone, but I did try to call him a few minutes ago. And—well, there wasn't any answer. Have you heard from him at all?"

Gram's hand covered her mouth, and her eyes began streaming tears yet again. I opened my mouth, but only a choking sound came out. It was Nina who spoke, finally.

"Cotton, this is Nina. Neil's sister." She took a breath, a shaky one, closed her eyes, swallowed, and started again. "You need to sit down. Seriously."

"I—I am sitting. Why?" Her voice rose. "What's happened? Tell me!"

"It's bad news. Very bad. There was—hold on." And Nina had to take a few breaths. "There was a forest fire. They were in a fire shelter, one of those aluminum things, but it wasn't enough."

"What do you mean it wasn't enough?" Her voice was a high-pitched yell. "Where are they?"

"They're dead, Cotton. They died in the fire."

I heard a kind of strangled sound and then Cotton must have dropped the phone. We all waited to see if she'd pick it up again. Nina blew her nose and took a few more deep breaths. Gram did her best to stifle her sobs.

Cotton finally picked up the phone again, obviously crying. As Nina did her best to explain that we'd need to wait for confirmation from the park service before anything else could happen, I found myself wondering how many times over the course of the coming days, weeks, months, years we'd find ourselves like this, weeping helplessly, going through boxes of tissues, unable to say Neil's name without weeping harder.

I tried to get myself to feel bad for Cotton. Truly, I did. But because of her, Neil had spent his last days on earth with her and not with us. Not with me. His promise to come home after the hike was as dead as he was.

There was, finally, confirmation by the park service. They found the two bodies, or the remains of them, and they determined that the body closest to what was left of the phone was Neil. Their teeth were so badly burned that dental record comparison was inconclusive. The park service knew of no other hikers in the area at the time of the fire, and Neil's description of their plans had been thorough, so the remains must have been Neil and Jeremy. Neither Gram nor Mrs. Ford requested DNA testing, though I don't know what would have been left to test, anyway.

The cabin was gone, they told us. If the guys had gotten back there, they'd still have been in the path of the fire, which had evidently made some sudden change in direction and intensity, almost like a tornado. I looked this up, the concept of a fire-nado, and was surprised that it turned out to be a thing. I read that temperatures inside a fire tornado—though I can't imagine how they know this—can get to nearly three thousand degrees Fahrenheit. That's hotter than volcanic magma, one article said. There's no fire shelter anywhere that would have saved Neil and Jeremy. And there was no way they could have predicted it or run from it.

I didn't realize this horror had reached the news. At our

house, we were barely paying attention to anything. But El Speed called.

"Hey, bro, um... Ellie just told me what happened to your brother. I don't know what to say."

I blinked and then closed my eyes. Then I swallowed. Then I coughed. "How—how did she find out?"

"Well—it's been on the news. I didn't see it. I've been up at the cabin doing some work. But she was at home."

Silence. It seems neither one of us knew what to say.

He found his voice first. "Ellie wanted to call you, but she wasn't sure you'd want to hear from her."

"Why not?"

"I guess because of how you guys kind of tussled over Neil going to Cotton's. And now—well, she feels horrible."

Horrible? She didn't have a fucking clue what "horrible" felt like.

He added, "She knows how much he means to you. I mean, meant. I mean—shit, this is awful."

"How would she know anything about that?"

"It was obvious, man. I mean, you talked about him the whole time you were here."

"I did not."

"Okay. Fine."

Did I?

I heard him exhale like he was trying to clear the air. "I don't suppose you know anything about a funeral yet. Like, a date?"

"They haven't released—" the remains. They hadn't released the remains. I couldn't say it.

"Okay, well, I just wanted to check in, you know. Let you know we're thinking about you."

"Yeah. Thanks. Appreciate it." I wasn't sure I did. Not yet, anyway. Mostly because other than this pain, I didn't feel much of anything.

It was nearly a week later before the funeral home Gram had chosen called to say they'd received Neil's remains, and we could schedule the funeral. Gram and Nina and I had already talked a little about that, about the arrangements and the preparation and the planning. It made me feel giddy, not in a good way, because I kept getting the strangest feeling that it wasn't much different from planning a wedding.

Jeremy's funeral would be the day after Neil's. Different churches. We would all be at both of them.

"That poor woman," Gram said after she hung up from a call with Mrs. Ford. "Jeremy was her only child, and her husband died seven years ago. She has no one. At least we have each other."

Nina did more than commiserate. Without telling us, she contacted Mrs. Ford and offered to help her organize Jeremy's funeral. I was stunned when I found out. This horror was bringing out sides of my sister I'd never seen before.

At some point, it dawned on us to consider having someone speak, other than Gram's minister.

"I don't think I could do it," Gram said. "I'm sure I'd fall completely to bits. Nathan, maybe you could say something."

I just gaped at her. There was no way.

"I'll do it, Gram." Nina to the rescue, again.

But that night, alone in my room, it occurred to me that I could at least consider saying a few words. It felt wrong for Nina to be alone up there. And if I dropped a few tears, so what? No one would mind. It would probably be weird if I didn't.

I wasn't sure I'd do it. But I did write down what I thought I would say, if I decided to.

A meeting we had with the minister, Reverend Talby, convinced me that I would stand with Nina and speak about Neil. During that meeting, we discussed what the reverend would say at the funeral. He suggested that he should include something about how Neil had died doing what he loved.

"No," I said, shaking my head. It surprised even me how firm my tone was. "No, he didn't. He loved hiking. He didn't love burning alive."

"Nathan," Gram started, but I interrupted her before she could say anything else.

"No. That makes it sound like a good thing. It wasn't a good thing. Nothing good about it at all." If anyone had pressured me, I was prepared to tell them about the sound of the fire, and about the screams. But it didn't come to that.

Nina came to the rescue again. "I agree with Nathan. Let's not say that." She sounded more polite than I had, but just as firm.

On the ride home, I told Nina I'd prepared something and would stand with her when she got up to speak. She nodded and tried to smile.

When the day of the funeral arrived, nearly a week later, I dreaded going to the church. One reason was obvious. The other had to do with Cotton.

She and her parents had arrived the night before. They stayed at a hotel, not with us, but Gram insisted we all join them for dinner in town. I tried to avoid it.

"They're treating us, Nathan. It's the least you can do."

"That makes no sense, Gram."

"Never mind. I should think you'd want to get to know the young woman your brother wanted to marry."

"They aren't going to marry now, are they?" She glared at me. "And they weren't engaged yet."

"Neil loved her. That should be enough. Now, go and change into something presentable."

Cotton's "pixie" face looked a little odd, perched atop the body of an athlete. She was at least two inches taller than Neil had been. Her parents were giants. They towered over us. It made me feel small and provincial. After all, they were from famous San Diego, and they looked like they had money to burn. I didn't know what to say to them.

Nina saved the day, again. She seemed to know how to talk to these California visitors, these beautiful people with the sophisticated clothing and the smooth tans and the blond teeth.

Gram and I were hopeless. She smiled unconvincingly and nodded a lot and, I think, tried not to cry a few times. Cotton didn't talk much; she dabbed at her eyes several times, which made me warm to her just a little. I barely spoke at all.

That night my sleep was restless. I kept waking up, legs kicking at something that wasn't there.

Sometime around six I woke up, sitting upright, back straight, legs rigid, teeth clenched tight. It hadn't been a dream. I wish it had. Because in my ears, just as though I'd been there, I heard the screams. I heard those screams I hadn't told anyone about. The screams of Neil and Jeremy dying.

When I walked into the church with Gram and Nina, I had no idea—never having been to a funeral before—whether I'd be expected to socialize with the Hazards again. I didn't actively dislike them, but every time I had looked at Cotton over dinner, I'd hated her for having stolen Neil's last few days from me. *That* was entirely her fault. And today, feeling even more raw emotionally, I didn't know if I'd be able to contain myself.

There were a lot of people already there. Like I said, Gram had lived in Concord all her life, and everyone who had known Neil had liked him. I glanced quickly around to see if the Hazards were already here. They were. Right in the pew behind where we were supposed to sit.

I saw that Mrs. Ford was already in the pew waiting for us. But then in another pew, I saw something I hadn't expected: the back of a blond head on a tall person I knew was El Speed. Ellie sat beside him. My eyes burned.

A single, gasping sob escaped me, and Gram took my hand and squeezed it.

There were hymns, and Reverend Talby talked about how long our family had been in the community and what a wonderful young man Neil had been, and then he introduced Nina.

She looked at me, our eyes locked, and I felt closer to her than I'd ever felt in my life. I nodded.

She shocked me by taking my hand as soon as we were away from the pew. We stood side by side in front of all those people, most of whom I had at least met. As we had agreed, Nina, now the oldest of our generation, spoke first.

I don't remember what she said; I could barely pay attention. But I remember thinking it was perfect, that it was very Nina and very Neil all at once.

And then it was my turn.

"My brother," I began, and then realized my voice was too soft. "My brother was like a father to me. He was kind, and patient, and he was the first person I told that I'm gay."

I waited through a slight stirring in the audience. I knew that would be a surprise to most of them.

"What he said, when I told him, was, 'You need to be who you are.'" I'd been tempted to mention that Jeremy was gay, but I knew better than to do that. I didn't even know whether his mother had known.

"That was the best thing he could have said to me. And it was how he lived, too. Neil was always himself. He always seemed very clear about the right thing to do. I've lost track of how many problems I brought to him, how many times I asked for his help, how many times his guidance made all the difference in my life."

I took a deep breath and lowered my head for a few

seconds. When I looked up again I couldn't see for the tears standing in my eyes.

"Neil wasn't perfect. But he was the perfect brother for me. For the rest of my life, whenever I feel confused about what to do, I will ask myself: What would Neil do? And I know," shaky breath here, "I will hear his voice."

I don't remember getting back to the pew. I sat or stood according to the program while tears leaked from my closed eyes.

Neil's grave was waiting for him, right beside where our parents' graves were. Each of us threw a handful of dirt and a white rose into the wound in the earth where Neil would lie forever. Cotton dropped a rose but no dirt.

It felt odd to go back to the church after the cemetery, but there was no way Gram's house was big enough for the number of people who would want to be at the after-party, as I thought of it. So that would take place in the church function hall. I rode with Gram and Nina again, but when we got there I looked around immediately for my friends. They were looking for me.

Ellie gave me a quick hug, and El Speed wrapped his large body around mine for a few seconds.

"I meant to let you know when the funeral was," I lied. I hadn't thought of it at all. "How did you find out?"

"Ellie made a list of the funeral homes in Concord and called around until she found the right one." Anything unpleasant I'd ever thought about her evaporated.

El Speed talked about the work he was doing at the cabin. Ellie was quiet but present; I think she was wondering if I was mad at her, but I didn't have the bandwidth to communicate my feelings.

After maybe forty-five minutes, it became obvious that someone was setting up a microphone on the low stage at one end of the hall. There were speakers, too, which I knew the church used for the occasional party. When everything was set, Reverend Talby took the mic. Cotton was on stage, off to the side, and I thought (unkindly, I admit) that black was not her friend.

"May I have everyone's attention?" Reverend Talby waited for relative quiet. "Some of you know that Neil thought the world of Miss Cotton Hazard. She has asked that we listen to a song Neil was fond of. Cotton?"

She looked a little shy, or tentative, as she took the mic. Then she looked right at me. The room grew absolutely still.

"Nathan, you said earlier that Neil was always himself. You were absolutely right. So even though," her voice broke up a little here. She closed her eyes for a second and then looked around the room. "Even though doing what he loved was how his life ended," and I flinched a little here, "he lived that life the way only he could do it. And his favorite song, by the band Cherryholmes, is about what to do with life. Live it. And that's the name of this song."

At the mention of a favorite song, my mind bounced around music I'd heard Neil play. His tastes had been eclectic, and I didn't land on anything. Someone on stage did something, and the music started.

It was immediately obvious that Cherryholmes played and sang bluegrass. I looked around for Gram and Nina; did this surprise them? It sure as hell surprised me. I didn't see them, so I just listened carefully to the words. Everyone around me seemed to be doing the same.

What my ears caught from the lyrics was how nothing in life will ever be just what we want it to be, and we need to accept that. But what cut into me, what left a groove in my memory, was one line: Go grab your life and live it.

I hadn't seen Cotton get off the stage, but as soon as the song ended she was right next to me. As I turned toward her she stepped forward and embraced me. I smelled a grassy, slightly sweet fragrance. It reminded me of Alden's mother. And then I heard her voice, quiet, intimate, in my ear.

"Neil loved you so much."

Then she released me and smiled, her eyes sparkling with unshed tears, and walked away. I watched, thinking she'd go to Nina and Gram with the same message, but she didn't. She went to stand with her folks.

It was just for me. That message was just for me. It was like Neil was speaking to me from beyond the grave.

There was an enormous amount of food left over. El Speed offered to help us bring some of it home, and then he and Ellie stayed and had a light dinner with us. Then Gram went upstairs, saying she was exhausted. We watched her leave, and then Nina went into the kitchen and returned with four bottles of beer.

"I had Gram get some beer for you and me, Nathan, but there's plenty to share."

I hadn't even known. My perception of Nina was changing radically.

At first everyone just took a few sips without speaking. Then Nina broke the spell. She waved the hand holding her bottle. "It's okay. You can talk about him or not."

Everyone seemed to relax, and Ellie took the plunge. "What was Neil studying at school?"

Nina didn't jump in right away, so I decided to risk a little humor. "I understand I might have monopolized the conversation at the cabin, saying things about him. I'm surprised I omitted that information."

Ellie and El Speed laughed, a little nervously, but that was okay. I filled them in, and then Nina surprised the hell out of me. "What's your favorite memory of him, Nathan?"

I stared at her, aghast; where had that come from? "Why me? What about your favorite memory?"

"I asked you first. And I'm the oldest now." She grinned and took a swig of beer.

I think it was a combination of her lording it over me

and of the humorous way she did it that helped me decide what to say.

"Okay, fine. I'm not saying this is my favorite, but—do you remember that Easter egg hunt we had, Neil's last year as a Cub Scout? Easter was late, and it was a warm spring, and the troop held this hunt event in a park. I forget which one."

"Rollins Park."

"Right." I didn't know she was right, but it didn't matter. "Anyway, kids under—what, eight, I think, which included both of us, were supposed to see how many candy eggs we could find under bushes and things. As I recall, you pooh-pooh-ed the whole thing and then got absolutely cut-throat competitive."

"And you found all of two eggs."

"But you didn't win, either. So here's Neil, trying his best to help me figure out where to look, but every time I headed toward where he'd suggested, there would be this dandelion. They were early, and everywhere, and lots of them had puffed."

"As I recall, you kept stopping to blow the seeds all over the place."

"And Neil kept trying to point me toward hidden eggs. He never lost his patience, even though I was much more interested in dandelions."

I grinned and took a swig from my bottle, watching Nina. Would she remember the rest of what had happened?

Her tone teasing, she said, "Very like you, Nathan, to go for puffy things and ignore the real object."

"Maybe my object was different from yours. After all, I had more fun than anyone else there. I freed so many fluff spiders!"

"You and your spiders...."

"What?"

"Spider Man?"

"Oh. Well," I leaned forward, elbows resting on my knees, "I saved a handful of the fluffs. You and I were in the back seat on the drive home, and you laughed at my paltry collection of eggs. So I blew those fluff spiders all over you!"

It didn't surprise me that El Speed and Ellie laughed. What surprised me was that Nina did. She laughed even harder when I added, "You should have seen your face!"

Nina went upstairs after that, without telling us her own favorite memory. The other three of us talked for another hour or so, and by the time they left, I was in the best mood I'd been in since before my trip to Concord Pond. Jeremy's funeral the next day was hanging over me, but my feelings seemed more manageable now. I'm sure the beer helped, but it wasn't about that.

I hugged both my friends before they climbed into the Forester and went back to their room at the Best Western.

Upstairs, the door to Gram's room was closed, but Nina's was open, and there was a light on. She was on the bed, sitting up and reading her tablet. I knocked on the doorframe.

She looked up. "A good time was had by all, I hope."

"It was." I almost smiled; it felt wrong, but it was tempting. I stepped in and sat down on her desk chair. The beer had opened me up a little, and something I'd never thought to ask her flew into my head.

"Nina? What was it about Daniel that made you realize you didn't want to see him any more?"

She set her tablet down. "Ah, yes. You mean the fellow who got you lost in the blizzard. That Daniel?"

I knew she was being facetious. "Yeah."

She nodded. "The man had loser written all over him. I can't say why I felt that, but I did. Did you, um, you know, did you like him?"

I shrugged. "I mean, I knew he was straight. But he was really sexy and interesting. He called me Nota Bene."

Nina barked a short laugh. "What was that about?"

So I told her. I told her about skiing with him, about the slalom race he'd ruined, about the karaoke, and about how he had apologized to me for his part in the disastrous hike.

Nina listened without comment until I'd finished. Then, "That puts a cap on something for me. I thought he might be bi, though I couldn't have said what made me think that. But, Nathan, I think he liked you, too."

We regarded each other with unspoken understanding. She was probably right, despite his protestation when I'd told him I was gay. Then I said, "Or maybe he just has a thing for Asians."

For the second time that night, Nina threw back her head and laughed. It was contagious, and with all the noise we made I was afraid we'd wake Gram. If we did, she never let on.

Neil's insurance was set up to be divided equally among any surviving immediate family members. It was about six weeks before the amounts came to us, and suddenly I had nearly seventeen thousand dollars to call my own. I knew it would go toward my education; our parents' insurance had helped only so much with tuition, and loans are a lousy way to pay for college. But Gram encouraged Nina and me to think of something not too costly to get for ourselves that Neil would like us to have.

I had no idea what special thing that might be. Then one Sunday evening I dropped something on the floor of my bedroom that rolled under it a little before bumping into a pile of stuff I'd brought home from school, things I hadn't looked at since then. I pulled them out.

Alden's black capes were in there. They took my breath away for a second, and I thought I might cry but I didn't. His notebook from *Eastern Standard* was there. And so was the Sarah Warren tapestry, the one with the rich, autumnal colors of mountain shapes all sloping together down to the deep blue of a lake in the lower right. I stared at it. And stared at it. And stared, until I could imaging Neil climbing those mountains, feeling so at one with the universe. And something he'd said the last time he'd been home came back to me, something he'd said during our conversation about why I hadn't ever hiked with him.

"I love the White Mountain trails," he'd said. "The rocks, the streams, the meadows and woods. I love the struggle when it gets super steep, and the way I feel when there's an opening in the trees and I can see other mountains in the distance. But what I really love?"

He'd looked beyond me at nothing, and yet at everything, and then brought his eyes back to mine again.

"The best part, Nathan, the reason I climb, is the profound feeling of perspective it gives me when I get above tree line, when I can see forever, and when I realize how very small—how infinitesimally small I am. You know, I could fall, I could break a leg, I could *die* on a mountain. And it wouldn't care."

I think I'd made some kind of scoffing sound at that point. "This is a good thing?"

"It's the only good thing. Because as small as I am at that precise moment, I'm also massively huge. I'm also part of everything there is. It's like I'm one with the mountain, and the next mountain, and the next one and the next one on into infinity."

His voice had taken on a breathy quality that I knew he was not doing for effect. I'd known it was genuine, and there had been no doubt in my mind that he'd believed what he was saying with everything in him.

Staring at the tapestry, I felt something like a hint of that existential experience Neil had described. And suddenly, like a flash of light, like a lightening bolt inside my head, I knew what I would do with Neil's money.

I would pick up the baton Neil had been forced to drop. I would buy myself a really good pair of hiking boots, and a really good frame pack, and a really good sleeping bag, and a white kerosene stove, and waterproof, breathable clothes and gloves, and a rugged watch that wouldn't freeze, and a compass, and a new edition of the White Mountain guidebook, and any other paraphernalia that I might need or want on a hike (not in the winter, but still). And I would hike.

CHAPTER SIXTEEN

It's now late September. Neil's favorite time to hike. And I'm back on Chocorua, just as Jeremy had said I should do.

This time, I'd made it to the summit, from Neil's favorite trail on this mountain: Champney Falls. I'd watched idiots send golf balls into the sunset. Then I'd found my way over to the Jim Liberty Cabin to see who would be spending the night there. Seemed like maybe two couples. Two straight couples.

It had been disconcerting to see how different it looked now, with the distant hills covered in the colors of early autumn, with the granite ledges empty of snow and ice, with people milling about in their brightly-colored hiking gear. There were even a few dogs running around. I'd sat down on a rock and contemplated the scene, reconstructing in my mind the day Daniel had nearly led us in a completely wrong direction. There were so many ways Daniel had led me in wrong directions. Even so, I'd found myself thinking fondly of him.

Late this afternoon, I'd done my best to locate the place where Daniel and I had made our makeshift camp last March. I think I'm pretty close. I've chosen a spot that doesn't have too much of an incline, and I've set up my new tent with the opening on the downhill side. I've unrolled my new sleeping bag and arranged it with the feet toward the tent door, and I've cooked myself some freeze-dried chicken stroganoff and some hot lemonade on my new stove.

This spot is on the north slope, so the light had been fading for a while as the mountain eclipsed the last rays of the setting sun. I'd sat on a fallen tree to eat my dinner and watch dusk settle in for real. With a mouthful of water, I'd raise a cup. At first I'd though I was raising it to Neil, but this whole hike is about him. So I raised it to Daniel. Or at any rate, to the memory of Daniel. Then I cleaned up my dinner paraphernalia in the last of the light and packed everything away. And now I'm sitting in the dark, at the open door of the tent, listening to the small sounds these woods make at night.

Neil had loved this. I'm pretty sure I could get to love it, too. When I get back to campus this fall, I plan to select another couple of mountains for my next hikes. I want to feel for myself that conviction Neil had described, of being part of the vastness, of belonging to the universe.

But even now, even as I contemplate that ultimate belonging, it still hurts if I allow myself to think of Neil for very long. I rub my face and check my fancy new watch; almost time to crawl into the tent. I decide to let my mind wander just a little longer. And guess where it goes.

Daniel. Why the fuck do I keep thinking about Daniel?

Well, maybe, a voice in my head mocks, *it's because you just climbed the mountain you followed him up, that he followed you down, and now you're sitting almost on the very spot where you nearly died inside his sleeping bag with him. D'ya think maybe that's it?*

Yeah, okay, fine. Whatever.

I picture his handsome face, his eyes—so sincere, so intense—seeming to hold secrets he might have shared with me. I hear his voice, the Italian-inspired lilt that had added to the feeling of intimacy and belonging I got whenever he'd said *Nota Bene.*

Yup. I'd been addicted to him. Even now, at this distance, knowing I'll never see him again and truly not wanting to, I want the feeling he'd given me. Almost given me. Because Neil had actually given belonging and love to me. Something about Daniel had promised those things—a promise he'd never quite fulfilled, a fulfillment it had been unfair of me to expect.

I stare at the dark branches of trees just downhill from me and then look over them into the distance. As dark as the moonless night sky is, the distant mountains are darker. They look like black holes that would suck into them anything nearby, to be lost forever in a bottomless emptiness.

A sudden connection to Alden starts somewhere in the back of my brain and shoots directly at my heart. It makes me sit up straight so quickly that I bump my head into the top point of my tent door. I'd read that the pleasure fentanyl gives you is greatest the first time you take it. But you take it again and again, more and more, because you believe it can give you that feeling again. You *have* to believe it, because you can't stand the thought that it will never again be attainable. And it gives you enough each time to make you believe in the promise of pleasure that's always just out of reach.

It seems likely that addiction to fentanyl, for Alden, would have been more powerful than my addiction to what I wanted from Daniel, or at least more immediate, more urgent. And yet the longing, the belief despite repeated disappointments that what I craved could be attained—Alden and I had had that much in common.

The promise I'd seen in Daniel was an echo of the feeling I'd gotten from Neil. But Neil's love, the belonging he offered, had been the real thing. I'd thought of Daniel as methadone before. But this idea of someone—or something—making you believe the promise of something you had, that you want desperately, but that you can never get again? That slays me.

In my head, I hear David Wilcox singing: "You can get what's second best, but it's hard to get enough." The truth of that hits me square in the chest.

And then another connection occurs to me. When I'd wondered what had made Alden *start* with fentanyl, I'd despaired of understanding that. None of the obvious reasons seemed to apply to the man I'd known.

Weren't the feelings fentanyl gives you—intense pleasure, euphoria, a powerful sense of belonging—also feelings you usually get when you're starting to fall in love with someone? I had felt them for Alden. Had he felt them for me? The response to fentanyl was said to be much more powerful than you'd get from any real experience. So had the euphoria he'd gotten from fentanyl meant that his feelings for me hadn't seemed like much?

Holy shit! What if his feelings for me had been like a pale imitation of how he felt on fentanyl? That hurt! It would have made me so unimportant to him in comparison with a fucking drug!

Worse yet, what if his feelings for me had just reminded him of how much more wonderful the *drug* made him feel? And what if it had been the comparative weakness of his feelings for me that made him go back to fentanyl? That hurt even more.

I clenched my eyes shut and ground my teeth. *This is not about you, Nathan.*

But there was no one else here. So, yeah, maybe it was about me. And it was about all that had happened in the past year: Alden disappearing into a black hole; my Neil substitute (that would be Daniel) getting me lost in literal wilderness and nearly killed; the real brother—the real source of love and protection and belonging—proving himself to be fallible after all by burning alive, dying on a mountain, which he'd once told me was ridiculous. His death screams still echo in my head.

So why hadn't I sought the same escape Alden had? Was what I'd learned about addiction enough to keep me from using? I still didn't have a clue why he'd started. Something he'd said, about needing to find worthiness, came to mind. Had Alden suffered from low self-esteem? Had he had a low opinion of himself? That wasn't the Alden I'd known.

But once he'd started, it must have been about that

stratospheric pleasure, that high that even fentanyl couldn't deliver more than once, that high that must have overshadowed even the euphoria of falling in love. I can't know whether I'd meant much of anything to him.

I find suddenly that I'm standing, and before I take two steps a tree root reaches out and grabs my boot. At least, that's what it feels like. Down I go, banging my knee on the ground and barely missing the exposed granite that scrapes the skin off my palm. I roll onto my back, cursing, rubbing my knee with my uninjured hand, and then I lie with my face to the stars while something gnarly pokes into my back.

This pain, the pain of realizing that I could never have meant as much to Alden as he meant to me, feels like placing your foot on what you think is a solid step below you, only to fall on your face when it isn't really there. It's like being kicked in the gut. It's like both of those things.

Love. Belonging. Security. Those are what Neil had given me, what I wish I could have gotten from my father. They're what I tried to get partly from Alden, and partly from Daniel, and though it wasn't their fault, neither of them had delivered.

Would I ever have those feelings again?

Once upon a time I'd thought maybe I needed a therapist to help me deal with being gay in a straight world. Now?

Now I need to understand addiction. And I need to understand how to believe in real love, the kind that isn't dependent on what I've accomplished or how thoughtful I am or how good I am in bed. I want to know how to avoid empty promises that deliver only pale imitations of real love, those black holes that make me afraid love will never come again. I need to understand the difference between the black hole of substance abuse and the black hole where you despair of finding love.

I need to understand need.

Deeply asleep, I remember no dreams and hear no screams. I wake up with my mind clear, as though washed with cool spring water.

I eat cheese and bread and drink water looking out at the mountains that had seemed so black the night before. I know the black will always be there, waiting. But I also know I don't have to go into it.

I pack up my cooking things, my sleeping bag, and my tent, and I heft my frame pack onto my shoulders. I turn in the direction I know will lead me back to the Champney Falls Trail—I've practically memorized the Mount Chocorua trail map by now—and I put one foot in front of the other, test for stability under my boot, shift weight, place the other foot in front of me, and repeat all the way down the mountain to the trail head, where I've left El Speed's borrowed Forester. And by the time I get there, I know what I want to do with my life.

As I throw my gear into the back of the car, I speak aloud: "Psych was the right major, for me, Neil."

Psych will lay the groundwork for my career. And I've decided that the focus of my work in psychology will be substance abuse.

Have I been at college only a year?

Seems like a lifetime.

The End

AUTHOR'S NOTE

One of the issues Nathan Bartlett (the main character of *On Chocorua*) explores is addiction—not just to substances, which is an issue for people he cares about but not for him, but also addiction to feelings. He explores the differences he can observe between substance use disorders in others and the purely emotional need he experiences in his relationships.

I have no personal experience of or knowledge about substance use disorders. I relied heavily on Patrick Frame (MSW, LCSW) of St. Louis, Missouri to guide me in how these disorders might affect someone on an emotional level, and on how Nathan's emotional need resembled addiction to a substance.

Many thanks, Patrick, for your conscientiousness and advice in representing these concepts as accurately, and as sensitively, as possible.

A Reading Group Guide

ON CHOCORUA (Trailblazer Series, Book 1)

Robin Reardon

ABOUT THIS GUIDE

The suggested questions are included to enhance
your group's reading of Robin Reardon's novel, *ON
CHOCORUA*, Book 1 of the *TRAILBLAZER* series.

DISCUSSION QUESTIONS

Note: The questions in this guide contain spoiler information. It is recommended that you finish the book before reading through the questions.

1. As a young child and then as a teenager, Nathan looks up to Neil and considers him mature beyond his years. How do you think Neil feels about being cast in the role of "little man" and then as a father figure to Nathan?

2. In what ways does Daniel Cooke remind Nathan of his brother Neil? Why is this important to the story?

3. Neither Nathan nor Alden says the magic words "I love you" to the other. Yet at some point Nathan believes he is falling in love with Alden. Do you think Alden feels the same?

4. Does what Nathan learns about how powerful fentanyl is, and how intractable addiction to it can be, surprise you? Do you know anyone who has experimented with it or has become addicted?

5. By January, Daniel knows Nathan is gay. Given that Daniel doesn't hesitate to go alone with Nathan on a skiing trip, continues to call him Nota Bene (which Nathan enjoys), and then takes him hiking, how do you think he feels about Nathan? What are the chances that Daniel is bisexual, even though he tells Nathan he is not?

6. Why do you think Nathan climbs Mt. Chocorua the first time? What about the second?

7. Over the course of the story, Nathan makes several statements—sometimes to himself, sometimes to others—to explain why he never went hiking with Neil, despite being

offered the opportunity more than once. Which reason or reasons do you think are genuine? Do you think Nathan is honest with himself about which is the most truthful?

8. Nathan sees a lot of truth in that line from David Wilcox's song, "Hurricane." It goes, "You can get what's second-best, but it's hard to get enough." Do you also see truth in it? Has this concept been evident in aspects of your own life?

9. What is your impression of Nina for most of the story? Does it change after Neil's death? And do you think she sees Neil as a father figure the way Nathan does?

10. Why do you think Alden started taking fentanyl?

11. In the final chapter, Nathan wonders if the extreme pleasure of fentanyl, a pleasure with which nothing in real life can compete, meant that Alden's feelings for Nathan were so much less intense that Alden could never really have loved him. Can you put yourself in Nathan's place? If you loved someone who was in recovery from fentanyl, would you be able to believe they loved you as much as you loved them?

12. After reading the final chapter, what's your impression of Nathan in terms of his becoming a hiker like his brother? Will he be able to step into Neil's hiking boots and claim for himself the moniker "mountain man?"

BONUS QUESTION:
There's something that's too big for Nathan in Interlude VIII, "That First Hike," and too small for him in Chapter Twelve. What is it?

If you enjoyed this book, please consider posting a review on the online sites of your choice. This is the best way to ensure that more titles by this author will become available.

If you would like to be notified when new titles are released, you can sign up for Robin's mailing list at **robinreardon.com/contact**.

About the Author

Robin Reardon is an inveterate observer of human nature, and her primary writing goal is to create stories about all kinds of people, some of whom happen to be gay, transgender, or intersex—people whose destinies should not be determined solely by their sexual orientation. Her secondary writing goal is to introduce readers to concepts or information they might not know very much about.

Robin's motto is this: The only thing wrong with being gay is how some people treat you when they find out.

Interests outside of writing include singing, nature photography, and the study of comparative religions. Robin writes in a butter yellow study with a view of the Boston, Massachusetts skyline.

Robin blogs (And now, this) about various subjects that influence her writing, as well as about the writing process itself, on her website.

Other Works by Robin Reardon

Novels
AND IF I FALL
WAITING FOR WALKER
THROWING STONES
(Published by IAM BOOKS)
EDUCATING SIMON
THE EVOLUTION OF ETHAN POE
A QUESTION OF MANHOOD
THINKING STRAIGHT
A SECRET EDGE
(Published by Kensington Publishing Corp.)

* * *

Essay
THE CASE FOR ACCEPTANCE: AN OPEN
LETTER TO HUMANITY
(Published by IAM BOOKS)

* * *

Short Stories
GIUSEPPE AND ME
A LINE IN THE SAND
(Published by IAM BOOKS)